The Legendary Awakening of Gerald Monkton

The Legendary Awakening of Gerald Monkton

Lyn Shea

To order additional copies of this book, contact:
Xlibris Corporation
0-800-644-6988
www.xlibrispublishing.co.uk
Orders@xlibrispublishing.co.uk
300646

Contents

CHAPTER ONE

GERALD AWOKE AS usual these days to the sound of Marjorie's merriment bubbling away in the room below his bedroom. She was entertaining (or being entertained by) her first client of the day.

He lunged out of bed. A tall man who was not so much overweight as out of condition; the sort of 'out of condition' which derives from a disinclination to life beyond the confines of duty and daily obligation.

Marjorie's speaking voice was becoming audible, the beginnings of some advice to the client whose feet she was pruning. Gerald heard the low, serious inflection in her tone and knew that she was concerned even at this early stage with more than the client's feet; she had moved to the more thrilling topic of the problems beyond mere anatomy. That Marjorie was a chiropodist was perhaps an accident of fate which aided and abetted her more prurient interest in the human soul and its emotions. The two factors were not mutually exclusive. For had she taken up a career advising the agonised instead of

tending their feet she could not have set about un-
raveling their inner-most mysteries with the blunt-
ness and vigour required more for the removal of
their corns.

Gerald watched himself in the mirror above the
en-suite basin and pulled a scathing mouth which
was somewhat disguised behind his beard and mous-
tache. Not a bad sort of face for forty something,
going on fifty, not a bad sort of face even now for
someone who had once been considered very hand-
some in the suave and semi-artistic style of the less
than rugged male who even so exudes a masculinity
which is suggestive of open spaces and things made
creatively from wood . . .

Marjorie's laughter echoed dimly once more
through the floorboards and around the joists and
was joined by that of her client, in a staccato and
lower pitch.

Gerald moved swiftly to the phone. Any conversation he had now would be obliterated by their enthusiasm for the humour and not alone by the sound
of their own voices. He dialled Elaine's number and
mentally chivvied her to pick up her receiver.

*   *   *

Marjorie lowered her voice and spoke to the client as if they were swapping state secrets in the lobby
of the Ritz Hotel where people were treated to the
utmost curiosity and attention.

"He's at it again, you know. . . ."

The client had leaned forward to hear Marjorie's
words but quickly leaned back again as Marjorie made
a sudden and untimely move with the scalpel in the
direction of her left ear.

"Another one on the go . . ." Marjorie inclined her head to the ceiling and to Gerald's absent form. "He thinks I don't know.."

"know what?"

"About this new girlfriend!"

"What! . . . besides the usual one. . . ?" The client watched her bare foot warily as Marjorie's mood swung from disdainful to determined and seemed to concentrate itself on the more painful area of her lower heel. "Another girlfriend alongside the usual girlfriend?"

Marjorie nodded vaguely and raised her brows as if agreeing to a general comment about the weather. The client looked embarrassed now, for although she had known Marjorie and Gerald for many years and had been a confidante of Marjorie's for half of that, it was still a prickly business; Marjorie seemed to relish these goings on, and the sinister overtones which this lent confused her. She was at a loss as to how to react or what comment to make, if any.

"Definitely a verruca.." Marjorie decreed, changing tone and tack, so that the client paused a moment or two to comprehend that this was a professional diagnosis and not the nationality of Gerald's latest girlfriend. "He's probably on the phone to her now . . . he thinks I think he's still in bed. . . ." There was a lull whilst Marjorie remembered her obligations as a chiropodist and the client observed these ministrations with hushed reverence.

"How long do you think it'll be, Marjorie?" enquired the client gravely.

Marjorie raised her head, red in the face from bending. "Oh . . . til she gets fed up of him!"

"No.." the client was irritable, "*the verruca!*"

"Oh, the verruca!" Marjorie paused on the brink of amusement but the somber gaze of the woman deterred it. It was not that the client was averse to witty interludes or oblivious to humour, but that verrucas were no laughing matter.

*   *   *

Elaine came to the phone with a swiftness of tread born of the knowledge that it would be Gerald.

He never varied his timetable if he could help it; he was not so much a creature of habit as a slave to monotony. She smiled a little as she lifted the phone. She loved Gerald's reliability—by which you could set your watch—the way other women loved the arrival of the florists van unexpectedly whilst painting the bathroom ceiling. Gerald and Elaine shared a world—indeed had created a world—where only they lived, a sort of time-warp in which they could exist side by side in their thoughts whilst apart. Not unlike Eloise and Abalard, Elaine always thought.

".Can you make today?" he asked her, and she hesitated fractionally because it was part of the adopted pathology more than the necessity to consider.

"..Yes!" she sounded as if she had made a mammoth sacrifice of time in a schedule crammed to capacity, whilst in reality she had nothing planned but the gardening.

"I'll meet you at.. what?.." he paused for politeness sake, not wishing to take her for granted or spoil the illusion of impromptu living in which their daring adventure relied upon moment-to-moment decision making and the seizing of random opportunities . . . "Twelve thirty? . . . One?" They usually met between twelve thirty and one.

"Twelve forty five" Elaine said, equally as impromptu.

"Okay then.." Gerald hesitated. It seemed a shame to waste the call now that all seemed safe.

"Is everything alright?" she enquired, aware of this need to utilise all that was given.

"Yes!.. fine!"

"Oh, good!"

"You?.."

"The news on my mother-in-law's health is worse . . . looks like she may have to go into a home after all, or stay with his brother and his girlfriend. . . . but I don't . . ."

Gerald tuned out for a second; all had gone extremely quiet in the downstairs surgery. He pulled away from the phone call to listen, Elaine's voice growing thinner and pervading the atmosphere like a radio in another room.

The client's car was still on the drive, he could see it as he stretched the phone wire to its maximum and peered from the bedroom window.

"Gerald? . . . Gerald? . . . are you listening?.."

Nothing could be heard at all from the surgery, so perhaps it was a delicate point in the treatment, demanding all of Marjorie's attention. However, that did not normally stop her verbals. There was a creaking on the stairs whilst Elaine's voice questioningly floated around his head. Then suddenly a door slammed, somewhere in the house, where opened windows admitted the countryside breezes that roamed and twirled and played havoc with one's nerves, even in the sunny broad daylight.

"I'd better go!" said Gerald to Elaine sharply.

"Yes . . . fine." concurred Elaine, and put her receiver down as if it were on fire.

*   *   *

Marjorie wrapped the client's foot in a warm towel and inclined the chair a few inches backwards for greater relaxation. "I'll get you a cup of tea, Christine.." she said, not allowing Christine a choice in matters. "Verukas can be quite painful!"

From the hallway which led off her surgery and adjoined the rest of the house, everything was quiet, so she picked up the phone receiver and was just in time to hear Elaine say: "Yes . . . fine!" and the line went dead. Had she been a mini second earlier she would have been able to catch Elaine's attention and make dramatic revelations and announcements which would take the wind out of their sails.

She went quietly upstairs and entered Gerald's bedroom without knocking. He was in his bathrobe and he wheeled around and looked at her with antagonism. Even so his voice was calm. "Can't you knock?" He turned away as if the answer were an irrelevance. And, of course, after so many years in a stale-mate sort of marriage it probably was.

"Was that Elaine you were on the phone to?" she asked.

He regarded his wall-mirror image mutely. Marjorie brazened him out, her round gray eyes fixing upon him obstinately. This was always the most maddening thing about him—the fact that he would answer presently, could not quite summon the courage to ignore her, but would not reply until he'd mentally covered all the angles. "Because I know about the latest one. . . . so don't think I don't."

"Marjorie.." said Gerald wearily, "its nine-fifteen in the morning!"

Had there been an audience Marjorie would at that point have turned to them and given an aside which said: *'see what I mean!'* Instead she hiccupped a laugh. "Why? . . . does it make a difference to who you're seeing and who you're not seeing?"

Gerald fiddled with his tie hanger unnecessarily and stone-walled her.

"A bit like vampires are they? . . . disappearing at sunrise!. . . . don't think I don't know what's going on, Gerald!. . . . I know about the new one!"

"What *new one?*" he inflected as much scorn into the statement as possible for someone who could not act or simulate.

"The arts director or whatever she calls her-self. . . . Donna!"

His hands froze on the tie hanger like the hands of an escapee shot dead at the fence and Marjorie, empowered, moved forward into the room and watched the back of his head. "Does Elaine know? . . . I'll bet she doesn't! . . . she doesn't know you at all really! . . . she's in love with a card-board cut-out!"

Coming to life once more, Gerald's hands began to smooth out the ties. "Marjorie, I'm not listening to this! You've got a patient downstairs"

"Client!" Marjorie corrected, "And don't tell me about my professional responsibilities!"

Gerald went on silently concealing his mortifica-tion behind a mask of feeble indifference as Marjorie nailed him with her intrepid stare until she had made her eyes water. "I thought you'd like to know that I know." she chirruped and left the room and banged the door shut, leaving behind her a lightness in the atmosphere which celebrated the relief of sad and familiar tension.

Gerald perched on the edge of the bed and pondered this startling revelation that Marjorie knew of his dalliance with Donna Lees. Gazing at the tree-tops in the near and distant hills for some twenty minutes he ruminated until eventually he decided that as long as Elaine did not know of Donna Lees he was worrying quite unduly.

*   *   *

In her office in the city Donna Lees was playing with her little silver and ebony puzzle, a present from an admirer. She watched her doorway intermittently, for she was waiting for the Managing Director to pass so that she could whisk out and catch his attention. The tiny silver balls ran hither and yon around the ebony face of the puzzle and then balanced nicely into place, just in time for the footsteps of the M.D. in the passageway. Donna rose and moved through into the corridor and exuded surprise. "Geoff! . . . just the man I wanted too see."

Geoff took her arm and smiled. "Walk with me to the lift, Donna! . . . I've got to make the station for ten thirty."

Donna relaxed immediately; a lifetime of seeing her own beauty appreciated had taught her to trust the omens when she was on the winning side. "I wanted to talk to you about the photographer I've met.."

"Oh?.." Geoff paused at the lift and attempted satire. "Is your personal life my concern these days Donna? . . . That's over and above the job description surely!"

Donna smiled obligingly. "He's a commercial photographer and I thought we might use him.."

The lift arrived and Donna stepped in ahead of Geoff to make sure he did not escape, but as Geoff never wished to escape from Donna it was not a hard maneouvre. "We have more photographers on the books than we need."

"Yes . . . but this one knows the sites . . . he's already worked for National and he's done the large tourist info guides.."

"And?.."

"He may be on to something!" Donna said in her diffident voice which had him eating out of her hand because it so belied her confidence and will-power.

"Such as?" Geoff held the button for Donna to alight before him on the ground level.

"A living side of history!"

"A what?"

They walked together through the glass doors of the building, Geoff nicely amused and with one eye on the time. The building was not large, but it was newly built and prefabricated and recently purchased at phenomenal cost from a large computer software company who had outgrown it in the first year of trading.

"I can't say more than that now.." Donna turned to Geoff and blinked her eyes which were large and luminous, clearly alive and working, despite her designer frames which sat midway down her nose.

Geoff stood thoughtfully—he was three minutes ahead of his allotted schedule.

Outside the building the discreet copperplate brass plaque said **'Heritage Matters . . . archivists and historical researchers'. . . . established since 1902. . . . affiliated branches in Dublin and Edinburgh"**

"You'll have to trust me!" Donna said, "I know what I'm doing here."

"You always know what you're doing, Donna!..but do I approve unless I know what its about?"

"You'll like the results!"

The M.D. regarded her detachedly, or as near detachedly as possible for someone whose wife was sleeping of her own volition in the spare bedroom.

"You'll like the reading figures!" Donna replied with the quiet assurance of those who knew their own worth and the infallible ways to sustain it.

"OK, see Bill Brightwell..fix a budget..but a low one, mind!"

Donna was already heading back into the building. "Of course, Geoff!. . . . This guy is not greedy . . ."

Geoff laughed and crossed to his car. A man who was not greedy where his living and his talents were concerned! He could have envied him, had he believed such types existed.

*   *   *

Gerald drove onto the winding road leading towards the Moors from where lay the small road on which Elaine would be situated, in the old phone box, or nearby it in very good weather. He was just thinking himself into the mood for seeing her (the way gourmets contemplate a dinner hours in advance) when his mobile rang. This was in itself cause for amazement because it was not reliable at all and only one in six calls got through. Which meant it rang about once every week.

"I have to see you to tell you what's happened." said Donna Lees

Gerald swung the car to the left to correct the steering wobble.

"Can you make this lunchtime?"

"When?..today?"

"Yes, this lunchtime would be today, Gerald.." Donna laughed—a wonderfully evocative and thrilling sound which tantalised him more than the sight of her naked.

"Well . . . I don't know if I can!"

"Oh!! . . . why?" She sounded devastated, out of all proportion to the slight disappointment to her plans.

"I'm on my way somewhere!..What time did you have in mind? . . . I mean what time do you call lunch?.." He was aware that he was babbling somewhat. The mobile was cutting in and out and the car was gliding all over the show. He shook the mobile and gripped the wheel and glared at the road ahead like someone in the throes of petrification. Life was getting too erratic.

"Lunch is between twelve and three isn't it, darling?..in polite circles! . . . depending on your day and who you are!"

Gerald never bothered to reply to these kind of remarks she made, he did not have the weaponry and knew when he was out-classed.

"So?"

"What?"

"Are we meeting or not?"

"I told you, I don't think I can get.."

"S'not Marjorie is it?"

"No!"

"So its Elaine?" said Donna, moderating her voice and becoming demure, not to seem jealous or unreasonable.

"Listen..give me a minute or so..I'll see what I can do!"

*   *   *

Elaine was almost unable to speak from the shock. She stared at the phone as if it had grown wings and flown in personally with the bad news. "..You don't think you're well enough?..Gerry..I don't quite..I mean . . . you were alright a while ago.."

"Some illnesses are very rapid and sudden." Gerald said, his voice frail and strained and containing no bass notes—the hallmark of the liar.

"Well . . . shouldn't your seeing me..I mean us meeting. . . . help you feel better?"

"Not in this case, no!" Gerald turned the car round. "I have to keep going to the loo."

"Oh! . . . Oh, I see! . . . I didn't realise..I'm sorry.." Elaine stared at the glass panes in the phone booth, which was so antiquated it might have been used in an old movie to summon police cars that looked like stately vehicles for royalty, except that on the upper advertising panels above the handset the graffiti scrawled upon the glass was very contemporary. Gerald's rambling excuses burbled along as she read everything before her to distract herself from the misery welling up in her insides. He had never before, *not ever,* turned back half way to meeting her.

Gerald felt like a heel. For a second he wanted to tell Elaine that he was sorry, that he had made it up, that he had seen the error of his ways and that he would never put any other woman in front of her. But it was only for a second and then he was gripped again by common-sense and the need to conceal his attachment to Donna. "I'll speak to you later then!" he muttered weakly.

"Yes . . . yes . . . take care of yourself."

She left the phone booth, forgetting to push closed the stiff aged door which always jarred just an inch or so before the jam, and trudged dejectedly back the way not ten minutes since she had arrived.

Gerald sat a moment and winced, he had earned himself some awful karmic retribution now for up-setting Elaine; he only hoped it would not come around Donna and the new dawn she could help him access in his flagging business. His expression was grim and fixed and as he maneouvred the three-point turn a high-pitched rasping sound alerted him to the fact that he had scraped his rear off-side wing on someone's gatepost.

*   *   *

"Its an opportunity made in heaven!" said Donna, her campari-soda held aloft, her bracelets speaking of foreign travel and indulgence. "No pun intended, of course!" she laughed, like a schoolgirl up to some minor prank by which everyone may be entertained and no harm could come.

But Gerald was still looking worried.

"I didn't mean to sound irreverent, Gerry," Donna said, gripping his wrist for a moment with her hand and exciting him more than a little, "I know its a sensitive subject which deserves respect.."

He nodded, sipped at his tonic water and gazed at the door of the pub, opened to the luxurious sun-shine. He was not at all sure what he was getting into but he sensed his need to gain entrance, whatever the price.

"You see, if what you say is true.." Donna began testing him, "if as you say.."

"It *is* true!" Gerald emphasised, as she had known he would.

"Well then . . . think how many people would love to know of it..need to know of it..we all need proof of the heaven worlds, Gerry."

He sighed in near exasperation. "It has nothing to do with the heaven worlds, Donna!"

Donna looked slightly abashed. "Oh..but ghosts and things..people always associate that with the heaven worlds..don't they!"

"Only the unlearned..the ignorant!"

"Of which half the world's population may be included!"

Gerald said nothing and seemed to her to have withdrawn from the proceedings, an effect which had she known him better she would have realised happened very frequently in his waking life, and was not contingent upon something she had personally evoked. She watched him for a moment or two. She was unsure, now, at this stage, whether she actually liked him. There was something cold about him, a distinct lack of warmth which was nothing to do with diffidence or aloofness or arrogance, but more to do with absence of feeling, or even interest. "Did you hear me?"

"Yes. . . . I don't know if that's right, but even so, more and more people are studying this kind of phenomenon!"

"Exactly!..quite!..that is my point!..you must forgive my crude way of expressing things, darling, as one of the 'unlearned'.. .Everyone's interested and everyone's clueless . . . there's a fortune to be made here!"

Gerry sighed and shifted his tall frame (which could be doing with some exercise beyond driving to assignations with his females) and looked noncommittal.

"And don't tell me money isn't the object!..I know that!..but Geoff Formby doesn't and its the likes of him we have to impress, I'm afraid! . . . its the way of the world!"

Gerald stared at the same point in the distance, his eyes glazed and his persona lack-lustre. As Donna again wondered what she saw in him out of the bedroom, he turned to her. "And have we impressed him?"

"*I* have!" she replied, adding emphasis on the first word, "and he has given me a budget . . . which I have yet to finalise with Bill Brightwell, but he will want to see the initial signs of impressive evidence by the end of the week..so I thought we could go up to that castle first and do a stint there!"

Gerald sipped the tonic, tasting it as an afterthought on the edges of his bearded upper lip tentatively, like a lizard at a watering hole, thought Donna with the fascination of the humanly curious and not necessarily the romantically dazed.

"They don't appear on command you know," he gazed at her with something approaching accusation, "I can't summon them like models on a photo-shoot.."

"No-one would expect you to, darling!..don't be silly!. . . . Even Geoff and Bill Brightwell are not that obtuse . . . we..*they* . . . simply wish you to do what you normally do so that what normally occurs may happen..if you get my meaning!"

Gerald nodded.

"But we have to hope it happens by the end of next week at the latest!"

Gerald cleared his throat, rather too noisily, and an aggressive undertone was pushed into the midst of the discussion.

"And let's be optimistic!..there's no reason why it should not..happen that is!. . . . is there?"

"Perhaps not." said Gerald. "We can but see!"

Donna gripped his wrist again and said: "Let's hurry..we have time to call home for a while if you like!"

Gerald breathed more easily; this was something which was at his command, over which he did have some arbitary control. He finished his tonic water rapidly and followed her out of the door into the glorious sunshine.

CHAPTER TWO

GERALD WONDERED, NOT for the first time, how he had allowed Donna to know so much about his work, and the extra revelations that had resoundedly begun to appear in his work. She had not so much taken over his agenda as exploited her professional position to the extent where his agenda had rendered itself at her disposal.

He had been a commercial photographer for twenty-five years. Ever since completing his apprenticeship in a civil surveyors office. Since that time he had worked consistently and well, without regret or cause for concern, gaining a place of esteem in the list of his notable colleagues, until several months previously, when he had attended a spiritual development class (simply out of curiosity because it was run by a Canadian girl whose first discipline had been that of photography and she had seemed to have interesting things to say about etheric interference, negative films and the supernatural).

It had changed his life, it had changed the way

he perceived life, the reality of the world out there, because he had begun to see cloudy forms and unexplained persons through the camera lens. At first he mistrusted this, and thought it an effect of his imagination after a pretty intense and impressive seminar in which Pearl (the Canadian) had convinced both sceptics and sympathisers of the existence of entities and such like (lay-people call them ghosts, she had said) in the etheric matter which was the substance much highlighted by the photographer and his equipment.

She had moreover shown people how to connect with and heighten the inner senses which materialise and call forth such phenomena via meditational techniques, prior to positioning themselves and looking into a view-finder.

She had charged, not unnaturally, a fairly high fee for doing this, and everyone expected brilliant results. Some were a little disappointed but not unconvinced; the testimony and enthusiasm of the more successful of their number sustained any flagging interest, for there were those present who had claimed to see all sorts through their individual lenses, from historical monarchs to vague shadow like forms which Pearl explained as 'subtle bodies'.

On the way home, Gerald had stopped the car and parked on the hills and watched the setting sun. Digesting what was perhaps the most memorable day of his life (not hard, given the unmemorable humdrum of his existence beyond the extenuating presence of Elaine). Then, seized with the need to prove and prove again, he jumped from his vehicle and got out his panoramic lens and adjusted it to his camera and pointed it at random towards the old abbey which lay in the dale below his parked car.

Scanning several yards from right to left and back, he took several exposures, and used a whole reel of film. He could not see anything out of the ordinary as he did the shoot, it was disappointing.

But in his dark room he had been amazed: faces, disembodied forms had floated, and almost gloated, on three of the twenty four exposures. He had enlarged these and sure enough they were—or appeared to be—human. Diaphanous and filmy they became more and more solid and visible as they grew in size or colour.

He took them to several colleagues he trusted, who surveyed them and gave different opinion. All said they could not explain them and agreed they seemed to be evidence of something 'else' beyond the physical. One of them said he did not want to have to see them again or talk of them, and Gerald was more impressed with this reaction than with the gasps and exclamations of others of his association who were utterly convinced and enthralled in the first two minutes.

Since that time he had set about on his own one-man exploration of this phenomena and had traversed the Pennines and surrounding areas studying and photographing many historic sites.

That had been eight months ago. And he had developed throughout that period skills which he had not previously known he possessed. The gift of some kind of psychic or mediumistic ability which allowed him to capture on film that which could not be observed with the naked eye.

*   *   *

It was on one of his days out, photographing a ruined castle, that he had met Donna. She was with a group of people, all taking quick shots of the place from many angles and scribbling furiously in note pads, and he had assumed she was a journalist.

It turned out she was a director of 'Heritage Matters' and was liaising with the Tourist Information Board to include the castle on the routine *not-to-be-missed-places-of-interest-and-rural-beauty* list for visitors.

She had watched him long and hard as he worked, impressed with his concentration and solitary adherence to whatever he was doing, and eventually he had angled his circular route of the site to coincide with her space.

She was obviously attractive, and not the kind of woman who looked like a less rugged version of the rugged out-of-door males surrounding her, not dressed in an anorak and sexless clothing.

"Free-lancing or recreational?" she had enquired, speaking first, confident of herself in a way, which did not at all surprise him.

He had stared at her with his tranquil, unassuming expression which females always felt to be sensitive and reassuring. He did not believe in plying women with words—women had enough words of their own generally and were not really interested in what men had to say, only with the way they themselves were perceived.

"What are you doing exactly?" a slight smile of suspicious irony illuminated her face.

Gerald had taken a long look at the hillside to the left of her head, his eyes scanning the landscape for guidance before taking a plunge into the heady and probable unknown.

And then he had told her, in great and graphic detail.

*   *   *

Elaine had that tiny frown which puckered her forehead between the brows, so beloved of him. He stared at it, rather than at her.

"..So were you really that ill yesterday? You look fine now!"

He shifted his dark eyes to her's and did not im-mediately respond.

She waited, as she always waited. She knew him well, after twenty years, and it was not wholly his com-ments she was listening to.

"I recovered very quickly.once I'd lain down and taken an alka seltzer."

The frown appeared again. He knew that she was doubting his word.

"It was a strange do . . . one of those forty eight hour things, I suppose!"

"But it's only been twenty four!"

"Hmmmm . . . though I did feel queasy the day before!"

He turned away, revolted by his own capacity for untruth.

Elaine turned away too. Something was wrong between them. It was in Gerald's other life, the one where anything might occur and she would know nothing of it. It made her feel helpless, and sort of unreal, like a ghost of herself.

She thought of the concept of being a ghost of herself, which led her to the issue of Gerald's new hobby, which did not please her, although she kept this to herself.

"I thought at first that it might have something to do with the spooks!" she said

Although Gerald did not like his 'light-beings' referred to in this manner he was more concerned with where her track was leading.

"What do you mean?" he asked, quite sharply for someone who hardly varied their tempo or raised their voice.

Elaine opened and closed her lips several times, and again the frown appeared and played around her brow in various shades of intensity, finally clearing to leave a pensive sort of expression on the whole of her face. "Well. . . . you know . . . I thought you may want to go and do something with them and not like to tell me!"

He rolled onto his side on the meadow and watched her, trailing a piece of long grass around her chin in the time-honoured way of lovers.

"Like what?"

This was meant to be ironic but it came out as a serious enquiry that required a serious answer.

"Whatever it is you do with them."

"You make it sound very sinister and ridiculous!"

Resisting the urge to say that in her opinion that was just what it was, Elaine looked him fully in the eye and reminded herself just how much they loved one another.

*   *   *

The castle that Donna wanted to photograph for explicit results lay in the depth of the Yorkshire Dales and was six miles off the main road.

They drove to it in the peaceful evening sunshine, the sun a glowing red ball at the end of another perfect September day.

They approached the desolated site with anticipation, both for different reasons of their own, and Gerald's car slid quite silently onto the ground surrounding the ruin.

Years of neglect and transient sightseers had left their mark in varying degrees of untidiness; litter which dated back to the last war and tangled briars and flowering weeds encircling the outer-perimeters of the fortress.

"We want shots of the inside and outside!" Donna urged with enthusiasm. "Perhaps we should do the inside before the sun fades completely . . . that way there'll be more interesting light and shade."

Gerald murmured assent—he was irritated at being reminded of the fundamentals of his own trade, but he was familiar with Donna's over-enthusiasm and had resigned himself to her more exuberant ways.

He assembled his apparatus with thoroughness and an adherence to the smallest detail. Donna entertained herself by walking about in the ground floor regions of the ruin and kicking loose masonry and running her hands over walls and peering closely at all the more curious things which begged architectural enquiry.

"Shall we see what lies up those stairs?"

"In a moment." Gerald clicked together his panoramic lens and his indoor camera. He was in no hurry to hurry the unhurriable. He was really having second thoughts about the jaunt, and indeed·the whole venture, but knew that there was now no turning back.

"You go if you wish!"

Donna came to him and ran her hands along his neck to his shoulders, standing behind him and exuding sexuality and excitement together with her Givenchy perfume. "Are you tense?"

"A bit..I'm always a little tense when I work."

"Yes, but this is not a normal session is it?"

"Isn't it?"

"Of course not..it's partly fun . . . and pleasure!"

"I thought you said they wanted results by the end of next week!"

"They do..but still . . . there's no need to get obsessive about it!"

Gerald wondered again what would happen if they got nothing on film, if the 'ghosts' as they would be termed, did not make themselves known.

"I think I will go up those stairs.." Donna took long and confident strides to the crumbling and winding staircase, "though I have to admit its a bit scary!"

Watching her, Gerald thought that he had never seen anyone less scared. Her need to dramatise and exaggerate annoyed him, it was an insult to everything he held dear, and a hindrance to the right approach necessary to the whole thing. He sighed and looked away from her retreating figure.

Minutes later her voice came floating down, echoing and cavernous and a few octaves deeper than usual. "There's the most fascinating font thing.." she said, "like an empty garden fountain . . . its slap bang in the middle of this upper chamber.."

He murmured and aimed his lens at the gaping hole where once had been the large double doors to the main building.

"What do you think it is?"

"How do I know till I see it?"

Moments of silence elapsed and only the dripping of errant water escaping from some orifice could be heard, to the background of the occasional sheep braying in the fields beyond.

"Oh, My God!"

He looked away from the camera lens and frowned in the direction of the staircase. He waited for more information; Donna might just become overzealous to the point of impeding the exercise if he encouraged her every observation.

"Gerald . . ." her voice was thin and reedy, "come here quick!"

"What is it?"

"There's someone in the window."

"Window! What window?"

"You know..the place where the window used to be!"

"Are you sure?"

Donna's voice returned almost to normal. "Yes, I'm sure! . . . are you coming or not!"

The stairs were slimy with moss and dampness and he placed his feet carefully as he ascended. Donna was standing a few feet into the chamber and staring at the north/western wall where the casement admitted the last of the glare from the sun. He trained his eyes to see the intangible, stilling his mind and breathing deeply, in the way he had been trained by Pearl on the seminar.

"What do you think?" Donna asked breathlessly.

"I can't yet see them!"

"Of course you can!. . . . you must be able to!. . . . you're saying that to wind me up!"

"I am not!" He was quite irritable; how dare she see something that he could not himself see! He was the one with the expertise in these matters, she was a rank amateur.

"It's a female I think.." observed Donna.

Gerald was now almost cross-eyed in the attempt to dampen down his vision and access the etheric matrix from which these emanations came. He was getting a headache and his eyes were watering.

Donna in the meantime was breathlessly still; he had never known her so transfixed. He watched her face for signs of fakery. He could tell nothing from her expression except that she was riveted and apprehensive. Her eyes were moving to right and left by no more than a two-inch span.

"Is it moving?" he asked with slight facetiousness.

"Yes. only a little!..it's inside the window as if looking out, but it keeps turning round slightly as if watching over its shoulder.."

Gerald peered again.

"I shouldn't keep calling it 'it'," Donna remarked, "I can see its female."

"What age?"

"Good God, Gerald! how should I know from this distance!"

"Well, is she an old woman or a young girl?"

"I don't know . . . the hair is long but that means nothing..she's not a crone if that's what you mean . . . but nor does she seem to be a teenager!"

Gerald let out breath rather angrily and shifted his weight. "You're making it up Donna!"

Donna wheeled round as if stung. "I am not!..how dare you suggest such a thing!"

He saw that his over-heated reaction came from jealousy and he was immediately contrite. "I apologise..its just that.."

"You're narked that you can't see it too."

"Yes.." he admitted, "and its odd because I usually do.."

"Do you think you're the only person in the world with these powers?"

"No..but you never before said you had them."

"How did I know till now!"

Donna began to watch the window again but her mood was spoilt by his petulance. "She's gone!"

Gerald looked at her for a long while, his eyes betraying his suspicions.

"You don't believe me, do you?"

"Yes..I don't not believe you . . . it's just that..it's just.."

"That you think I'm making it up!"

"Well, you could have imagined it!"

"Yes..I could!. . . .just like you could at those seminars!" She turned on her heel and made for the crumbling staircase.

"Be careful!" he called to her. "Those steps are treacherous!"

She did not reply and he could hear the click of her heels on each mossy stair

*   *   *

They sat in his car and kissed, a little distantly. It was completely dark now.

"I'm sorry." Donna said. "I didn't mean to be so. . . . usurping!"

"S'not your fault!"

"Yes, but it must be galling.."

Gerald looked away and into the darkness

"Perhaps if you had just taken shots . . . it might have shown up!"

"I suppose it might!"

"Why didn't you?"

Gerald was unsure how to reply.

"Because you needed proof with your own eyes!" Donna supplied, "before wasting film!"

"Yes!"

"Shall we go back tomorrow?..you're bound to see something soon! . . ."

"Not necessarily!"

"How do you mean?"

"Well . . . she might be someone on your wave length, someone from your history . . . and may only be accessible to you.."

"Is that how it works?"

"Sometimes!"

"Sometimes? It either does or it doesn't!"

"There's a lot you don't understand!"

"I'm sure." Donna said, ready for conciliatory gestures to save the friendship.

"We could come back the day after tomorrow if you want!"

"Whenever." Donna agreed with cool unconcern.

She was on to something so hot here and she did not wish to appear too covetous. She needed time to think about it all.

*   *   *

Gerald parted from Donna an hour later. Having taken her back to her car several miles along the main road towards Rotherham, he quickly swung his car round and headed back to the castle.

It was almost dark when he arrived. Others might have been scared but Gerald was not, he loved the atmosphere and the potential for the unexplained.

The token pay-gate, which seemed to be manned

at some points during the week-days and not at others, was locked and held a sign showing the normal
hours for going around the ruin and the price, which
was nominal. The token gesture of the gate was literal as far as Gerald could tell, for it was possible to
'storm the battlements' from a few different angles
and gain admission to the castle without actually laying siege. He did not know who the owners of the
ruin were or who held responsibility as far as the
public was concerned. It was one of those cultural
efforts so beloved of the English which thought it
should represent history in some way but did not wish
to go big-time, or even properly corporate. So it set
out its stall in the most modest way possible and hoped
to make a few bob when the weather was right. It
even had a courtesy box (made of an old rusting oil
drum into which people were expected to drop their
donations, if the pay-gate was not manned) before
entering through the small make-shift door, of fairly
modern origin, which lay next to it. Without hesita-
tion, Gerald went to the upper level and looked
about him for the best camera-angles. He was not
able to see the floor or the corners of the chamber
properly now for the growing darkness, but he aimed
the camera at the brighter area emanating from the
western window aperture.

It was after he had spent an age adjusting the
lens that he saw her: a lady of ample proportions,
dressed in clothes which might have been from any
era between the sixteenth and nineteenth century.
Her hair was long, as Donna had said, and a dullish
and undistinguished colour. She was turned
sidewards as if tired of watching the countryside from
the window but prepared for any developments there
even so.

He snapped shot after shot, using up one whole reel of film, and moving on tip-toe from place to place so that the exposures would be in varying perspective.

Finally he shut his camera lens and packed away his gear, and humming gently to accompany his own solitary movement, made his way back out to the car: even he was a little unnerved by the eeriness of the blackened landscape around him and the strange sounds within the silence.

He threw everything into the boot of the car and unlocked his door with alacrity, jumping in and driving away at a more reckless speed than he usually employed.

He thought about Donna..

Donna was obviously graced with the sight. How amazing! He would not have thought it. He would have imagined her to be so earthed in the earthly that it would take a blinding flash of lightening and the appearance of all the saints to convince her of anything above the usual 3-d.

He was also slightly annoyed! Donna now would be a force to be reckoned with. It was one thing to have her on board as an ally, or a sponsor, but as a fellow-psychic she might just prove to be too much!

CHAPTER THREE

ELAINE LOOKED AT Gerald with the dove-like quality which he had initially fallen in love with all those years ago. How many was it? Probably twenty or so!

"I just thought we could go to Southport or somewhere..after we've had lunch . . . like we used to..seeing as Graham is in Leeds and you don't have much work on"

"I didn't say I didn't have work on.." Gerald protested, laughing in that slightly outraged way which was also gently reproving. "I said I wasn't working full out at present!"

"Sounds like the same thing to me." said Elaine, petulantly. "We always used to go places when we had the time . . . so we didn't feel like we were..you know..simply..being lustful!"

Gerald chuckled and pulled her closer to him in the front of the car. "Being lustful?..us!"

She kissed his mouth briefly, feeling that it was almost pointless from that angle, given his beard growth and the position of his head.

"I have things to do!" he said, still using the patronising tone as if she were outrageously demanding of him something he had not agreed to give.

She pulled away from him and frowned.

"What?" he said, "What are you looking like that for?"

"You're up to something." Elaine became serious. "Something you don't want to tell me about!"

"Am I!"

"I think you're seeing someone else!"

Gerald's laugh was harsh and clipped like that of an amateur actor hamming it up so that the audience would know he was a fraud.

"I think you might have another woman.."

"I do!" he said and looked at her, impishly attempting whimsy. "You!"

"I mean besides me!"

She was acquiring that small and distant demeanour which rapidly overtakes women when they are faced with the unknown and the threatening.

"Don't be silly!"

"Is that the best you can do?"

Elaine now seemed to be scanning him for signs of the unreadable, like somebody who has caught an important headline on a newspaper across a train carriage and forces their vision to span the distance by sheer effort of will.

"What do you mean, *is that the best I can do?*"

"Gerry, stop echoing everything I say and answer my questions!"

"There's nothing to answer!"

"There must be!"

"Why must there?"

"Because I know I feel something!"

"Like what?"

Now he had Elaine's psychic powers as well as Donna's to deal with! It was becoming a joke! But it had to be borne, because once they were onto the scent there was no stopping them and it was theirs by right. He considered whether he should try some romantic coercion, like affirming how much she meant to him, or telling her how wonderful she was! but he could not bring himself to be so hypocritical, it would make him feel ill.

"So we're not going to Southport then?" said Elaine, after a few seconds, as if this was the main focus of concern and her other accusation had not been spoken.

"No!" he said, and wondered how she thought he could take her to Southport after that little altercation; with his discomfort and her suspicion. Of course, were he not a liar he would not have discomfort and therefore he should perhaps continue with a charade or a bluff, to save *her* discomfort. He was in a paralysing turmoil of mind and emotion and looked as if he had turned to stone; pale beneath his beard growth and grim with worry.

"Fine.." Elaine took on the angelic and martyred look which attempted to hide disappointment and make all this seem like another event within the rich tapestry of life, whereas in reality it was like a slow sick feeling in the stomach which took with it all purpose and energy for the rest of the day.

*   *   *

Later, in the dark room, he discovered that only three exposures on the reel of film he had shot revealed any evidence of the female 'light being'. But that was good enough to convince Donna's colleagues and others.

He took the reel to Donna's flat the next day a little before eight in the evening and they examined them together on the verandah in the mellow evening light.

"If they stand up to scrutiny in normal daylight such as this, they'll print out well!" Donna said.

"I know." Gerald replied, rather testily, did she think she was talking to a novice! And then a thought struck him. "What do you mean, 'they'll print out well?' . . . print out where?"

"In the magazine..next month.."

"What magazine?"

Donna widened her milky grey eyes and stared. "Our magazine!. . . . *The Heart of Heritage*. . . . the quarterly publication we own!. . . . what else did you think I meant?"

"I didn't know you were printing them in there!" Gerald sank to one of the wicker chairs which was too low for normal humans and felt as if he were sinking and sliding into some nether-world beyond the terracotta pots of petunias and miniature roses and freakish little marble ornaments adorning her verandah garden. "I thought you were using them as publicity . . . and general data about the castle."

"We are!..but in the magazine!. . . . how else do we reach great parts of the populace?"

"Yes, but . . . but we haven't discussed my fee . . ."

"Oh, don't worry about that darling!"

A browsing wasp disturbed Gerald's concentration and hovered confrontationally in front of his left eye..he waved it away and it backed off, zig-zagged and bounced back. It was all very well for her to tell him not to worry. People in her line had been saying that since Caxton invented his presses.

"Donna . . ."

"Yes?" she turned her innocent gaze to him.

"You can't just. . . . you can't just expect.."

"What?..expect what Gerry?"

"Me to hand over those shots to you like that. . . . they're worth a great deal!"

"I know..and we will pay you handsomely.."

"How much?"

"I don't know until I write the editorial and consult Bill Brightwell!. . . . Don't worry, I'll ring you to discuss terms!"

"I should hope so!" said Gerald, allowing himself a brief show of hostility in the face of professional manipulation.

*   *   *

Marjorie meantime paced the studio in which Gerald worked and played and generally avoided the normal responsibilities of married men of his years.

In turn perusing strips of negative film and his business correspondence lying on the desk, she looked around for signs of the personally unusual. Of course there were none; Gerald being altogether too careful to betray himself in any way to casual observers-or prying sabouteurs-and she did not search with much intensity of purpose.

She was just about to abandon the investigation when her eye alighted upon a letter from Donna Lees. It was type written, with a post-script scribbled in fountain pen. It was naturally this that Marjorie was interested in.

Screwing up her eyes to decipher the terrible

writing, she at last made out some words. . . . *I* something. . . . *not cheat you.* . . . something. . . . *you can..*something. . . . *you are.safe with me in that way..*something *secret.* . . . and then clearly *'don't fret pet'*

Marjorie dropped the letter back into the desk drawer . . . *don't fret pet!!* She sat down in Gerald's swivel chair and stared from the window. The pair of them were scheming to go off together. . . . *you are safe with me..*could only mean she was telling him he was in good hands for the future.

The body of the letter contained terms and suggestions regarding Heritage Matters and its affairs and Gerald's photographic services.

Marjorie sat a long while and surveyed the countryside. Then she toured briefly the dark room in which the films were developed—a small room hardly bigger than a toilet—and sat again to read the letter, or rather the sub-script. She could still not read the words which had eluded her before. Even so she was satisfied with what she did read. It was more than revealing.

*   *   *

Donna was awake half the night thinking about the whole phenomenon. It was quite mind-blowing! She had almost accepted the fact that she had something of the gift of clairvoyance—it hardly surprised her at all, perhaps because it seemed to be an extension of something already existing rather than a miraculous breakthrough or an accomplishment after great effort. She doubted it, of course. It may after all have been a flash-in-the-pan, a one off. She needed to repeat the experience to be sure.

But in the meantime she had to wear her business-head and deal with the matter of the hot-shots that were Gerald's photos. Three beautiful exposures of the female she herself had seen in the castle. A female who could not be anything other than 'ghostly'.

She arrived at the office early so that she could commandeer some of Geoff Formby's schedule before it became choked solid. He looked at her expectantly as she sailed into his office, that sad sort of longing look which she had grown accustomed to as being part of the script they had between them.

He watched her hands as she removed the glossy exposures from the file, hands wich were flexible and magical . . . hands he imagined would know how to thrill him.

She laid down the photos following on from outer shots of the castle, like a story with footsteps leading to the climax.

Geoff cleared his throat as his mind framed the word 'climax'. He had to retain a sense of proportion here, not to say a calm exterior. "What is she?"

"A ghost!" Donna said plainly, in a voice which invited no query.

Geoff gawped at the misty figure, and then back up at Donna, and then down to the photograph again. "You sure?" He looked at Donna for signs of humour and none were apparent.

"I saw her myself!"

Geoff was not a man to say too much in the face of the unknown. Bluff and hearty he might have been, but he was no lightweight. He retained a stolid silence until he had assembled his thought processes enough to separate the various issues involved here.

Donna was aware of this, all the while staring at

the female on the photos from different angles, moving her head from one side to another, like a specialist from Sotheby's trying to price the priceless.

"So, is this what all the mystery was about then?..ghosts..and spirits and things?".

"Yes." Donna said, again in a tone which gave nothing away but brooked no argument.

"So, there's more of this kind of thing in the offing?"

"Definitely!"

"I didn't know you had that sort of. . . . whatd'ya'm'callit, Donna!"

"Neither did I!"

They both stared at the glossies. Geoff searching for a way this had been faked and wondering why it seemed so real!

Before they could say anything further Bill Brightwell appeared. Donna straightened up immediately and walked to the window. She did not like Brightwell overmuch

Brightwell examined the photos with Geoff Formby and was told briefly that the female was a spirit.

"Ghost!" Donna corrected, with her back turned.

"Oh," said Geoff, feeling rebuked, "sorry"

Donna turned around to see the look of slight derision on Brightwell's face..he was intensely stupid unless money and figures were concerned, in her opinion at least.

"Its a fake of course?" Brightwell said. "That's what we're paying this guy for, is it?..to rake up the interest on the pretense of supernatural forces around the sites etc!.."

Donna composed herself before speaking. "It most certainly is not..on both accounts, Bill!"

"You don't mean these are genuine?"

"I suppose given my former statement that must be what I mean.."

Geoff darted her a warning look: he did not see the need to annoy people unnecessarily. Whereas Donna saw no need to placate them unnecessarily.

"They are very good.." Brightwell said cautiously, intimating that their fakery was unimportant.

"They're brilliant!" Donna asserted. "One could not hope for a better result . . ."

"I think they may be subjected to rigorous scrutiny and the debunkers will move in.."

"They can scrutinise all they like," Donna said, "there is nothing to hide..and therefore nothing for them to find . . . beyond what they see!.."

"Do the owners of the castle know about all this?" Geoff asked.

"No.." she was blasé,` "I don't even know who the owners are! . . . Its not one of the famous places . . . its only eeking out a living by the skin of its teeth!"

"Then why the interest?" Brightwell said.

"Why not!. . . ." Donna cast disparaging eyes on Brightwell whose attention was elsewhere. "The countryside round about is our territory and tourists flock there!. . . . Local businesses will benefit..sponsors will be among them..who cares who the owners are!"

"Possibly the owners!" said Brightwell scathingly. He envisaged litigation scenarios here, if someone wasn't diligent.

The conversation continued well into the morning, with Geoff Formby squashing his complete schedule for the day in favour of plans for the correct engineering of this latest castle investigation.

*   *   *

Marjorie entered the phone box with trepidation, the haunted but slightly gormless look of the
guilty written on her features. The phone booth was
just within the small parade of shops built to the rear
of the local village. The parade of shops boasted a
contemporary design and a twenty first century aspi-
ration but earned the reputation of being dog-in-
the-manger alongside the old and staid village habi-
tation.

The phone box smelt and Marjorie wafted her
hand in front of her nose, pulling an aggrieved face
as she lifted the receiver and read the instructions—
it had been a long while since she had used public
phone boxes.

Someone had written 'cock-sucker' on the little
mirror above the phone apparatus and Marjorie was
somewhat offended and alarmed by this. She paused
to read other similar debauched comment, scribbled
and printed in various places around the booth, and
it became, after a moment or two, quite soothing to
her nerves. Enough so to allow her to attempt the
actual process of making the call.

A mere two chirrups of the ringing tone and
Elaine answered her phone. Marjorie placed the
Kleenex tissue across the mouthpiece of the receiver,
the way people in films did it, and consequently there
was a few seconds pause.

"Hello. . . . hello.." said Elaine rather frantically.

"Hello there!" Marjorie's voice had assumed the
deep tones of masculinity, or as near as she could
manage.

Elaine was intrigued, wary, disbelieving . . . holding her mug of tea in one hand and blinking rapidly. "Yes..what is it..who is it?"

"A well-wisher!" said Marjorie in the exaggerated and deep drawl.

Elaine froze momentarily to analyse the semantic meaning of well-wisher; it was not a phrase one heard very much outside of literature. "What do you want?"

"You should know something.."

"What?.."

"Gerald is deceiving you!"

For a moment there was nothing at Elaine's end and Marjorie felt utterly stupid; suspended in that non-responsive void where her own daring and silliness became glaringly obvious to her. Then Elaine suddenly demanded: "Who is this?".

"Never mind!" said Marjorie, "just ask him about Donna!"

She rammed down the phone receiver and fled the box, as if the whole world knew what she had done.

*   *   *

Bill Brightwell, Geoff Formby and Donna Lees had retired to the Shepherd's Rest a little way out of the town to discuss the matter of the castle ghost over an extended pub lunch.

"I think maybe in the long run the only way is to buy the castle.."

"Buy the castle!.." Brightwell looked at Formby over his beer. "Buy the castle! . . . have you any idea how much castles cost?"

"No, but run down castles like that can't be much.."

"Don't talk bloody stupid." said Brightwell and huffed into his glass. "Run down castles like that!. . . . it's a ruin..it's supposed to be run down!"

Geoff Formby looked at Donna who winked at him quickly and smiled. She turned to Brightwell with more amicability than earlier in the day. "What you have to remember, Bill, is its inherent value long term!. . . . tourists will come in droves if I publicise this now."

"Nine day wonder, surely!" said Brightwell, not about to be won over.

"Not necessarily. . . . look at Loch Ness.." Formby pointed out.

"Loch Ness . . . Loch Ness is a lake not a castle!"

"He means the legend..the creature!" said Donna

Brightwell sighed with forebearance, they had been discussing this bloody castle now for three hours.

"One blasted ghost does not make a legend..it makes for a bit of interest . . ."

"But there may be others.." Donna said

"What? at the same castle?. . . . how do you know?"

"Gerald has seen them!"

Brightwell looked over at Formby who offered: "Gerald the photographer!"

"Donna, how many of the houses have you done write-ups for and how many have legendary ghosts?..and how many of the buggers ever put in an appearance for the onlooker?"

"This is different.." Donna was dismissive, as if having to talk about it were not the right way ahead but something she subscribed to as a gesture of good-will. "I have never seen the ghosts before!"

"So! . . . just because you see them doesn't mean everyone else will!"

"No, not everyone..but it means that at least this

one is here to see! . . . if I can see them, others with the ability will see them!"

Brightwell again looked at Formby; he was out of his depth and the subject was not one he knew how to handle.

"She's right!" Formby said, "Look at Priory Hill! . . . Reckton Abbey! . . . Fillers End!..Raynham Hall! . . . Research all that stuff and look at the profits on them! . . . If you're talking small ventures they need to be consistent and steady. . . . nothing is ever lost by cashing in on the availability of what is found in there!"

"Yes..I know..but what about the owners?"

"Leave the owners to me!" said Donna, as if this had been obvious all along.

"I still say we should put in an offer for the site!" Formby contemplated a small cigar, unlit in his hand for the past fifteen minutes.

"Oh, for Christ's Sake.." Brightwell summoned the waitress for the bill. "We could end up with a can of sardines."

"Yes, of course we could . . ." Donna watched both men in turn and smiled. "There's no need to go to those lengths yet . . . I can walk in and out of the place at will!"

"But you can't charge an entrance fee can you?" Brightwell intoned.

"No, but I can employ other means of production!" said Donna and lifted her bag and thought it a good time to go to the loo in order to break the flow.

She had other irons in the fire, stewing nicely. If these came to fruition she could leave Heritage Matters out of the deal entirely.

*   *   *

Elaine sat on her second best sofa in the dining room annex and studied the floor, tracing the pattern of the carpet with her gaze. It was hypnotic. Several dozen times she had followed the pattern of tiny rosebuds to their obvious starting point in the circular design of rosebuds nearest her vision, faded now from many years wear to a shade far from that of their former glory.

The news from the 'well-wisher' regarding Gerald's infidelity had rooted her to the spot. Not that it was such a surprise. She had known for a while that something was going on. The shock value lay in the fact that others knew too, and the possible identity of the so-called well-wisher had almost taken precedence over the fact of his faithlessness.

It was too sinister for words. To have someone prying into your inner-most secret and then keeping their identity from you. She wracked her brains to consider who it might be. There was no-one she knew of. It must be on Gerald's side. But she was sure Gerald had told no-one. Beyond Marjorie!

Not that he had actually told Marjorie directly, he had more confessed to it when Marjorie accused him of it, all those years ago . . .

Interspersed with her cogitations over who the caller could have been came the vague memories of the events of those times. Her friendship with Marjorie which had led to her meeting with Gerald, Marjorie's horror at discovering their attraction for each other all those years later. The scenes and the recriminations, the threats and the shame. The tears she had shed. The pleading Gerald had done for her to leave Graham. The fear she had felt at having to do so, the ambivalence of mind . . . the anti-climax that had settled upon them when no action was taken, and the obvious affair which had ensued as a result . . .

She had tried to reach Gerald but his mobile was off. She dared not ring him at the house now. She only ever rung there in emergencies. Usually, he was the one to ring her. He was the one with the power. But that was the way she liked it. She did not want the power, it was too much responsibility. Had she taken the power she may have to alter her life and make decisions, and she did not want to do that. She wanted things to happen of their own accord, as if fate, or some higher deity, had taken charge. But of course nothing happened like that in real life. It happened only because people made it happen. You were given so many chances and you had to seize them or see them go to waste. Between a man and a woman, Elaine knew, there was a time and a tide. And if you missed the tide you missed the time, and you had to wait for the tide to come again, and often it did not. Like at Southport Beach where the sea never came in.

Elaine was caught in the middle of a web of events, past and present, to which there was no sensible conclusions and the clock ticked on, until it was seven in the evening and Graham arrived home.

He looked at her dolefully. Graham was doleful at the best of times. Seldom smiling, he graced every occasion with his cynical, stolid presence and seemed as if the world held no surprises for him—no joys either—but certainly no surprises.

"Any dinner?" he enquired, removing his tie as always as he picked up the mail from the hall table.

"No.." Elaine hesitated and thought of an excuse,

"I've been out." she said lamely, it was the best she could come up with in her current state of mind.

Graham tutted and thumped upstairs.

If she drove over to Gerald's now she could possibly attract his attention by parking and entering the farmland at the back of the house and creeping up to the back fence and hoping to see him in the window of his studio. She could wave and jump up and down and make herself conspicuous. Of course Marjorie might see her first. But then again, so what?

Except that a confrontation with Marjorie was the last thing she wanted. If it went wrong, as it invariably would, she would feel worse and be devastated for two whole days until she saw Gerald again.

In her heart of hearts she did not want this situation to go on the way it was. She wanted it to change. Maybe this was the start. Maybe the 'well-wisher' was sent from God, as a blessing in disguise.

Graham came down the stairs and into the dining room annex. He looked at her with his mournful gaze and allowed moments to elapse unremarked.

"What are you sitting there like that for?" he said eventually.

Elaine sighed.

"What's up?. . . . have the goldfish died or something?"

Graham's disparagement of Elaine's gardening enthusiasm was a familiar weapon. If things went well in her garden he always found fault, and if things went badly he blamed her and belittled her.

"No..they're fine!"

"What then?"

Elaine rose, like someone waking from the dead. "I'll get a pizza out of the freezer!" She went into the kitchen and stood in front of the fridge, unable to proceed.

If the well-wisher had informed her, he may well have informed Marjorie too. Perhaps it was someone about to blackmail Gerald.

"What the hell's up with you?" Graham appeared behind her and caused her to start. She put a hand to her heart to steady herself and he sneered slightly.

It was at times like this when you realised how far apart you were from someone you were supposed to be married to. It was at times like this when you realised what an idiotic mess you had made, and what a coward you were. No, worse..a hypocrite!

"I'm a little under the weather.." she said, sadly.

Graham stepped in front of her, causing her to step back—the gesture was not so much hostile as rude. "You're always under the weather, Elaine!"

"Yes.." agreed Elaine dully, in that voice which made men like Graham want to hit women like Elaine.

*   *   *

"You see, we're onto something so good here.." Donna put her legs under her on the chaise-long in her lounge and leaned forward slightly towards Gerald in the chair opposite. "You do see that?"

Gerald did not immediately respond. She was moving too quickly for him.

"If we play our cards right we can set up photographic sessions for lots of amateur photographers and ghost-hunters and all of that.." she gripped his left knee and squoze it firmly, massaging the inner-leg with her thumb.

Gerald swiveled his eyes and studied her darkly. "They're not necessarily the same thing . . . photog-

raphers and ghost-hunters.." he tried his best to ignore the physical sensations she was causing, and the
temptations these gave rise to.

"I know that . . . but it doesn't matter..in the end
all ghost-hunters have to use cameras don't they!"

"No . . . only if they want to carry the proof over
to others.."

"And we do!"

"Do we?. . . ."

"Of course! . . . how else are we going to make
this pay?" Her hand had now risen and her fingers
were deftly manipulating a sensitive spot on his thigh.

"Making it pay isn't the prime function here . . ."

"Oh isn't it?..it certainly is mine!" said Donna,
coldly, and let her hand fall away from his body, leaving a bereft and deserted feeling somewhere in his
being. He then rose, rather tentatively; an argument
was brewing if he didn't make an exit.

Donna caught his arm. "Listen..don't rush off like
that. . . . you know what I mean!"

"Frankly, I don't, Donna.."

Donna herself rose and went for the wine bottle
to re-fill the glasses.

"None for me..I'm driving!"

His whole manner had begun to sound rather
pompous, and she detected it, like the hint of breath
odour, and in the same way it repelled her slightly. But
he sat beside her and placed a hand on her arm,
innocently, in what he hoped was a one-person-to-
another manner.

"Thought you were leaving!" she sounded playful, but he knew she wasn't.

"I am..but I don't want us to fight."

"Neither do I . . . but don't slag me off just for
doing my job!"

"I know!..I'm sorry!"

"Gerry..if no-one ever considered money and profit, very few good things would ever see the light of day.." her manner had that brittle edge, curbing her annoyance and holding onto it so as not to let rip.

"A capitalist at heart, eh!" said Gerald weakly.

"No..an economist." replied Donna with marked tolerance.

Gerald really was a bit pedantic, and rather dull of himself, but she did not want to lose him either.

"What I saw the other day was wonderful..but I have to keep my feet on the ground ..and I have to make it pay, or leave it alone."

"Talking of payments, you haven't given me a price for those shots in the castle yet!" His voice had a weedling and rather high pitched note and Donna was irritated but saw that he was now manageable again.

"Haven't I! ..what an oversight.." she disengaged herself from his clutches and moved to the small bureau; a priceless item of furniture like all the rest in her apartment. After a lot of rummaging and fiddling she wrote out a cheque and came back to him and handed it over.

Gerald looked at it and then looked again. "This is surely too much?"

They looked at one aother.

"Oh, I see!. . . . its a bribe!..its peace money.."

"Maybe something like that.." she flopped down into the nearby chair, "but don't go on about it! . . . More to the point, we have to go back out to the castle this week and do more work!"

Gerald nodded, his mind on the fee. "Are you sure your magazine can afford it!"

"Gerry.." her voice was more than a little weary, "I am not in the habit of getting the magazine into debt!"

It was only on the drive back home that he realised what an evasive answer that had been. The magazine had little to do with Donna's off-shoot schemes, and he saw that nobody had any control over what Donna was planning or doing within Heritage Matters or outside it.

*   *   *

On arriving home, he parked the car in the side drive and made his way to the kitchen door. His mind was full of misgivings about Donna, and the state of his financial affairs, but from the side of his eye he thought he saw a tall hollyhock move a full three yards to the left of his vision and some fifty yards down near the fence. Most probably he was tired and hungry and weaker than he thought.

As he approached the conservatory door—which always stood open at this time of night in the summer—the hollyhock rendered him a smarting blow to the back of his head, and he fell to his knees on the lawn, more from shock than harm.

He looked around to see the hollyhock on the ground to his left, its long stem trailing a human being, swathed in a cotton coat with a hood.

Squinting into the darkness, his closer inspection seemed to reveal the human as Elaine.

CHAPTER FOUR

GETTING ELAINE BACK in the car without Marjorie seeing was fair nigh impossible. For one thing, Elaine was babbling in a high pitched voice which carried like grand opera in the stillness of the night. And for another, Marjorie was entertaining several of her cronies in the kitchen overlooking the driveway. Why she had to entertain in the kitchen God only knew!

As Gerald ushered Elaine into the passenger seat of his car, one of the cronies rose at the kitchen table, a glass of wine in hand, and immediately spotted them. She froze for a second and studied their antics.

Gerald now expected Marjorie to come rushing out and assail them both with some deadly weapon in the way of kitchen equipment, but nothing of the sort happened. Whether the crony had thought she had imagined it, or was even now advising everyone, was a mystery which formed a tension of such proportions that he felt he may as well plunge his car into the Leeds to Liverpool Canal while he and Elaine were in it together.

"How did you get here?" He backed the car out onto the avenue.

"In a taxi.." her teeth were chattering; although it was a summer evening the long wait for him combined with the misery and the lonely vigil in the darkness at the bottom of his garden had made her cold and fraught. *"Where were you..I thought you were never coming.."* she began quietly crying "I thought you'd gone for good!"

"Don't be silly.." It was the best he could do in the way of comfort since his hands were employed on the steering wheel. "Where would I have gone?"

"I don't know..but you might have decided to make a fresh start and just disappear..after all if someone's blackmailing you.."

"Elaine . . . why would anyone blackmail me?"

"I don't know . . . but you don't get well-wishers calling up from the goodness of their hearts!" she dissolved into a frenzied bout of weeping, interspersed by comments on the direness of her life. So he tuned out whilst he thought of what best to do.

He would take her to an hotel an hours drive away!

Five minutes down the motorway he felt he had some semblance of calm and his concentration was not doing badly considering events.

"What's all this about a well-wisher?" he made the enquiry gently, and it was apparent that he'd not listened to any of her anxieties.

"He said you were deceiving me..and to ask you about Donna!"

Gerald was devastated. He dropped a good ten miles from his speed and tailed into the slow lane and stared at her. She was wretched now, pulling and tugging at a tissue and looking mournfully at her hands. Of course she had had hours to absorb the shock.

"Who was he?"

"Gerald, I don't know!. . . . do you think I'd not tell you if I did!. . . . he wouldn't say..he just said he was a well-wisher!"

"A well-wisher!"

"Yes!"

"A nutter probably"

"Who's Donna?"

"I dunno!"

Elaine undid her seat-belt and turned her body and stared at him long and hard.

He waited . . . in the way he was waiting for Marjorie to circle overhead in a helicopter with a long-range rifle and blow his head off; he had left the realm of everyday mundane effect now and had entered the surreal where you could expect anything and it was better if you did.

"He was telling the truth, wasn't he?" Elaine fell silent.

He left the silence to hang there, it was not his to control

"Well? Wasn't he?"

"About what?"

"About this Donna!"

"About Donna maybe..but not about me deceiving you!"

"But if there is a Donna..you must be deceiving me!.you must be seeing her.."

"Yes but for purposes of business.."

"Business?"

"Yes . . . professional stuff!"

"You mean..you mean she's a client or something?"

"Yes..that's exactly what I mean.."

"You mean, she pays you to do work?".

"Yes. . . . handsomely actually!" His voice rose on
this point of truth and seered through the atmospheric gloom like a cheerful firework.

Elaine sniffled and wiped her nose and perked
up a fraction, suspended between the need to clutch
at any old straw and the need to delve deeper.

"Well, why would he say you were deceiving
me?.."

"I dunno!"

"He must know a lot about you.."

"Why must he?"

"To have my phone number!"

Gerald said absolutely nothing as Elaine stared at
him. There was nothing to say. Whatever he said now
would be grist to the mill. He was not one for thinking on his feet at the best of times. Behind the wheel
of a car was even harder.

"Perhaps this Donna gave him my phone number.." said Elaine after several more miles.

"Where would she get it from?" he frowned at
the empty stretch of motorway, feeling himself to be
less a culprit and more a hapless co-victim.

"Perhaps she went through your wallet!"

"What for?"

"I don't know . . . maybe she's trying to blackmail
you!"

"I don't carry your number in my wallet..I carry it
in my head. . . ."

He turned into a motel car-park, the sort of soul-
less motel owned by a consortium. He wanted only

to sleep, but he suspected that a long night lay ahead of him.

*   *   *

Christine Walters sat down again at Marjorie's kitchen table and looked perplexed. Fortunately no-one noticed, they were busily laughing at the colourful topic of Wendy Grantham's husband's attempt to use a condom for the first time in their married life.

Christine Walters decided to say nothing of what she had just seen. Marjorie's obsession with Gerald's other life was already too morbid and did not need fuelling. It was obvious to Christine that the female form he had been bundling out of sight had been waiting for him, for reasons one could only speculate about. That Gerald was a tormented soul, married to Marjorie, was not in dispute. On the other hand, why he did not do something positive to terminate the marriage was very much in dispute, the talk of local dinner parties!

Christine Walters personally found gossiping and mud-raking very disturbing She was not malicious, nor was she a sensationalist. She was a discreet and sensible woman. If it was ever necessary, she could describe what she had just seen to any designated person perfectly adequately for her own conscience.

She turned back to the comic discourse on Wendy's husband, who worked with her own husband in their recently launched pet-food delivery service, which was doing very nicely thank you but taking up more hours than any mortal should have to work. No wonder he couldn't manage condoms with any success! Being probably too tired to see straight half the time!

*   *   *

Donna awoke knowing what she was going to do. She gave it a cursory review whilst in the shower and driving to work, and then walked into Geoff Formby's office. She was late so he was already esconced and pouring over drafts of the latest publication on disused churches.

"Sit down.." he indicated nonchalantly, her rather determined attitude not escaping him.

"Listen, Geoff. . . . forget all we said yesterday about the castle . . . I'm doing it on my own."

Geoff raised his eyes. "What?..buying the castle?"

"No..of course not buying the castle!..The ghost thing!. . . . I'll manage it..as a separate issue to the company!"

Geoff threw himself back in the chair and slung the pencil over the desk. He gazed at her with his red-rimmed eyes which were indeterminate in colour..not eyes to inspire love in another person, thought Donna gazing back, but perhaps pity or concern.

"I have to say, that's not very ethical, Donna..!"

"Why not? . . . the company have not bought me body and soul!"

"It was company resource you used to research the place..fund the photos. . . . company time!"

"Yes, but its out of the usual scope of the company . . . let's face it . . . its not run-o-the-mill stuff!"

"Beside the point!"

"Yes, but Geoff, we spent all yesterday trying to reach the point!"

"Precisely!"

"And we could not . . . not one on which we could agree. . . . I have seen a way to proceed here..and I don't think you should begrudge me that!"

"Well, maybe I don't . . . personally . . ." Geoff subsided into the chair again, like a dead weight, "but the others might!"

"The others can screw themselves!" said Donna and rose and smiled at him, a friendly and sincere smile, before leaving the office.

*   *   *

Gerald was busy persuading Elaine to leave the sterile comfort of their motel room.

"Listen. . . . you have to go back!"

"Why do I have to?" Elaine's face was mulish, staring at the ceiling, flat on her back and neatly composed, like a tidy talking corpse.

"Because its not sensible to leave everything you own now.."

"Not sensible!. . . . inconvenient to you, you mean!"

"To everybody!"

"Everybody! what do I care about everybody?"

Not unnaturally, they had been talking for most of the night. He was exhausted, although Elaine looked as if she possessed the same amount of energy this morning as she had in the garden last night swinging the hollyhock.

"I cannot abide to live with Graham now..not after that awful phone call.."

Gerald cast about in his mind for some way of understanding. He did not see that the disturbing phone call made any difference to Elaine's home-life. He decided it was a female thing, which only a female might understand.

"Do you think you could try and see the phone call as a separate issue?"

"To what?"

"To your stuff with Graham.."

"What if they call again?"

"Threaten them with the police!"

Elaine tried to imagine herself doing this, but then she was honest enough to see that she would be too interested in what they had to say.

"Because it is an offense, to go around making calls of that nature!" he added.

Elaine thought that Gerald was rather naive. Rather trite in many ways. "I don't know how you can say things like that!"

"Like what?"

"In that banal way . . . as if we were talking about unwanted double glazing sales-people or something!"

"How do you want me to talk about it? . . . I wasn't there was I!"

Elaine was prompted to raise herself on one elbow. "What difference does that make?..you sound as if you don't believe me!"

"Of course I believe you.."

"Well, it doesn't sound as if you do.."

"Elaine, I believe you..why wouldn't I believe you?"

"You may think I'm just saying it to get you to leave Marjorie!"

He turned his head sharply to watch her. Their gaze locked for several seconds. Moments of truth, as noisy as the aftermath of a clanging bell.

"I didn't say it for that.."

"Of course you didn't.."

There it was again—that trite, patronising inflection. He was not totally convinced by her.

A trolley full of linen trundled by outside the window, obscured from ground-floor observation by blinds. It was being pushed by someone with a heavy tread, moving at a snail's pace.

Elaine's eyes were challenging. Gerald stroked his beard lovingly and considered things, not daring to take his gaze away from her confrontational stare. . . . perhaps she had made it up! He knew of no man who would know anything about his business, he was not a mans' man. He did not associate with men unless professionally, he certainly did not confide in any. Why would any man ring up Elaine with this information. But then again, how else would she get the name of Donna?

He decided that Donna must be behind all this in some way. She was the only person who knew of the affair with Elaine—he had told her, one night in a passionate fit of soul bearing, inspired by her worldly understanding and his need to appear worldly himself.

Donna was the only person, besides Marjorie . . . *MARJORIE!!*

His eye contact with Elaine faltered under the realisations and possibilities inherent in this new thought, and he spontaneously followed a visual route around the small uniform room which tailed his random suspicions.

"What?" said Elaine, perceptively. "What have you thought about?"

"It was Marjorie.." he said slowly and watched Elaine's trusting face going through a gamet of reactions, "it must have been!"

"Of course it wasn't!!..it was a man!"

"It was Marjorie imitating a man!"

"Of course it wasn't!. . . . Gerry, will you be sensible!"

She flopped back onto the pillows and into the corpse like posture again. She did not want it to be Marjorie. She found it too intimidating. . . . or too deflating. She wanted it to be a mystery which gave them impetus to move their lives. Because when things go stale it is only fresh and unknown energy which opens up the access to change.

Gerald harboured these thoughts without divulging them. "You must go home, darling!..where else are you to go?"

"I'm not moving.." she said, more mulishly than ever, her mouth pushed forward into a stubborn pout. "You go if you wish!..I'm staying here. . . . until I've decided on a plan of action!"

"What sort of action?" Gerald rose and stretched, he was as stiff as a board and as tired as hell.

He had still to develop some film and get them in the post and then meet Donna at the castle.

"Away from Graham . . . I keep telling you!"

"I don't see how the call from Marjorie changes things with Graham..how does it alter anything?"

"You either understand or you don't.." Elaine's calmness bestowed displeasure.

Gerald sighed—it was too ridiculous for words, but he had no way of explaining or contradicting, he lacked the necessary insight to see where she came from on the issue.

"I'll pay for another day then." he agreed wearily, "but you'll get bored lying here by yourself."

"I shan't ..I've too much to think about!"

"I'll come back this evening then, shall I?" Gerald said.

He felt the situation was unreal, he was still in that realm where the reality of everyday life had disappeared.

Elaine raised herself to look at him, her eyes wild and scared. "I should hope you will?"

"Of course I will!"

Out at Reception he told them that she was staying because she was working on an important project for her firm. The man at the desk looked a little disbelieving; he felt that this was not the truth at all, but then he was used to all kinds of stories from all kinds of people, and at the end of the day it was really not his business what she did as long as she did not wreck the room.

*   *   *

At nine thirty Elaine's husband rang Marjorie who was just about to start treating Christine Walters.

"Its Graham Ridley" he said, without preamble.

"Oh yes!.." Marjorie's voice was like the inside of the fridge and Graham felt a surge of anger at having been put in this position.

"Is she with him?"

"I beg your pardon!" Marjorie said, unhelpfully. "Is who with who?"

"Elaine! . . . is she with him?.."

"How do I know! . . . they don't keep me abreast of their schedule!"

"Well, where's he now?".

"If you don't mind, I'm with a client!"

"I don't give a fuck if you're with the entire royal family!. . . . Unless I know where she is I'll have to report her as a missing person!"

"I can't help you!" Marjorie felt a great sense of

joy that something was amiss, something she could get her teeth into, but she continued to exude only cold indifference.

"Look..Marjorie.." Graham lowered his voice as two of his colleagues came into the office, "why don't you just throw him out?. . . . that way he'd take her and we'd all get some peace!"

"He doesn't want her!" said Marjorie with relish. "Don't imagine he does . . . he's toying with her.."

"I don't care what he's doing with her! . . . he's doing it!. . . . They're making fools of us!..You may like it but I don't!..I want it sorted!"

"That is not my problem.." Marjorie's voice was losing its cool a little, like a badly fitting dress slipping off the shoulder. "What do you expect me to do about it?"

"You know very well what goes on . . . you should confront him on it . . ."

"I don't care to discuss my marital situation with you, Graham!"

"I don't know why the fuck not Marjorie, you discuss it with half the village. . . ."

"That is not true.."

"Of course its true! . . . I'm constantly over your neck of the woods . . . its the talk of two pubs to my certain knowledge! . . . Now just tell him to take her off my hands or leave her alone completely.."

"*He's not taking her anywhere..*" Marjorie's reply was strident—the dress had not just slipped at the shoulder it had fallen down around her waist. "*He can't bloody well afford it . . . so you can get that idea out of your mind straight away!. . . . wherever they are they'll be back..you can put your money on it. . . . now can you leave me to get on with my daily business and don't come onto my phone again abusing me and using bad language..*"

"You stupid fat cow!" Graham raised his eyes to note that several people in the office were observing him closely.

* * *

Marjorie rushed back to Christine Walters and resumed her position on the low seat at the foot of the client chair. "That was him . . . the husband!"

"Husband of the existing one or the new one?" Christine thought it apt to play with words a little to dilute the intensity.

"The existing one!" Marjorie's face had about it the enthralled expression of someone who has just received riveting news. "Of course he's gone off with her . . . and he's been gone all night..but I wasn't telling *him* that.."

"Perhaps its time you did something about all this.." said Christine idly.

"Like what?" enquired Marjorie, a barbed quality entering into her tone.

"Well. . . . whatever it is that couples do when they're not getting on!"

Both women were aware that this last was an understatement, and that in being so the subject was more a topic of embarrassment than the drama Marjorie tried to make of it. However, Christine's overriding concern was that Marjorie's hand was shaking as she treated her foot and the tender flesh surrounding her varuka.

"I am doing nothing!" said Marjorie in quiet, firm voice. "I am not playing into their hands!. . . . After all.." she raised her head from the varuka and noted Christine's pained expression—as if she thought Marjorie capable of amputating her toe by accident, "its not me who is dissatisfied is it!. . . . I am not having an affair!"

"Perhaps you should.." said Christine, pretending not to feel stressed. "What's sauce for the goose.."

Marjorie made noises of disdain and threw her ample weight around on the seat. "Do you think I want another man on my hands . . . an affair is the last thing I want!"

'And probably the last thing you'll get' thought Christine uncharitably.

Her hand was steadier now on Christine's foot and Christine breathed more freely. She thought of Gerald in the garden the night before and the woman he had been hustling down the drive, either against her will or because she needed support.

Marjorie said suddenly. "You know she used to be my best friend don't you?"

They looked at each other.

Christine enquired: "Who?..the existing one?"

"Yes!"

"No..I knew only that you were acquainted with her.."

"We were closer than that. . . ." Marjorie seemed completely restored to normality now and worked deftly on the veruka, almost as if she were creating a tapestry or a piece of sculpture. "Can you imagine that!. . . . I don't know which one of them I felt most betrayed by!"

"I can imagine!. . . . I can imagine it was awful.." said Christine with plain compassion.

"It rocks your trust..that sort of thing!"

"Yes, its bound to, Marjorie.."

"It makes you so you don't want to take any more risks!"

"Yes.." Christine paused, "but life is one long risk..overall!"

"Perhaps..but they don't have to be emotional ones unless you choose them to be!" said Marjorie, philosophically, and wiped Christine's foot with a disinfected pad.

"I'm not sure. . . ." Christine placed her foot back in her shoe, "I think most things become emotional somewhere along the line!"

Marjorie removed her latex gloves and picked up her diary. "Next week should be the last one you need. . . . then I'll see it again in six weeks to check it!"

"Thank you, Marjore!" Christine handed Marjorie a pre-written cheque.

On her way out she paused and said: "You're not worried then? . . . about Gerald going missing?"

Marjorie looked up sharply from her instrument tray. "Missing!..he's not missing. . . . he's with that slut . . ."

"Well..you will let me know if he doesn't turn up won't you?"

A surprised expression appeared on Marjorie's face, followed by amusement—she walked to the door with Christine. "I didn't think you were that concerned, Chris.."

"We are friends, Marjorie..why wouldn't I be?"

"I thought for a moment there you were on his list of candidates!"

Marjorie's laughter was hearty, as usual, and seemed to follow Christine down the path to her parked car.

*   *   *

Gerald hastened trudgingly towards the castle entrance and joined Donna in the gloomy, rain-laden afternoon. A wind was blowing, heightened by the exposed hillside position of the site.

"You look, not to put to finer a point on it, just terrible!" she said and scrutinised him closely. "As if you've been pulled through a hedge backwards and been awake for several days without sleep.."

"I feel it!" he concurred and led her through the opening to the inner site. "I had to deal with one of Elaine's problems.."

He was about to divulge more—he felt the need to off-load, but then he remembered he could not trust Donna. She might, after all, be behind the well-wisher call, although he couldn't for the life of him see how or why! Still he was guarded.

"She strikes me as being one of those feeble sort of women.." Donna said as he unpacked his camera.

"You've never met her," he replied defensively, "how would you know?"

"For heavens sake, Gerry. . . . I don't need to meet her . . . I can tell from the bit you've told me! . . . women always know these things about each other!"

"Do they!" said Gerry with suspicion.

The afternoon unfolded into sheeting rain. But then several sight-seers arrived. They walked politely around the periphery of where he was photographing, tentatively asking innocent questions and trying to see what it was he found so interesting as a photographer, and obviously a professional.

Heartened by their general attitude to his presence, Donna attempted an experiment.

She turned to a couple of Australian women and

announced: "There's a ghost in this place!..did you know that?"

The women were immediately enthralled. They moved closer to the camera as if the ghost were somehow attached to it by invisible threads.

"Yes . . . we saw it the other day and took several reels of film . . . didn't we, Gerry?"

Gerald was reluctant to join in this floor-show and murmured assent whilst ignoring them in favour of his view finder.

"Is that what he's doing now? . . . looking for the ghost?" asked the youngest of the women.

"Yes . . . in a way!"

Gerald had his camera on a tripod. They moved to stand near him to see if he would reveal more information.

"Could we have a look?" said the elder, expectantly.

"There's nothing to see." said Gerald, thinly concealing irritation. He glared at Donna, who gazed back at him with raised brows and a smug expression.

"Let them have a look, Gerry..don't be mean!"

The two women took it in turns to see through the camera which was carrying a panoramic lens attachment. The surrounding hillside seemed shrouded in mist and eerie and about to render apparitions and ghoulish things at any moment. They made sounds of interest and murmurings of satisfaction as if they had seen an army of ghosts.

Gerald was now greatly disconcerted. That Donna had encouraged these people to expect the unexpected and to enter into some fantasy whereby ghosts might appear on demand offended his sense of moral rightness in ways he could barely express. He made futile gestures at her to discourage other comments she was making to other people coming into the chamber.

Soon there was a little gaggle of folk all with inside information about what was going on.

Quite obviously, they were fascinated. One man laughed skeptically while his wife regaled them with the occasions on which she had seen ghosts herself and how psychic activity ran in her family. Donna was pretending to be impressed. The chattering and animated noise resembled a zoo or a garden party. The castle had seldom seen such vivacity since the sixteenth century.

"We are having an open day here on Saturday!" said Donna to the general crowd. "If any of you would care to come.."

Gerald stepped back from his camera in shock. "What!"

Donna ignored him

"We are part of 'Heritage Matters' . . . you've probably heard of us! . . . and we are promoting legends and myths and heightened awareness to these things as a general educational feature this year!. . . . We run small seminars aimed at giving people the experience of sampling the atmosphere around ghosts and psychic phenomena . . . not that we promise you'll see anything, but you can try.."

There was a heartening response and people began enquiring how much it was, and whether they could bring friends.

Donna produced a notepad and stepped to the font-like structure in the middle of the chamber. "Leave me your phone numbers..and I'll contact you in the next forty eight hours and give you exact information . . . I have not finalised details yet.."

There was a clamour to write in her pad, and she stepped back and produced some more biros and pencils from her large Gucci bag.

Some of the crowd dispersed and went on their way so that a gathering of perhaps five or so were left to wait their turn to enlist for Saturday.

Gerald pulled her to one side and stared at her. "What are you doing?"

"Weren't you listening?" she replied hotly. "Its obvious what I'm doing!..I'm running a pilot to see what's what and how it goes!"

"Oh, are you! . . . and how are you going to do it?"

"You'll see..later when we go through it with a fine tooth-comb!"

"I don't remember being consulted" Gerald said, angrily.

Donna disengaged her arm from his clutches and made to join her audience. He held onto the sleeve of her silk jacket. "I am here too, you know!"

"I know!"

"Then maybe you could do me the goodness of asking me before you launch into these things.."

She sighed and snatched her sleeve away. "Grow up, Gerry!" she said, flatly, and moved into the little throng.

Gerald turned to see a man approaching from the staircase. A wizened little man of about sixty five, ill-shaven and wearing a ludicrous woollen hat which took no discernable shape but covered his curly gray hair, all except the sides, where tufts of it escaped around his ears and face and gave him the appearance of one of Santa's elves.

He strode across to Gerald and indicated his camera. "What do you think you're doing!" His speech revealed his yellowing and decayed teeth and turned his mouth into the shape of a snarling bull-mastiff.

Gerald stepped away from him, automatically, as to a repellent horror. "Ask her!" He pointed to Donna who at that moment turned and saw the man.

She approached, smiling, and extending her hand—she was quick to spot human reaction a mile off and instinctively knew him to be attached to the castle authority in some way.

"Donna Lees," she said sweetly, "and who might you be?"

The man ignored her and looked at her hand as if never having seen one before.

"What are you up to?" he asked, turning his head to one side and assessing her from one eye.

"I need to talk to you about hiring your site for the day," she said, "presuming it is yours to hire.."

"None of your business!" said the elf.

"Then why are you making my business your business!" said Donna, still smiling charmingly. "I simply need to talk to someone in authority.."

The elf looked at Gerald, as if Gerald should be held personally responsible for everything but could not be trusted with the role. He weighed Gerald up and down and eyed his camera, which was impressive and expensive. Then he switched to Donna, eyeing now her costly clothes.

"Come over here then.." he inclined his head towards the back of the chamber. "I expect I can come to some arrangement if you make it worth my while!"

"I feel certain you can!" said Donna facetiously, smiling ingratiatingly at him, as if to some icon of masculine beauty.

Gerald gritted his teeth. He regretted ever having associated himself with Donna Lees, but it seemed there was no way out. His photographs would appear in the magazine in three weeks and his name of course would be with them. He could not disclaim at this point. She had him exactly where she wanted him.

Eventually the decrepit custodian left Donna and made his way back towards the stairs, casting a filthy and disparaging look at Gerald as he did so. He was so engrossed in this facial grimacing that he almost collided with the younger Australian woman dashing back up the stairs. He stepped adroitly out of her way but teetered off towards the thick stone wall and slightly lost balance. He cursed under his breathe and waited to see what would happen next.

The girl dashed up to Donna. "I have just seen the ghost!" she said excitedly.

Everyone present turned to look at her. Donna smiled tolerantly, hesitant to believe.

"Yes . . ." she looked around at the interested faces, "a woman in old-fashioned garments with long hair like a girls!"

Donna looked at Gerald with a small suggestion of triumph. Gerald tried to smile politely. He was at the point of physical exhaustion, what with one thing and another.

The custodian lurched forward like an animated puppet, revealing again his dilapidated teeth as he called to Donna: "Here . . . I want a word with you, missy!. . . . If there's many more of these ghosts I want a rake off extra to the agreed fee!"

He had lowered his voice, which involved him leaning in to Donna in a confidential manner that enabled her to detect the contents of his alcoholic lunch and the years of dental neglect. She turned

her face away, diplomatically. "Of course!" she concurred. "But it has to be said that she has just spotted the only ghost seen here by myself or Gerald..so
don't get your hopes up!"

Knowing when he was bested, the little man
backed off.

CHAPTER FIVE

"WHERE'VE YOU BEEN? . . . its nearly eight o'clock!"

Elaine appeared not to have moved since the morning. Except that she wore a towel around her head, turban-style, denoting that she had washed her hair.

"I'm sorry..I got delayed doing shots in a castle.."

"I thought you weren't coming.."

Slow, silent tears were coursing down her cheeks again, and Gerald sat next to her on the bed

"It's alright..I'm here now.."

"I can't go back!" she said between gulps.

He groaned and stretched himself out full length. He was so exhausted he felt he may lose consciousness.

"Well, I don't know where you'll go.." he said, callously.

Elaine said nothing. She did not know where she would go either. There seemed to be no solution.

"I can't go back to him. . . . I just can't!.." She

continued with a diatribe, slow at first and then gathering in speed, a litany to her married hell with Graham. It seemed to continue for hours and Gerald faded in and out of oblivion. "So, I thought I'd go to my sister's.." she at length announced. "It's a bit of a drive..but you'll have to take me!. . . . Gerry, are you listening?" Elaine turned to him and shook him slightly. "I phoned her. . . . she says to arrive anytime before midnight . . . Gerry?"

Gerald turned on his side and began to snore. No amount of prodding him or calling his name or shaking him would arouse him. She fell back angrily onto the bed. She had rested all day and was quite energetic. When she thought about it, he had probably not had much rest at all.

She watched him while he slept, a sleep like someone drugged, and dreaded the thought of not being able to wake him in time to get to Glossop for midnight.

The planning behind her leaving home was little to do with her unbearable life with Graham. She had lied. In reality, it was to do with the fact that she believed if she didn't leave Graham she would lose Gerald to this other woman, this Donna. She did not really believe that Donna was simply a client. It was time that she and Gerald did something with their affair, beyond meet twice a week. Clearly Gerald had too much energy to spare. Although looking at him now you would not have thought so. His mouth open in that goldfish pose adopted by heavy sleepers, prostrate on his back, fully clothed, in need of a shave, he seemed more like someone's grandfather than someone's lover.

Back in the days before she and Gerald had become a habit, in the days when they had looked at each other yearningly across rooms full of friends, she had believed that one day they would be together in a homely and final sense. She knew that it would be some time in the future, in the unforeseeable future. But she knew it would come to pass.

Now she felt that it would never be, in that part of herself where a person's total truth resides, she felt it would never be. Gerald did not feel strongly enough about it, and therefore she herself had lost impetus, ground down by the endless routine of evasion and snatched hours and hopeless hoping.

But Gerald and she were the illusion she needed to keep her going. Everyone needed a dream. It was no longer about sailing off into the sunset with him, it was about simply keeping him from a rival, securing him in the usual routine which had become their lot.

Watching him sleep, she realised how far she had slid in the positivity stakes, subtly passing the demarcation line which marked negativity and not even realising it. How desperate one had to be to go to these lengths. Leaving one's husband and going to one's sister's..not as a prelude to anything else but just as a way of sustaining the little one had.

* * *

Marjorie rushed to the phone, dropping armfuls of bindweed pulled from her shrubbery and moving in through the side door at lightning speed and snatching up the kitchen phone.

It was Graham Ridley again. She held the receiver away from her ear and decided not to speak and only to listen.

"Have you seen him yet?" demanded Ridley, as if they had not had their altercation earlier in the day.

"Yes." said Marjorie, some perverse urge driving her against her own resolve.

"And?"

She did not speak.

"Did he have her with him?"

"Of course not!" she was once more jolted by the stupidity of his question.

"What did he have to say?"

She left an acre of silence into which he was forced to dive.

"Listen . . . if I don't hear from her soon I'm reporting the matter to the police and I'll incriminate him in it so they'll be forced to eliminate him from their enquiries . . . and then you'll be involved!"

"Not necessarily!"

Marjorie saw that this was becoming a game and going off at a tangent. It was out of her control unless she hung up or consented to communicate in a straightforward manner.

"Okay so that's what I'll do then. . . ."

"Please yourself what you do . . . but you'll be wasting everyone's time!"

Ridley hesitated in the act of terminating the call. "Look . . . do you know something or don't you!"

"I know she's been with him!" said Marjorie and her voice drooped at the end of the sentence, betraying the sense of remorse normally hidden behind her bluff exterior.

"How do you know?..did he say she had?"

"He didn't have to . . ."

"Why? . . . could you smell her on him or something?"

The question was meant to be sarcastic, but it held within it the grain of truth which made liars of them both where their bravado was concerned.

"Something like that!" said Marjorie airily. "I'm sorry I can't tell you he was wearing her knickers!"

Ridley groaned, as if this was too disgusting from the mouth of a woman, or the lips of a wife. She had thwarted him. He knew it. His male pride was thinner than her female endurance.

"I'll go then if you don't mind!. . . . I have better things to do than worry about those two!"

Marjorie hung up and smiled at her reflection in the shiny window pane, as if she were not such a failed person after all, as if she could congratulate herself for being up and about and on her way to shower and dress in time for her meeting with her favourite group of people from the local conservationist group.

*   *   *

"Why are you doing this?" Gerald asked Elaine as they drove into the silent country night. "Why are you going to these lengths all of a sudden? . . . has he hit you or something?"

"No.." said Elaine, "I told you all about it but you weren't listening!"

"I was asleep for God's Sake!. . . . Elaine, I've been awake for forty four hours out of forty eight.."

Elaine said nothing and stared from the window at the varying shades of blackness beyond. "We're not going to make it! . . . We won't make Glossop before midnight!"

"So, let's go home then!"

"No!" her voice was strong and abrasive, a tone he seldom heard her use. "I've told you I'm not going back.. and stop trying to talk me into it! . . . I wouldn't do that to you..I would support you in your determination whatever the cost!"

"Elaine, don't shout.." Gerald winced and Elaine thought briefly how he lacked stamina and something else that she couldn't quite name which she would prefer her man to have.

"Just drive to Glossop. . . . I'll sleep in their shed..there's a disused garden swing there and I'll sleep on that till they wake!"

"Garden swing!.." Gerald's voice also became shrill in its disbelief. "You can't sleep on a garden swing, Elaine!"

"It's not exactly a swing in the ordinary sense of the word..it's one of those long canopied seats made for two people . . . its upholstered!" Elaine added, as if this made it deluxe and sought after in the wee small hours of the morning.

Gerald did not argue. He felt now that he had tried his best. He was beginning not to care where she slept or where she went. It was exhaustion, and who could blame him? He would feel differently about most things after a good eight hours sleep. Of course he had to get to her sister's yet without dropping off behind the wheel. He turned the radio up to enliven him and Elaine reached out and switched it down. "For Heaven's Sake! . . . how can we talk with that!"

"I need to concentrate on the driving..I don't have the strength to do both right now!"

Elaine turned the volume up again. "Fine!" she said. "I'll make plans on my own then shall I!"

"Do what you want.." Gerald said under his breath. "I'm past caring!"

*   *   *

Donna rose at dawn that day and drove to the castle to experiment and explore on her own. She was anxious to see what would reveal itself without Gerald present.

She stood in the south side of the ruin where there was precious little wall and the daylight poured in through the gaping apertures. It was still a rather unnerving experience for her, and she shivered a little as she stood, both from a sense of anticipation and a sense of trepidation which made her feel colder than the September morning warranted.

She stared for a long while at the horizon through the largest of the apertures and narrowed her eyes and looked about her every now and then as if expecting to be joined.

An hour passed and nothing happened. She was beginning to feel exhausted. No wonder they kept all night vigils, these psychical research people. But presumably they nodded off now and then to refresh themselves and had somewhere proper to sit.

Sinking onto the dank floor, she folded her coat beneath her and leaned against the chamber wall. She lit a cigarette to cheer herself up and have something to do, but she was not an early day smoker and its biting, acrid taste did not cheer her at all. She should have brought a flask of coffee, instead of which she had brought a tin of coke. She drank from it and it simply made her feel gaseous. No breakfast and little supper the night before told on her constitution. She leaned back and closed her eyes and hummed a little, and drifted into a kind of mindless vacuum that was not sleep but not alertness either.

Some time passed but she had lost track of it.

When she next opened her eyes it was because of a
rustling sound, the kind of rustling that happens
when people drag in foliage or tree branches from a
garden to an enclosure. She could see nothing whatever. . . . perhaps the little elf person had risen early
to do something to the land round about. She leaned
back again and re-accessed her vacuum.

The rustling grew louder, accompanied now by
murmurings. She opened her eyes a second time
and glanced towards the staircase and it was then
that she saw them: a group of about six young girls,
in what looked to be tunics of a greyish and indis-
criminate colour. At first she thought they were visitors, until they walked right by on the other side of
the chamber and ignored her.

She called to them. "Hello there!. . . . what are
you doing out at this time!"

There was no response, they did not even pause
or flicker or look in her direction.

She stood up abruptly and called again.
"Hello . . . look at me please!"

They continued a roundabout walk of the chamber, peering downwards at the floor, some distance
from her position against the wall. She moved towards them and was hit by the icy pocket of air forming a band around their perambulations.

She stepped back immediately, repulsed and
afraid. "Can you see me?" she said feebly.

It was apparent that they could not. She approached a little further and was deterred then by a
strange sensation, like an irradiating force resembling
some kind of ultra sonic frequency.

She flattened herself against the wall again and
waited. . . . They walked, engrossed in their stuff,
oblivious of everything else.

Obviously they were more of Gerald's Light Beings.

For a few seconds Donna had a doubt about her sanity. Her urge was to flee the place, but her ability to do so was not forthcoming. She was quite weak— not with fear, but with the kind of shock which accompanies the arrival of the unexpected coupled with the miraculous. She lit another cigarette and still the circle perambulated and murmured, and then one of them laughed out loud and said something which was not discernable.

She called to them again. "Girls! . . . can you see me at all? . . . are you at all aware of me?"

Nothing happened, they did not in any way show recognition, it was like looking at them on a cinema screen.

Donna had lost count of the time—it felt like an age but it could only have been moments—when a car pulled up below at the keep. A car with an exhaust that needed badly to be repaired. She glanced towards the largest aperture and listened. A door slammed and then all was silent.

When she looked back the circle of girls had gone. They were nowhere to be seen. She called to them again and nothing happened.

She walked slowly to the eastern window and looked down. The elf had arrived and was unlocking his money-hut and muttering in disgruntled tones. Perhaps he was a Light Being as well! Although a denser 'light being' she could not imagine. She flattened herself against the wall and designed in her mind ways to make an exit without attracting his attention.

Eventually, some half hour later, he disappeared to the west of the building on foot, carrying what looked like a kettle. Donna made her way to her car, which presumably he had noticed on his way in. Her feet felt strange beneath her and the world looked and felt strange altogether. The incident had disoriented her, and she felt she could not trust what she saw around her as being solid or reliable. It was an unnerving feeling and one she thought might stay with her forever if she did not get some down-to-earth human company and everyday noise around her.

She drove back to the city, at a careful speed, and memorised what she had just seen as best she could before attempting to dismiss it from her mind so that normality might be resumed.

*   *   *

Gerald crept into the house the back way and heard Marjorie with a client in the surgery. It was just turned eight-thirty. He made his way to his bedroom but the floorboards creaked and Marjorie appeared—like an undercover agent in a cheesy film—as he reached the doorway.

"Has she gone back to him?"

The venom in her voice seemed to crackle in the air.

"Has who gone back where?"

He did not turn round—her face in one of these situations was too much to bear at this time in the morning. All red and bloated with suffused rage. The veins on her neck perilously close to the surface of her skin.

"Don't come that with me, Gerald! . . . you know very well what I'm referring to.."

He opened the door and made to step in. "I'm afraid I don't Marjorie.."

Marjorie lashed out and grabbed hold of the back of his jersey; the wool stretching to form a balloon-like erection between her grasp and his body. "That's the worse part of it you know, Gerald..your denial!"

Her voice had assumed now the hollow daring of the gleefully martyred female, the sort who did terrible things to gain vengeance. He was aware of this and clueless as to how it should be addressed before it became Hollywood-style danger.

"He's been on the phone..twice . . ."

"Who?.." he turned around in pure body reaction. "Who's been on the phone?. . . ."

"Who do you think?. . . . Graham Ridley! . . . looking for *her!*. . . . and he was abusive and threatening."

The colour draining from Gerald's face gave Marjorie the satisfaction of a confirmation.

"What did he say?" he asked lamely, unable still to look at his wife's distorted expression.

Clearly Marjorie was not going to answer—this particular dialogue was her arsenal.

"If she doesn't appear again soon he'll report her as a missing person and incriminate you!"

Her final satisfaction lay in the way Gerald closed his eyes and frowned, as if he had been hit by a blast of painful reality. She studied his disheveled appearance. It was quite disgusting, it made her want to throw him out and bolt the doors against him. His grubby shirt collar, his hair mussed rather than untidy, as though he had risen straight from some resting place, like a dosser or one of those people who live in garages and pretend everything is normal.

He went into the bedroom and shut the door,

leaving her standing on the landing, her case of instruments in her hand, ready to do her round of house visits to the elderly and infirm in outlying areas.

He sank onto the bed and moaned to himself, the vision of Graham Ridley as he had last seen him, as livid in face as Marjorie was just then, cursing him and threatening him and thumping his car roof with tightly controlled fists to add emphasis to everything he said.

After dropping Elaine at her sister's he had slept briefly in his car. He could not sustain the thoughts of Graham and Graham's obvious wrath, let alone what to do about it all, before being overtaken by complete and utter oblivion and the welcoming arms of sleep.

CHAPTER SIX

GERALD WAS AWOKEN after some five hours of unbroken and refreshing sleep by the sound of clanking and rattling outside the house and in the proximity of his bedroom window. His first thought as he sat upright and was assailed by hazy memories of recent life events was that it was something to do with Graham Ridley! And then he realised that Graham would know that she was not here; no-one would believe him capable of bringing her here because there was Marjorie!

He sank back down into the bed again and was drifting with the speed of a traveller on the Edinburgh to London express back into sleep, when the thought struck him that Marjorie might have told Graham that Elaine was here, simply for spite. He sat bolt upright once more as the clanking became louder. He dived out of bed and crossed to the window and looked tentatively through the curtains.

The window cleaner was in the act of adjusting his ladders against the bathroom sill.

Once back in bed he tried to re-board the Edinburgh to London express. But the phone which he was vaguely aware of ignoring all morning began to ring on the bedside table, and this time his brain totally engaged the sound of it and brought him to full consciousness.

He picked it up.

"Come over to the castle as soon as possible!" Donna said, without preamble, in her usual *the-world-just-awaits-my-command* manner.

"What?" he was grouchy and did not mind revealing it.

"The castle!..just get there today with your camera, Gerald..and I'll meet you.."

"What time today?"

"As soon as . . ."

"I can't just come like that, you know!"

"Why not?..what are you doing?"

"Sleeping!"

Donna let out a shrill of laughter, sarcastic and insolent laughter.

"Its okay for you to laugh but I've hardly had any sleep for the past three nights."

Donna's laughter became a mere gurgle of amusement. "Perhaps you shouldn't be such a ladies man, Gerald darling!. . . . You know! . . . don't bite off more than you can chew!"

"I need another three hours sleep!"

"Alright..I'll see you at about six then, at the castle!"

She hung up as if there was to be no more question about it.

Gerald swore and lay back down and thought about the complications of his life as they came crowd-

ing in on him like the chorus-line of a musical comedy anxious to utilise all of the stage.

*   *   *

He was late setting out for the castle but did not
care! In fact it was better; better not to allow Donna
to summon him to meetings she had decided should
take place.

The traffic was heavy around the M6 and he
waited patiently to enter the slip-road. Into the near
side lane came Graham Ridley's company car, stolidly concealed in the middle of a convoy of similar
company cars all fighting their way home.

Gerald was oblivious of him and drove toward the
castle, easily tailed in his own older bright red hatch-
back, bemusing Ridley by the turns he took towards
the forest and the countryside once they had left
the motorway.

Donna was walking around impatiently in the
upper chamber . . . she had obviously had some sort
of interchange with the elf, who was attempting his
ineffectual sweeping up near his money-hut and
looking intermittently towards the castle main doors
(which had been simulated to the earliest possible
date by a reproduction craftsman at great
expense..despite the fact that entry could be had by
all the gaping holes in the masonry around the fortress) as if he expected Donna to emerge any second and continue some acrimonious debate.

She swung about when she heard Gerald's foot-
fall on the stairs and marched towards him, her long
linen trench-coat swishing about her legs, her expression pensive. "I thought you'd never get here!"

"I got delayed.." Gerald lied.

Donna took his arm and led him to the window casement. "Listen . . . you won't believe what happened early this morning!..I have seen more ghosts..'light beings' or whatever they're supposed to be.."

Gerald's face darkened with disbelief, he looked at her with a wry and cynical gaze.

"We must set up the camera and wait till morning."

"Till morning!.. are you mad?"

"It was morning when they appeared.. about six I would say..I had been dozing . . . anyway I thought that's what psychical researchers did.. held vigil all night in haunted places!"

"Don't use that word!" said Gerald, irritably. "Its so misleading and trite!"

"Which word?" queried Donna, re-arranging her expensive coat impatiently.

"Haunted!" said Gerald quickly, as if he would be struck down for repeating it.

Donna sighed and shook her head—if she had to watch every utterance she would be quite inhibited on Saturday. She assumed a different expression entirely as if turning over a page in her mind to a fresh chapter and began on a description of the morning's occurrences.

Gerald listened to the account of the group of girls, and Donna's amazement and the length of time she had stared and then been interrupted by the elf's car. At length it ended and Gerald had to make some rapid decisions.

"We can't stay till morning," he pointed out firstly, "it'll be freezing and uncomfortable..where will we sleep?"

"I don't mean wait literally. . . . I mean set things up in rehearsal and then return at dawn.."

"Where from?" he asked, guardedly.

"My place!" Donna said decisively. "Its nearer."

She twinkled expectantly at him, her eyes welcoming and seductive and her silky ash blonde hair swinging over one cheek so that she looked like a young girl.

Gerald felt twinges of arousal at the thought of what Donna and he shared when not on the track of metaphysical publicity.

"Well . . ." he deliberated with himself and made noises of indecision and uncertainty.

"Well what?" she hopped about from one foot to another, her hands deep in her trench coat pockets, her large leather pouch bag dangling from one shoulder. "What could be more apt!..more convenient! . . . not to mention more important! . . ."

"I cant leave a camera set up . . . it won't be safe.."

"Course it will..I had a word with the elf..he says a camera will be safe..no-one comes here at night..except us."

"How does he know that?" protested Gerald. "He's not here then is he?"

Donna pursed her mouth and looked towards the casements. "Well, no . . . but I suppose he has a fair idea."

"He'll say anything now that he knows there's payment in it for him!"

"I don't think he'd risk us losing valuable equipment, Gerry!. . . . he'd see that as counter-productive to his little earner.."

Gerald considered things, walking about the chamber. "Where were they then..these wenches?"

"Here.." Donna walked to the centre of the chamber and imitated the movement of the ghosts. "Walking round and round ..like this..like some kind of ritual dance or procession!"

Gerald began to be fascinated despite his disbelief. In truth he did not want to believe her. He was jealous now. Envious that she saw the Light Beings more easily than he did. She had the natural gift and didn't even value it properly, just took it for granted, hadn't had to work for it, or spend years developing it, but had discovered it quite by chance, by courtesy of her meeting with himself.

"Okay..I'll erect the camera and leave it covered and that way we can enter and whip the cover off and position ourselves with as little fuss as possible."

"Brilliant!" Donna clapped her hands, smiling her effervescent smile which won the hearts of most men. "And then we'll go and drink some wine and eat something and get a few hours kip and return."

*   *   *

They left in Gerald's car, leaving Donna's in the castle grounds, and took the main road towards Rotherham. As they rounded the bend five hundred yards from the castle perimeters they were tailed again by Graham Ridley, who was now utterly baffled at Gerald's choice of a hiding place for his wife.

He was, of course, absolutely sure that the woman with Gerald was Elaine. It was too dark to see clearly, but it was clear that a female person sat beside Gerald as he drove, and it sure as hell was not Marjorie, since Gerald had been alone when he left his house the previous afternoon. It was obviously Elaine, although Graham did not remember her looking as glamorous in profile as she now looked passing at a fair speed in the passenger seat of Gerald' car.

He considered matters deeply as he kept a careful distance behind Gerald on the drive back to Donna's flat.

Since he was unable to park anywhere near the main entrance of Donna's apartment block without being entirely conspicuous, he had an even worse view of Gerald's escort as she alighted from Gerald's vehicle some thirty minutes later. He saw only that his wife looked better from a distance than she ever did close up. But he was distracted from the proper understanding of this concept by the uncertainty of where he actually was and who owned the apartment that Gerald and she had just entered.

*   *   *

Elaine wiped dishes with monotonous movement and dull eyes. Staring at the kitchen shelves above her sister's sink.

Her sister nudged her. "Elaine . . . did you hear?.."

"What?..no..sorry . . ." Elaine spun around and faced her sister. "What did you say?"

"I said . . . 'you are going to go back to him at some point, are you'?'"

Elaine slid her eyes back to the shelves, furtively, as if caught out in some kind of deceit. She shrugged by way of answer.

"You must have an idea whether you want to make a go of it again!"

"I don't.." said Elaine, and began wiping more plates.

"You must know whether you left to give him a

shock..or whether you left because you'd had enough!"

"It was me had the shock!"

Elaine had said it before she realised. She felt she wanted to retract the words and she clamped her teeth together with a harsh gnashing sound and stared at the wall with her lack-lustre eyes.

"How do you mean? . . . what shock?"

For a full two minutes Elaine could not reply. She was conjuring with the pain of going into it all and the need to avoid offending her sister by withholding vital information about her private life.

Her sister stared at her with a blend of sympathy and discomfort. When people talked about shocks you never knew what to expect!

"I found out.." Elaine was tentative and put out the toe of her shoe and touched the edge of the white floor inlay as if it were water.

"Yes?..you found out?.."

"I found out that Gerald had been seeing another woman!"

There was a total silence for a few moments and Elaine found it hard to look at her sister.

Eventually her sister cleared her throat daintily. "I might have known it was something to do with him!"

Elaine sank miserably to a chair at the kitchen table. "I know you don't like him! . . ."

"How can I dislike him? . . . I never met him!. . . ."

"You know what I mean..you don't like the idea of him!"

"He always seems such a wimp to me!"

Elaine picked up a tea spoon and played with the sugar in the sugar-bowl. "That's a bit unfair Amanda!"

Amanda remained silent.

"He has not had the chance to show himself in his true colours to you or anyone in the family!

So how can you possibly judge him?"

Amanda was very careful to keep her voice neutral, almost whimsical. "It may be something to do with the fact that he has not made the slightest effort to change his *difficult* circumstances in the last ten years and more!"

"Maybe I haven't encouraged him to!"

Amanda stacked the crockery in the cupboard. Elaine would have to say something of this sort in order to defend him. Amanda was a black-is-black-and-white-is-white sort of woman and did not want to have to start understanding these complex issues.

"He'll have to do something now though won't he?" she said, and looked at Elaine pointedly.

"Will he?" Elaine met her eyes with a hang-dog expression.

"Of course . . ." Amanda's voice rose a few octaves, "if you don't go back to Graham you'll have to go somewhere..he'll have to have you!"

"Not necessarily.." said Elaine who was more miserable at the thought of her own sister not wanting her to stay than at anything else. "I can look after myself!"

"Don't be stupid!" said Amanda in finality, with the kind of controlled animosity that adult elder sibling display in the face of younger sibling folly.

*   *   *

Donna twined her legs around Gerald as he leaned over to check his watch on the bedside table. Her legs were encased in shiny blue stockings, a sort of sapphire colour with lacy cuffs at the top to hold them in place. "I'll sell these shots all over the world if they're good.." she said and her eyes were as luminous as her stockings while she tipped back her head on the satin pillows and watched the concealed lighting in the ceiling.

Gerald twisted sharply. "What do you mean..sell them all over the world?"

"How many languages would you like it translating into?" she replied, her legs tightening around his waist; two exotic snakes with ulterior motives.

"Now just a minute.." Gerald felt himself wilting in the romantic act. "We haven't even got them yet and you're selling them!"

"Its the way my mind works, darling!. . . . I always go ahead of myself in these matters! . . . it keeps me at my commercial best!"

"I thought you were doing this open day thing on Saturday!"

"I am..that's a separate issue!"

"But supposing they take photos of their own on Saturday and sell them first!"

"That's why we get ours done tonight . . . and copyright them..we make no bones about the fact that the ghosts are our property!"

"I wish you wouldn't use that word Donna!"

"Which word, 'property'?"

"No, 'ghosts'.."

"Oh, well..whatever.."

Gerald felt he should have more opinions than he had at present, and more objections, but his mind would not work clearly. It was full of his other life issues, like Elaine and her current position and Graham on the warpath.

*   *   *

Meanwhile Graham was wondering what best to do—whether to settle down in the car and sleep till morning when Gerald would eventually emerge, or whether to drive off and review matters before taking further action.

In the event, he fell asleep at the wheel and coming to some four hours later he felt he might as well sit out the next few hours until Gerald and she emerged, or just Gerald alone.

He was surprised into action by the sound of voices and then the slam of a car door just as he was pouring himself some coffee, his attention on the flask at his feet. He jerked upright in alarm and spilled hot coffee on his foot. He was in time to see Gerald putting his car in reverse and getting ready for departure.

From his left hand off-side position in his own vehicle, Graham could again see a female figure in Gerald's passenger seat, but this time she seemed to have some kind of hat or hood over her hair. No wonder; it was barely turned five a.m. and a distinct autumn chill tinged the day.

He fiddled anxiously with the lid of the flask in a clumsy desperate attempt to get it all back together. By the time he had succeeded in securing it Gerald's car had left the landscaped forecourt of the apartment block.

Graham reversed his own car in a manic fashion and sped towards the main road. He kept a careful distance behind them, and it was very easy since there were so few cars about at this time of the day in this neck of the woods.

It surprised him somewhat that they were head-

ing towards the castle again. He began to recognise
the route from the night before, the bleak moorland scenery and the same country roads. From what
he had made out last night in the dark, the castle
was a ruin. But most probably he had overlooked
some kind of domain or habitat belonging to it which
could be the only thing that took them to the God
forsaken place.

By the time Gerald's car had pulled into the deserted grounds the sun was fully up, and would have
been visible except for a grey bank of cloud which
threatened to mar the weather for the day, by the
look of the sky.

Having parked up Gerald alighted from the vehicle and Graham slammed on his brakes, turned
off his engine and vacated his own vehicle in a great
hurry; he would go the rest of the way on foot.

He ran pell-mell down the rutted, mudded,
stoney footpath to the courtyard where Gerald and
she were now. Moving stealthily and remembering
his army training, Graham jogged silently on the balls
of his feet so as not to be heard. Gerald and she went
forward together, talking and laughing, past the
money-hut and round the side of the castle to where
there was an aperture of some three foot breadth
allowing access to the castle itself.

They stepped into the dank enclosure where the
difference in temperature and light assailed their
senses and for a mere second or two halted their
progress while they acclimatised.

It was then that Graham made his presence
known. Springing forward through the same aperture and leaping up behind them, he lunged at the
woman he thought to be his wife and gripped her

upper arms. "I think we'll do some talking don't you? . . ."

Donna screamed and the pale blue hood of her cashmere woollen jacket fell back, revealing her blonde hair. Realising his error, Graham immediately let go of her, but Donna naturally was greatly shocked. She swung around the second she was free and lifted her arm and brought it into Graham's face with full force, hitting him with the weighty solid silver bangle on her wrist.

This redoubtable piece of jewellery caught the side of his head, the clasp tearing at the sensitive skin beside his right eye. He jumped back, putting up tentative fingers to feel the slow trickle of blood. "You bitch!" he said, and stared at Donna with incomprehension.

"Who the bloody hell are you?" Donna screamed. "We haven't any money if that's what you were after. . . ."

Graham gaped at her open-mouthed, still unable to believe she was not his wife. Then his gaze moved to Gerald who had been frozen to horrified silence by the suddenness of events. He was stunned by the blow from the bracelet into a state of inarticulation.

"Don't just stand there, Gerry . . . do something!.." Donna was glaring at Graham as if afraid to take her eyes off him. "Phone the police on your mobile . . ."

Gerald saw that Graham was obviously in some pain from the blow but was trying not to let it deter him.

"Where is she?. . . . where's Elaine?"

"I don't know." Gerald lied.

"*Elaine!*" Donna now stood between them. "What's she got to do with this?"

Gerald and Graham stared at each other in silence.

"Look, Gerald..if you don't call the police I will!"

"No need." said Gerald. "You've blacked his eye and got the best of him.."

"Got the best of him!..what are you talking about? . . . he could be armed for all I know . . . bloody maniac!..leaping out of nowhere and grabbing me like that!. . . . There are laws against people like him. . . ."

"Where is she?" Graham asked again. "Where's she gone? . . . Otherwise I'll call the cops..and I'll say you did this!" He mopped at his injured face with a hanky and waited for the other man to reply.

"She's at her sister's!" Gerald said, meekly.

Graham looked once more at Donna, as if she may contradict the information, and then back to Gerald. "You're a shit, Monkton!. . . . not content with one..you've got her as well.." he looked disdainfully at Donna.

"Do you mind!" said Donna, effecting outrage. "We're colleagues! . . . how dare you conjecture on things you know nothing about. . . . jumping to salacious conclusions!"

Graham's hand trembled slightly as he rearranged the blood-soaked hanky. He looked Donna up and down from head-to-toe and back again. "She your posh tart then is she?"

Donna moved towards him as if to retaliate and Gerald caught her sleeve and tugged her backwards.

"Well, why don't you do something with him?.. instead of standing there..letting him insult me like that!"

"Leave him!" said Gerald, quietly. "We've nothing to gain by making this worse."

"You've not seen the worst yet.." Graham sneered, and with a last look at Donna—who no normal male would deny was worth a last look—he turned and walked out of the chamber.

*   *   *

Donna lit a cigarette and inhaled deeply, shaking a little now that it was over but exuding fury in her every move. "What's going on, Gerry?..who exactly is he?"

"Elaine's husband!"

"Elaine's husband!"

"Yes. . . . she left him the other day!"

"Oh, bloody marvellous! . . . for you I suppose?"

"Not exactly!..I don't know!..I can't tell..she doesn't make any sense on the subject when I ask her!"

"Then if not for you..for who?"

"No-one, I suppose!"

"For you then!" Donna stated.

"Look, I'm sorry!" Gerald turned to her and attempted to take her into his arms.

"Get the hell off me.." she shrugged him away expansively, so that Gerald—fearing assault with her deadly bangle—stepped back from her with a remorseful and shamed expression concealed partly behind his beard but evident in his eyes.

"He thought she was with you! . . . He thought I was Elaine!"

"It would seem so!"

"Seem so! . . . it was so..you could have got me killed!"

"Donna, don't exaggerate.."

Gerald was weary; with his early morning wake-

up call, his torrid entanglements, his tie-in to Donna's
mad schemes. "Let's see if the camera is okay!"
    "Oh, the camera! . . . of course! . . . silly me! . . .
The camera..let us by all means see if the camera is
okay . . . never mind if I'm okay!"
    "That camera is worth a lot of money!"
    "Of course.." Donna was near to explosion point:
the stupidity of men, and especially men like Gerald
Monkton. Graham what's-his-name seemed to have
more about him as far as men were concerned. Perhaps Elaine didn't know when she was on to a good
thing. Swapping feisty Graham Caveman for the likes
of wet Gerald Anorak!
    In the upper chamber the camera was in tact
and everything was as they had left it.
    Gerald uncovered it and looked through the view-
finder mournfully. "Nothing will happen now," he
said, "not after that fracas!"
    "How do you know that?" Donna demanded. "Do
you know how their minds work?..assuming they have
minds!"
    "No..but it stands to sense!"
    "Whose sense?..yours! . . . perhaps they see be-
yond the stupidity and cupidity of mere mortal men
like you! . . . perhaps they enjoy a bit of a tasty situation, upstairs!"
    Gerald dived towards his camera and took ref-
uge. Unable to stomach the blasphemy that may yet
leave Donna's mouth. Donna's mood was out of control now—her tongue with it—liable to become as
lethal as her bracelet.
    She withdrew to lean against the old cold stone
wall and smoke, and sulk. She was rapidly becoming
disenchanted with Gerald. Not only was he boring in
his everyday conversation, he was professionally pomp-

ous in the extreme, and without a flicker of initiative in times of crisis. She sank to the floor again, in the same pose as yesterday morning and allowed her mind to wander to thoughts of a Canadian she had met last month on a journalists convention: the head of a geographic journal based in Vancouver, with hair the colour of natural wheat and a jawline to die for.

Gerald was happy enough doing God knew what to his precious camera and generally fiddling about with his equipment

An age had passed and Donna was wondering how she could terminate her personal association with him without putting paid to their professional opportunties.

And suddenly they were there, in front of her, the circle of girls! She blinked hard to make sure she was not hallucinating, and there they remained, doing much the same as they had the morning before. She stood up slowly, as if she might disturb them, never removing her eyes from them.

"*Gerald!*" she hissed his name, her voice barely above a whisper, so that at first he did not hear.

She repeated herself, a little louder, and he looked around at her.

She inclined her head towards the girls. Gerald followed her eyes and then squinted into the gloom of the middle chamber. He could see nothing at all. He looked at Donna, as if Donna would somehow make them appear before him.

The girls were now performing some kind of circular movement, akin to dancing, some ritual or devotional rite, or something. Donna did not dare look away in case they disappeared. They were dressed again in tunics, but again the clothing seemed to be of no distinguishable colour, as if it were made of some substance giving the illusion of opaque transparency.

Donna frowned at these inconsistencies and her concentration was avid in the still and quiet damp chamber.

"Are you seeing them?" Gerald asked, his voice very low.

Donna nodded.

"Where are they?"

"Right in the middle of the floor..watch my gaze!"

He moved forward as if this would improve matters.

"Don't!" Donna said loudly, and then raised her hand to her lips, at once contrite and scared that she had disturbed them. But of course they were completely oblivious of her, as they had been the day before.

Gerald was watching her closely, frowning, feeling annoyance and something else beginning in his brain. "I think you're making it up!" he said, as pleasantly as his envy would allow.

"Of course I'm not. . . . focus!..try a little harder!"

He sighed, biting back retorts of an acrimonious nature. He peered and strained his eyes and still he saw nothing.

"Get the shots.." Donna whispered. "Just shoot at the middle of the floor!"

"I can't see what I'm shooting!" he complained, reluctant to have to prove anything at all by camera which was not within his own range of sight.

"Just bloody well do it . . . who's paying for this!"

"The light will disperse them," he said, "the flash will kill the frequency!"

"*bloody well do it, Gerald!. . . .* we're not here for our health!"

Gerald took the shots, convinced that she was fabricating the whole thing and that he would prove her wrong in the developing of the film.

He was right about the light from the flash. As she watched them slide this way and that, gracefully weaving and twirling, in a circular movement, all the while Gerald taking shots, they became thinner and less visible, until at last they had dissolved and were no more to be seen.

Donna felt a little sad, as if something of value had disappeared from her life. It left a cold and lonely atmosphere, like the scene of a celebration when the guests have departed.

She could not speak of what she had seen. It was too much to take in and she needed to retain it in her mind's eye and her memory for as long as possible without disturbance. She wanted to be alone with it, to think and reflect. It was after all one of the most amazing things she had ever witnessed.

It might change some people's perception of life, it might make them go religious or have a spiritual re-birth or whatever. It might make some people lose their sense of perspective and get all hung up on it. But Donna was not *some* people. She was a public relations woman par excellence. She needed only a few hours to digest it properly, to imbibe it and take it on board and let her system get used to the idea. Then she would make it part of her material life, make it pay, make it worthwhile, for others as well as herself.

She could make this place another Borley Rectory! Folk would come from all over the world to see. They would flock in their thousands. The possibilities were endless and mind-blowing.

"You're very quiet!" Gerald said as he loaded the equipment into the car.

"What do you expect?" she replied. "I've had a life changing experience!"

"Oh, yes." said Gerald, in his most patronising manner. "I forgot about that!"

Donna looked at him sidelong, a filthy look which he did not see.

CHAPTER SEVEN

ELAINE LET HERSELF in to her home with her front door key and went through the usual routines in the hall; putting the keys in the dish assigned for the holding of keys, turning off the burglar alarm, saying soothing things to the cat, checking for mail on the hall table, glancing at her own sad reflection in the gilt-edged mirror above the radiator on passing.

It was as if she had done these things so many times that her life was a blur wrapped in the procedures attendant upon entering the house, and that after the procedures all other experiential memory seemed to stop. It most probably did, since to a large extent her life had closed down some eleven years ago, or the parts of it which did not include Gerald.

All was quiet, and she wished to God she could afford to keep it that way, to live alone, to not need another person to make life affordable. A husband who was not a proper husband, but a prop.

Eventually the room became very cold, and she

had to leave her perch on the edge of the armchair and get up to switch on the central heating.

It felt strange to be back, even though it had only been three days ago that she had left. But she had been convinced she wasn't coming back. She had been convinced that Gerald would find it necessary to leave Marjorie and set up home with her somewhere. But Gerald had not. Gerald had acted as if none of it were his problem, as if nothing had changed, beyond his need to rush off to some old ruin and take photographs of light beings.

Elaine personally did not believe in Gerald's light beings—she thought they were something he had invented to make himself more imortant, or to find a new business angle. She did not understand his interest in it all and did not take much notice when he explained little bits to her. It was too bizarre, and it was the kind of thing you either felt drawn to or repelled by. Elaine personally felt repelled. She did not want to have to share any of that with him. She wanted him to enjoy himself and to be happy, but she did not wish to have to share in any of it. But now it seemed he had found someone who wanted all of that with him. In the guise of this Donna woman.

Elaine felt she had lost the war. It was not so much the sense of defeat which troubled her, but the sense of injustice, because she had not even known that the war was about to start. She was completely unarmed and defenceless against attack.

She walked into the kitchen and opened the fridge. The cat appeared on cue and she fed him, with the leftovers of a chicken that Graham had obviously bought for himself. She drank some milk out of the bottle, nibbled at a digestive biscuit and looked at her tradescanthia drying in its pot above the sink on the window ledge. She watered it without feeling any pity; she had no pity left for the plants, only for herself. Surely that was healthy! In magazines she read they said that loving oneself was of paramount importance. Did that include pity?

She chewed the second biscuit and stared disconsolately from the window. The next door neighbours had erected some strange sort of structure in her absence, it looked like a miniature marquee, on their back lawn, but she could not be sure.

It was a very sad thing when your own sister was disinclined to giving you shelter, and made no bones about the fear she had of you becoming a liability. That was more sad even than the thought of your lover not supporting you when you left your husband.

Idly, Elaine drifted around her house and inspected things she had known for years, things she had looked at everyday of her married life, items people had given her for wedding presents. It was a bleak kind of inventory, filled only with such things that other people had chosen and not beloved objects she had chosen for herslef. Because, of course, she had lost interest in it all years ago and not bothered to remain house-proud to the extent of caring what went on the walls or in the corners which held the knick-knacks.

She was deep into the abyss of this mental domestic misery when she heard Graham entering the door. His keys went down with a clang into the brass dish and a few moments passed before he entered the lounge. When he did it was apparent to her that she should not have come back, that she should have stayed away, anywhere but here.

"I don't know why you've bothered to return!"

He was sporting some kind of bandage thing on

his face, the kind of thin gauze with tiny strips of plaster that only trained medics administer. The first aid person at the office no doubt.

"What happened to your face?" Elaine asked, softly.

"I met with an accident.." Graham's eyes glittered in a way which disclosed his deep and burning resentments. "I had a little contretemps. . . ."

"A what?"

"Forget it!..anyway its not your business!"

"No, of course not!"

She moved to pick up her plate and cup and go to the kitchen and he stepped into her path, blocking the door.

"You back for good are you?"

"Yes."

"We'll see about that!"

Elaine went silently into the kitchen.

"I pay the bloody bills here, you know, not you! . . . you'll stay if I say you can stay!"

"I have rights.." Elaine said and her voice was a feeble drone at the base of her throat. Her legs were shaking, not from fear but from the insurmountable distress at the thought of being so unwanted, so powerless and having no real place to go.

"You're making a fool of me, Elaine! . . . you and that bastard!..I will not put up with it any longer!"

Elaine looked around her, her eyes searching some answers, resting here and there on the kitchen effects.

"I know why you're back. . . . it's nothing to do with wanting to come back..it's because he doesn't want you.."

Elaine began to cry, tears forming which remained unshed, making her eyes appear large and wild as she fought to hold them back.

"And do you know why he doesn't want you?" Graham came close to her and spoke to her in the kind of voice which is only possible from people who know their power. "Because he has somebody else besides you.."

Elaine felt herself crumpling . . . her legs like jelly, refusing to support her. She allowed herself to sink down and held onto the units with her out-stretched arms to keep from reaching the floor. Her tears were flowing freely, without sound, and cours-ing down her face and making a nonsense of her eye makeup.

"I've just seen her and him . . . with my own eyes . . . a blonde. . . . tallish and sophisticated. . . . the business . . ." Graham helped himself to a can of lager from the fridge and drank from it. "I tell you what girl. . . ." he paused to take a swig, "not wishing to offend or anything, but you'll have a job compet-ing there . . . unless you get down to one of those clinics!..but then again, where are you going to get the money from!"

Elaine felt her world close down to a pinhead. It was undoubtedly one of those moments when if death were summonsed by the mere wishing for it, she could now shuffle off the mortal coil. But these mo-ments are not cognitive whilst they are in flow, they are not recognisable as anything but black holes from which we struggle a second at a time, and then wish we hadn't bothered.

*   *   *

Gerald was developing the negatives of the film from the castle, allowing them maximum time in the solution to bring the black and white exposures to their fullest. His studio was in the back of the house, accessed by a door from the hall leading out into an annex structured to blend in with the architecture of the modern detached house, but possessed of another entrance from the driveway.

If he looked from the small window and through the slatted blinds he could see Marjorie in the lounge, re-arranging the cushions on the sofa and thumping upholstery to rid it of dust. He had not spoken to her since the conversation about Graham Ridley, and he wondered if Ridley had been back in contact with her, and whether they were in any way in cahoots. They both had axes to grind, axes of a large and powerful nature.

How long could he and Elaine survive the maelstrom! They were already playing on borrowed time! Things had changed, but he did not know how, except that it had something to do with Donna in his life. The woman was like an omen, the siren who lured men to their deaths on high seas in pursuit of lustful and untold heights of pleasure.

Eventually, in this colourful reverie, he found that he had allowed enough time to pass to inspect the film.

What he saw shocked him. All of the reel had developed and revealed blurred but discernible females holding hands and positioned in a circle, the exact images of what Donna had described.

He felt a moment's great surge of gladness, swiftly followed by a surge of alarm that he had not seen with his eyes what the exposures now revealed. Obviously he was losing his gift. Certainly it had waned! Perhaps Donna had robbed him of it. Perhaps in her finding *it*, he had to sacrifice *it*. That was patently nonsense, but he could not help but pursue the thought.

He held for the moment the idea that he would pretend the films were blank, so as not to encourage her into any more investigations, to prevent her from exploiting her talents further. Then he decided that he could not do that without risking the wrath of the subtle realms who clearly wished this work to be done. Maybe something up there wished her to develop the sight. Perhaps if he did anything underhand something would be lost forever and he would not regain it. He would be as he was before Pearl's seminar—bleak and without hope, without access to other dimensions. And without the chance to make these work for him in his everyday life.

Once the exposures were dry he began to digitally enhance them by computer. He was almost afraid of doing so now, so sensitive had the subject become in his mind.

The enhancements showed quite clearly the girls, six of them, in a circle-dance or some other form of movement. Their faces clearly differing from one to the other but not with any recognisable features. Except for one, whose strength of persona made him wonder if she were not a live mortal interspersed in the otherwise surreal assembly. She had on her features a smile, radiant and almost mischievous, bearing the human qualities of slight embarrassment or uncertainty, as though she were coming back from a late night out and trying not to be noticed.

Gerald stared at her for several minutes, and then

again at the other five who were as zombies next to
this colourful sister. They seemed to be waiting for
her to take the lead. She was directly facing the camera, as if she were aware of it, but not aware of the
photographer. It was accidental of course, her position in relation to the camera! . . . or was it? The other
girls seemed to lean towards her without actually
looking at her, as if they were somehow acknowledg-
ing her presence as the strongest link or the leading
member of the group, like an orchestra aware of the
presence of a conductor even while engrossed in their
individual endeavours.

Gerald watched the films for nearly forty five
minutes. He was totally enthralled, quite fearful,
unable to think what to do next. Only another psychical researcher could help him to shed light on
things now, but left to Donna they would be with the
world media for maximum hype and publicity, in the
vulgar fashion which had befallen all newsworthy information in the current age, besmirched all over
the tabloids and wondered at, or ridiculed; left open
to criticism and debunking and those who could not
rest until they had uncovered the source, or proved
the fakery, or tied the castle owner into multi-million pound contracts to use more of his premises.

At the thought of multi-million pound contracts
Gerald stood up abruptly, parting reluctantly with
the exposures as he locked them in a drawer. He
would not let Donna see them just yet! She would
have to wait! He might even say they had not turned
out. That would serve her right! It might even make
her sever all connection with him, and then he could
take the exposures and use them for his own purposes, more discreetly . . .

He glanced from the window to see Marjorie

polishing the furniture. The slant of the studio window blinds meant that she could not see him, even if she wished to do so. He was safe from her relentless scrutiny. He pondered on whether to go out of the studio door to his car or whether to use the door annexing the hall. If he went out of the studio door he could not collect his coat which hung on the hall stand, but if he went through to the hall Marjorie would hear him. He would have to stay coat-less and risk it not raining whilst he went again to the castle on his own. But then he recalled he had a travelling rug in the back of the car and he could put that around himself if necessary.

He crept from the studio and locked it, and had started up his car before Marjorie noticed.

She came quickly to the front door and mouthed something at him about money, but by that time he was almost out of the driveway onto the avenue, and he stared at her from his car window as if he had not noticed her waving some kind of invoice in the air like a flight controller on an airfield.

*   *   *

Once in the castle grounds he looked around, scanning the horizon and surrounding areas through his panoramic lens and watching for signs of either Donna or Graham Ridley. The early evening weather was as grey and misty as the day had been at its start, and swirly clouds carried on a light wind threatened heavy rain later on.

Donna, it was to be hoped, was safely in a shareholders meeting at Heritage Matters.

He climbed to the upper chamber and was not long in assembling his camera, the likes of which he was using only for telescopic sight purposes, when the elf appeared and stood at his elbow.

"What are you doing today? . . . looking for U.F.O.s?" the elf laughed, polluting the nearby environment with alcoholic breath.

Gerald smiled obligingly and said nothing. He was of the opinion that if you ignored people like this they went away. They thrived on response and the lack of it repelled them quicker than anything.

"I told that wench of yours the other day . . . I said she could have the castle whenever she liked..provided she let me know . . . and gave me a percentage!"

"Percentage of what?" said Gerald airily, driven to speaking for the first time by the thought of the elf laying claims to the profits from his light-beings.

"Whatever it is you make from these 'ere jauntings.."

"Which jauntings?" said Gerald again. "Saturday, do you mean?"

"Yes, and the rest of it she has planned?"

Gerald straightened up from his camera and stared at the elf. "What's your name, by the way?"

"Its Alf" said the elf, and Gerald almost laughed out loud at the similarity of the real name.

"Pleased to meet you, Alf!" he extended his hand. "I'm Gerry!"

The elf shook his hand.

"Thing is, I don't know what other plans she's told you of..so you'll have to enlighten me, Alf!"

"Well..you know the garden parties and the moonlight musical evenings with mid-night fireworks? . . . all of that!.."

Gerald smiled, as if it had slipped his memory.

"You must know.." said the elf suspiciously.

"Yes..yes . . . but I have so many other things on the go, I get absent minded.."

"Well known are you?" said Alf "Like them celebrity photographers?"

"Not quite!" said Gerald good humouredly.

"Anyway . . . as I was saying, I'll expect a rake off from all of it . . . I told her and I'm telling you now!"

"Right, Alf..I hear you! . . . that's fine!"

Gerald began to change his zoom lens for his panoramic lens and hoped that Alf would see that he was not wanted, but Alf remained and looked on in fascination at all Gerald's equipment.

"Of course, if she brings that many there's a mess.. my superiors will have something to say about it..and I can't handle the litter problem single handed.."

"Who are your superiors?" said Gerald without much interest.

"The owners"

"Yes, and who might they be?"

"Now that would be telling!" said the elf merrily, and moved away, limping for some reason on his right foot as he made towards the staircase.

Gerald grimaced as he viewed the moorland . . . moonlight musical evenings!! It made you want to throw up!

*   *   *

Elaine tried Gerald on his mobile for the fifth time that day. His mobile was not very good; he only persevered with it because his cousin had given it to him. *His cousin, of course, was female! No doubt she was hopeful of a dalliance with him, if not already engaged in one! Or perhaps the proud owner of a past close encounter which had not quite gone away!* Elaine had these cynical and distressing thoughts every few minutes now, they simply would not leave her alone.

She had not bothered to dress throughout the day, there seemed to be little point. She would only have to undress again at night. And it wasn't as if she had been out anywhere. Not even to the shops. She was not due at her part-time job till tomorrow afternoon, since she had told them she would be gone for an indefinite period and not to count on her return. They would welcome her back naturally, with few questions asked, for it was the kind of position which they did not easily fill.

She felt that life was not important enough now to warrant demarcation in time between morning, noon and night. It was all one long dreary bout, with nothing to enliven it or relieve the monotony. She pottered about doing bits of things, and made cups of tea and listened to the radio while staring at the t.v. screen: the garrulous rantings of afternoon disc jockeys and the visual impact of a nun walking around the Cathederal at Chatres! It was quite surreal. Life had lost its sense of purpose and normality.

At length Gerald answered his mobile. She was taken by surprise, because when you've been dialing and re-dialing a number on and off for three hours you sort of give up the hope of ever having a reply.

"Gerry. . . . is that you?"

"y-ee—ss—he—ll-ooo." Gerald's line was filled with static, and it sounded as if he were talking from a mountain summit.

"Its me!" Elaine announced dully.

Gerald did not speak for a second. He was not sure because of the appalling reception who 'me' was. It was one of his women folk and that much he did know.

"Its me, Gerry! . . . Elaine!"

"Hello sweetheart!"

"Where are you?"

"In the castle!"

"Again?"

"Yes..a lot to be done, you know!"

"Are you alone?"

"I am!"

"Well, listen . . . I need to see you!"

"Why?"

Elaine paused in painful disbelief. "Because I haven't seen you for four days.."

"I'm a bit pushed, Elly!"

Elaine held the receiver tightly and tried to think of what one said to one's lover in times like these. One's lover was supposed to want to see one for the hell of it. If one had to point out that they had an obligation to keep to a schedule it impeded the forces which made them want to be your lover in the first place. They may as well be your husband, or your dentist or someone like that.

"Elaine.." Gerald shouted into his mobile, "are you there?"

Elaine stuck the receiver to her ear again. "Yes!"

"Did you hear me?..I said I . . ."

"I heard you!" Elaine said, raising her voice to match his.

"I thought you'd gone!"

"Never mind, it doesn't matter.."

"I'll see you tomorrow, shall I?" Gerald offered questioningly; sweets to bribe a truculent child.

"If you like!"

"Of course I like! . . . don't you like?

"Not as much as I like today!"

"But, Elaine, it just isn't possible . . . I've got all this work to do!"

Elaine's voice dropped to a mere whisper. "It always used to be possible. . . . before Donna!"

Gerald was stunned into speechlessness.

"Its true, isn't it!"

"Elaine..you're bing unreasonable!"

"Of course I am..I love you.." Elaine said, without guile.

Switching the mobile to his other ear, Gerald turned to see the elf approaching, his woollen hat pushed to the back of his grizzled hair. "That's a lovely thing to say, Elly . . ."

"Some folk waiting to see you at the gate!" announced Alf briefly,

Gerald frowned at Alf. Who could be waiting for him at this place at this time of day when no-one knew he had arrived?

"I'll have to go, Elaine! . . . I'll call you back later!"

"No, don't!. . . . Graham's in doing his paperwork tonight!"

"Tomorrow morning then?"

"Okay!"

Gerald hung up without any sweet farewells and then realised his omission. But the thought of people awaiting him down below was too disturbing and too intriguing.

Alf had gone down ahead of him and Gerald followed, a little uncertainly.

*   *   *

In the forecourt stood a man with a voice-activated tape and a camera. "Gerald Monkton?" he extending his hand. "Guy West." He offered Gerald a card which pronounced his professional status as that of journalist.

Gerald stiffened. "You're a newspaper man!"

"Correct!.. Miss Lees told us it would be okay to come out here. . . . we were not expecting to find you on the spot, however, merely to take preliminary shots."

"Preliminary shots?" Gerald repeated and snapped his jaw shut before he could make himself seem even more gormless.

"We're doing features currently on the paranormal and sightings around the U.K of strange phenomena ..its a weekly feature scheduled to run for a couple of months!"

"Who's 'we' exactly?" asked Gerald.

"The Sunday Facilitator!" Guy West smirked at the impactful sound of the statement.

A second man had come around the corner of the castle and stood silently next to Guy West, and West offered no introduction.

"You can forget it!" said Gerald excitedly. "You're not shooting anything in this location.."

The two men looked at each other briefly and then back at Gerald

"she had no right . . . she should have consulted me first..I'm the photographer contracted to work for Heritage.."

"Yes, but Miss Lees is not working for Heritage on this. . . ."

"*I will not allow it!*" Gerald closed his eyes to add emphasis and stood back. "But if you care to have a look round help yourself..you won't see anything.."

It had occurred to him that the average person would see nothing of his light-beings, and they could stare all day and not be any the wiser. These guys would be clueless. But they might cover it all in text, which would be as bad.

He turned his back on them churlishly and began to fiddle with his own heavy duty Olympus, leaving them in no doubt of his feelings on matters. They wandered off and began examining the various parts of the castle. In several minutes they had returned

"So, you don't want to negotiate?"

"No!"

"Miss Lees seems to think you will."

"Miss Lees is wrong!.."

"Seems we wasted our time and yours!"

"Dead right!" Gerald felt starchy and out of character.

"Okay . . . we'll say goodbye!"

"Yes..have a good trip!" said Gerald and searched frantically for Donna's mobile phone number in his wallet, discarding bits of useless paper and memos and ploughing through old parking tickets and receipts for out of town lunches. Wishing he had been patient enough to master the art of storing numbers in the phone apparatus.

*   *   *

Donna herself was busy completing preparations for Saturday. She knew that Saturday would be small-fry next to what was possible but she wanted to see the general reactions of a broader section of people to the whole possibility of the phenomenon and the general adaptability of interested parties under such circumstances.

Donna might have found spiritual realms, but she remained a marketing person at heart!

She had purchased a number of special sets of

goggles, the likes of which enhanced the ability to see subtle bodies etcetera when worn. She tried them out now, turning off her lights and closing the curtains and peering relentlessly about her, into corners and above shelves and into mirrors, to see if they would have any immediate effect. They did not. But perhaps indoor domestic settings were not the best place to use them.

When her mobile rang she was a moment or two remembering where she'd left it..it seemed to be fairly near but not in the room. The aura-goggles had completely disorientated her. She ripped them off and stumbled towards the hallway, tripped over a furry mule she had left carelessly in the doorway that morning, ricocheted back into the door frame and banged her elbow.

The pain was excruciating and she swore and doubled over. The phone continued to ring.

She caught sight of it on the ledge near the bathroom door. She made towards it but it stopped ringing. Replacing the aura-goggles she went into her covered verandah and tried them out in the gathering dusk. It was not much more successful, but after a while she felt she could see changes in the atmosphere and the etheric in front of her seemed to glow, as a prelude to other things perhaps! Rather like the monitor on the computer lighting up prior to access.

The mobile began to ring again. Taking the goggles off once more she realised her elbow was hurting rather acutely and may actually stiffen if she did not take a bath or rub on some liniment.

She dashed to the mobile and answered it. "Yes?" she snapped, her 'public relations' reflexes as deadened to harmonious responses as her elbow.

Gerald could tell in an instant that the war zone had been entered. Not only from his own feelings on matters but on her acrid greeting. The cool between them which allowed pleasurable warmth had disappeared. "Gerald!.." he affirmed.

"Yes." she replied, as if to a stranger.

"Who the hell are these men?"

"Are we talking more ghosts?" she asked sarcastically.

"Journalists!"

"Oh, yes! . . . They will get us good coverage in exchange for an interview."

"Forget it! . . . its not happening!" said Gerald, with unaccustomed forcefulness.

"I beg your pardon?"

"I told you, Donna..its not happening!.. I will not permit a circus!"

"Who said anything about a circus?..really, Gerald, you do over-react to things!"

"The press always means a circus!"

And before she could retort in any way Gerald terminated the call. He walked about and practised his breathing techniques to calm himself. But nothing much was working for him. It had grown quite dark now. The elf was sweeping up near his money-hut. Not that anyone had been through this afternoon to make a mess of anything.

Gerald turned from perusing the vacuous darkness of the surrounding hillside through the casement and there behind him was the stronger sister (as he thought of her), the light-being who had stood out from the rest on his exposures. She was watching him from the middle of the floor. No sign of the rest of her little troupe.

Gerald stood for a couple of seconds and stared

back at her. She could certainly see him, it was obvious from her expression.

"Welcome.." he said, with gentle and deeply felt respect.

She smiled, a merest flicker, and then moved to the far wall and melted—in the time-honoured fashion of her world. He was heartened by it. He would have liked her to stay longer but he was heartened that at least one of them had taken the trouble.

Although he lingered in the castle and walked around for a good half hour, concentrating intently and focusing his mind and his vision, he could see nothing more of any of the girls, or any other member of the discarnate fraternity. He packed his camera carefully and made to his car.

As he was leaving the forecourt and passing the money-hut he heard movement. Expecting something paranormal he turned to see the two reporters taking pictures of the castle walls and sizing up the ruin.

"I beg your pardon." said Gerald, with his new-found directness. "I thought we agreed, no deal!"

The two men ignored him, beyond a cursory glance in his direction.

"Am I talking to myself?"

"Could be!" The one who had introduced himself as Guy West lowered his camera momentarily.

"There are copyright laws, you know!" Gerald announced.

"So there are! . . . but not where we're concerned!"

Gerald was at a loss. He was feeling angry plus foolish, and the combination was not conducive to situation management.

"You have no permission.." It was all he could think of to say and he knew it was feeble.

"yes, they do!" said Alf, manifesting from the rear and some unknown hiding place. He beamed his decayed grin at all concerned and then addressed himself to Gerald. "leave 'em be..they can stay.."

"On what terms?" said Gerald.

The elf pushed back his woolly hat with authority. "On the terms that they've made it worth my while." he said, and screwed up his gnarled face into something simulating amusement, before limping off to his invisible habitat.

*   *   *

Elaine slumped into the armchair and watched the silent t.v. screen. All was rapidly becoming lost. Despair had completely swallowed her. And then Graham entered.

"I'm surprised you're still here!" His nastiness was written clearly on his face.

"Where else do you expect me to be?" Elaine felt her tears rising. She made for the staircase in the hall.

"Anything to eat?" enquired Graham, nonchalantly.

"No.."

"Useless, aren't you!"

"You can't expect me to cook for you with your attitudes."

"Oh, *my attitudes!!.*" He took of his suit jacket and raised his brows in fake astonishment. "*My attitudes!* . . . what about your own?"

"I'm perfectly fair with you . . . civilised towards you . . . I don't abuse you all the time and sneer at you!"

"No . . . you just have affairs with other blokes!"

"One other bloke!" said Elaine, spontaneously, for the first time in a decade alluding to her illicit relationship with Gerald Monkton. She froze with alarm at the slip she had made.

"So, you do admit it then?" Graham came into the doorway and watched her carefully.

She was at a loss for words. She had made a verbal error, of the worst nature. There was no point in lying.

"It's never stopped has it.?" Graham said. "It's been going on for all these years..even after you said it had stopped!"

Elaine felt she need never speak to him again; he had all he wanted in the way of information now.

"I'm right, aren't I?"

She shrugged and looked hopelessly at the carpet, at the floral pattern that was etched on her brain from months and years of being stared at.

"I am right, aren't I Elaine?"

"S'pose so!"

"Well, perhaps you can leave then . . . now that its out!"

"No, I can't..I don't want to ..I have nowhere to go!"

"That's your look out.."

She turned to climb the stairs and heard him follow her

"*What do you think we'll do?..*" he was shouting a little, a prelude to loss of temper. "*What do you imagine we can do now?..now you've admitted it finally and the game's up?*"

"It wasn't a game.." she said levelly. "It was not a game..and really it did not concern you.."

"I see! . . . pardon me! . . . I am only your husband!"

Elaine walked into the bedroom—she would have to go back to Amanda's now. At least for a bit. She would have to swallow her pride and Amanda would have to put up with her.

"You have never rated me have you? . . . not since the birth of Carl!"

"That's right!" said Elaine, again quite levelly, her mind on other matters. "I expect that's right!"

"I was just a meal ticket..a way of keeping the wolf from the door..while *he* was the hearts desire!"

Elaine stood uselessly at the side of the bed they shared and wondered what she would be doing two weeks from now, two months from now, the rest of her life!

When she looked up from her perusal of the bedroom carpet—which was also horribly familiar— he was in front of her.

She had not seen him move and she was off-guard when he hit her. She felt the whole left side of her face turn numb. She felt dizzy and sat on the side of the bed for a second before he grabbed her hair and hit her again.

CHAPTER EIGHT

SATURDAY MORNING AND Donna was apprising
everyone of what to expect, giving them the low-down
on how to develop the right frame of mind for the
day's event. Gerald had not arrived. She would not
be surprised if he did not show. Tough! She really
did not need him.

There were perhaps eight people assembled, all
with cameras, all wearing the sign of great anticipation about their persons. The two Australians were
the most enthusiastic, not bothering to disguise their
obvious excitement.

"..Now, don't expect too much of the day.." began Donna in her sunniest and most intimate manner, like a female vicar addressing newly weds in the
vestry, "..or of each other. . . . just relax . . . because
your own energies will have an effect on the etheric
energy and the possibility of sightings.." she paused—
Gerald had told her not to call them that, it made
the light-beings sound like spacecraft, he said—but
what the hell! People had to have some frame of

visual reference. "Allow yourselves to be normally poised.. but with a greater depth of awareness, if possible.."

"What do you mean?" asked one member—an elderly gentleman who was mostly there to accompany his wife, "*a greater depth of awareness?*." he looked at Donna as if she were using an alien tongue.

"I mean, just allow your mind to be open!"

The man looked at his wife, as if she might throw light onto the nuances of whatever strange state the woman was alluding to. His wife did not, she shook her head briskly and frowned with devout concentration at Donna. Donna smiled at them both radiantly, as if they were dear souls with a joint handicap that had little to do with her address and all to do with their marital union. "..So, I think we need to begin with a few breathing exercises.." she checked her watch. Gerald was supposed to be doing this part, it was his department. "We need to breathe deeply to change our perspectives..alter our consciousness . . . we need to rid our minds of all other concerns.."

"Is it alright if we suck a mint?" said the elder Australian. "It helps me to concentrate!"

"Of course," said Donna, "but not noisily, if you can avoid it."

"Well, no, for heavens' sake.." replied the Australian, patently offended

The rest of the assembled crew looked at the Australian with pity and a mild amount of amusement.

*   *   *

Gerald did his best to comfort Elaine. They sat outside Amanda's terraced cottage and awaited her arrival. He felt sick every time he looked at Elaine's bruised face. "You should go to the police." he said again. "You should report him!"

"I don't think so.." she replied softly.

"But, Elaine, you can't let him treat you like this!"

"He's never done it before!" she looked up at Gerald with imploring eyes.

"That's not to say he won't do it again!"

"If I went to the police they'd go to see him.."

"They may even arrest him.."

"Yes, but then he would tell them . . . about us . . ."

"So?"

"It would be down on record, and I couldn't stand to think of that for the rest of my life!"

Gerald was silent. This was a female logic and he was lost.

"They would come and speak to you perhaps!"

"hmmm" said Gerald.

"There's no telling what he might say about you . . . or me..or us!"

"hmmm"

Elaine was irritated with all this hmmm-ing and looked at him sharply.

"I don't know what to suggest!" he said quickly.

"You could suggest we live together!" she said, feeling she had little to lose now.

Gerald sneaked a glance at his watch. He was not going to make the first part of the event at the castle. "Elaine..all of this needs thinking about!"

"We've been thinking for ten years!"

"No..we've been loving for ten years..it's not the same!"

"What's there to think about?" Elaine said and unconsciously touched her bruises, gingerly.

Gerald sighed and straightened his jacket as best he could in the car seat. Where in Gods' name was Amanda!

"You always said you did not want to leave the marriage because of Carl.."

"I know..but that was then..and Carl's grown up now!"

"I know..but what I mean is..we hadn't planned on it!"

"You mean, you hadn't planned on it." said Elaine, rather acidly.

"Alright..I hadn't planned on it!. . . . I have a lot to sort out and a lot to lose.." He had become a trifle ratty. He surveyed the row of cottages, which ran steeply down into a main road.

"Of course..there's Donna to be considered!" Elaine announced.

"Donna doesn't come into it" said Gerald with asperity.

Around the corner then came Amanda's youngest son, a lad of thirteen. He cycled onto the narrow pavement abutting the houses and looked up and saw Elaine in the car. He cycled alongside and she wound down the window.

"Hello, aunt Elaine!"

"Hello, Michael!..where's your Mum?"

"She's doing Church crèche duty!"

"Oh!. . . ."

Michael eyed Gerald as if he were a spectacle of great interest because his mother referred to Gerald as 'that philandering bastard'. Gerald stared at

Michael pleasantly until Elaine effected introductions.

Gerald nodded to Michael and Michael grinned a sort of half greeting; he had never seen a 'philandering bastard' close to before. He thought it was something of a disappointment.

"I'll come in, Michael..if that's alright.." Elaine reached for her bag from the back seat.

"I'll get the bag." said Gerald a little testily.

Michael had no idea whether it was alright or not but moved his bike so that she could open the car door. Gerald had alighted and was fishing in the back of his large hatch-back to retrieve Elaine's overnight-bag, which he then handed to Michael as if Michael were a porter, and Elaine automatically gripped the handle-bars of his bike to lighten his load. She thought that Gerald was wrong to give the bag to her nephew in that manner. But then she thought now that Gerald was wrong in many things and it was too much to think about, because it might just prove to be the straw that broke the camel's back.

Michael took out his doorkey and hefted the bag onto his shoulder, looking sidelong at the 'philandering bastard' in case he might not get a close up view of another one for a long time. He was not that surprised by Elaine's arrival; his mother had pronounced her liable to come back in the near future.. what with her inability to properly sort out her life and all . . .

Elaine and Gerald were left on the narrow pavement outside the cottages. Elaine still holding onto Michael's bike.

"So..you can't see it as being a possibility?" Elaine asked.

"What?" Gerald swivelled his gaze from the house

next door where the net curtain was moving faintly and someone was obviously secretly watching. "See what?"

"Us living together!"

"Look, Elaine..I can't talk about it now..I've got to dash!"

Elaine had tears in her eyes again, her eyes were swollen from crying, her face pale and drawn. She looked the epitome of a battered wife. Gerald could hardly bare to look at her at all. His compasion was great but his nerves were shattered.

"What could be more important?" said Elaine with great humility and a vulnerability that made him inwardly cringe.

"There's a seminar at the castle..for photographers..I'm supposed to be leading it!"

Elaine put her hand to her mouth in consternation, then realised she was joining him in minimising their relationship and she straightened her back as if for battle. "Are they all waiting for you to start?" she asked casually.

"No..they'll have started.."

"Without you?" she quizzed, sensing the possibility of a lie.

"No..Donna will have got it together!"

"Oh..Donna!.." Elaine squared her frail shoulders. "I might have known..you'd better rush then hadn't you!"

"Listen..Elly..its just a days' work! . . . Donna is the public relations woman for Heritage Matters!"

"I don't care" said Elaine, and looked around to where the next door neighbour was still twitching the curtains. "I don't care who she is..you'd better just clear off to her then!"

He reached out to give her a kiss and put his

arms around her but she dodged his grasp and let the bicycle down to the ground and ran through the opened front door of Amanda's house and slammed it quickly.

Gerald was left standing there, feeling foolish under the gaze of the mysterious neighbour and the impossibility of the whole situation. Almost immediately the door opened again and Michael came out and gathered up his bicycle and looked at him with a darkling youthful sort of animosity, and Gerald tried to smile politely but was met with a stony implacability which did not permit any familiarity whatever.

*   *   *

When Gerald arrived at the castle it was well onto lunch time but things were moving ahead very rapidly. It seemed that three of the participants had seen vague outlines and hazy forms and one said that they had just seen the ghost of a monk as they came out of the make-shift toilets that Donna had had shipped in at great expense.

Gerald took it all with a pinch of salt. If they wanted to make things up to please their avid imaginations it was no skin off his nose, after all they were paying for the privilege of deluding themselves.

There was an avid—not to say intense—atmosphere to the proceedings, as would be expected of course, by laymen. Donna had no doubt contributed to this and built up a genre or theme which lent itself to stereotypical expectations.

Ten minutes from breaking for lunch, which they planned to take in the nearest public house, the elderly gentlemen of the rather cynical frame of mind came huffing and puffing up the staircase after visiting the porta-loo. He was white about the gills and with a frantic expression around the eyes.

He whispered to his wife, who could hardly control her irritation at his sudden need to claim her sole attention, while the others goggled at him. He gripped her elbow and pulled her back from the assembled group. "Esme!" he said, in a stage whisper and began to mutter and hiss down her right ear. Esme nodded rapidly throughout whilst keeping her face neutral. Finally she pulled Donna to one side and whispered down her ear in a similar manner to that of her husband.

Donna smiled delightedly and stepped back into the circle. It seemed the gentleman had been fortunate enough to have a sighting of one of the circle of girls; the one espied by Gerald only the other day.

"Mr Blackwell has just seen a light-being.." Donna proclaimed to everyone, "and I myself must admit to knowing exactly who she is..because I have seen her, in company with other of her ilk on a couple of occasions.."

The general acclaim was edifying. The frozen assemby, agog with curiosity, fell into animation immediately, oohing and aahing and chirruping excitedly . Donna smiling at their separate comments and remarks, turning this way and that to note the various responses, in the way of someone who has just shared the glad tidings of a lottery winner or the birth of an infant.

Gerald frowned and hovered a little way to the back, reluctant to enter into something which might become too frenzied or unmanageable.

"What was she like?" said one of the Australians. "Describe her!"

Mr Blackwell cleared his throat and his face

flushed a dark shade of red. He floundered through gruff half-assembled descriptions. "Sort of . . . well..sort of old-fashioned! . . ."

"Old fashioned? . . . do you mean quaint?.."

"No, no . . . he means of another age!" someone proclaimed

"Well, yes. . . . but that could be said of anyone existing over twenty five years ago..what age for example?" enquired another.

"I don't know.." said Mr Blackwell to the last querent, rather offendedly. "I'm not a ruddy historian . . . I'm a market gardener!"

"yes..you do know Arnold.." interjected Esme encouragingly, as though to one of her grandchildren rather than her husband. "Just tell everyone..we're all here to share these things.."

"Well.." Arnold moved ploddingly back and forth as if surveying rows of beans. "She was dressed in a tunic thing..very shapeless!"

"What sort of tunic?" asked a girl with dreadlocks and a ring through one eyebrow and a nostril. "Long or short?"

"Long!..sort of!" replied Arnold, regretting now that he had divulged his revelation at all.

"And what else?" prompted one of the Australians.

"What do you mean, what else?..isn't that enough!"

"She means, can you supply any other detail." Donna said, ingratiatingly the diplomat.

"Well..she had long dark hair and a sort of Mona Lisa smile!"

"Do you mean she looked Italian?" enquired a young housewife in their midst who had never done anything of this sort before in her life and considered it the bravest thing she ever might do.

"No..that's not what I mean..I mean her smile was kind of .."

"Wistful?" supplied Gerald from the rear.

"Yes," Arnold turned on him thankfully, "that's exactly what I mean!.... have you seen her too?"

"Yes.." said Gerald, calmly, "couple of days ago as a matter of fact!"

There were gasps and exclamations and they began to dissipate and murmur and a couple of them moved hurriedly in the direction of the outer castle and the porta-loos.

"We'll break for lunch presently.." Donna raised her voice. "There'll be plenty of time to inspect. . . . can we just have a little pow-wow before then?"

They generally ignored her. Those who hadn't flown off to spot the tunic-clad wench were avidly discussing Arnold Blackwell's luck or power or charm or whatever it was that had caused the ghost to reveal herself to him alone.

Gerald looked across at Donna with a wry smile. 'see what happens' his face said, in an unmistakable I-told-you-so-manner.

"They'll calm down in a while..it's good that they're all so enthusiastic!" she told him.

"Oh, its wonderful!" Gerald retorted, and Donna felt that if she did not move away to be on her own she would probably hit him; turning up hours late, looking sardonically down his nose at everyone and making off-colour remarks! He was rapidly becoming the most unreliable and unprofessional person she had ever had to do business with.

*   *   *

In the nearby land, some few hundred yards away from the castle and to its rear, in a converted barn, sat the elf with his employer—the owner of the castle.

"What exactly are they up to, do you say?"

The elf shuffled edgily and pushed his woollen hat this way and the other whilst contemplating words. "Sort of . . . gazing at things!"

"What? . . . parts of the structure?"

"No. . . . invisible things!"

"Invisible things!. . . . how can they gaze at invisible things?"

"You know . . . so's they become clearer.."

"No, I don't know!. . . . I don't know, Alfred, what you are talking about..can you be more specific?"

Alf was terrified of authority, and especially the kind of authority on whom he was dependent for his living. He shuffled with greater discomfort and scraped his ill-clad feet around the office floor, like a truculent school-child awaiting home-time.

"You know.. like ghosts and things.."

"Oh! . . . do you mean they are researching historical psychic phenomenon?"

"Yes..that's it!" agreed Alf.

"Well, well!. . . . and what is it worth to you?"

Alf became evasive, almost to the point of catatonia, and gazed at the ceiling, his feet still beating a loose tattoo on the floor tiles.

"Did you hear?"

"I 'eard . . ."

"Well then?"

"I expect they may have bunged me a couple of quid!"

"I expect so too! . . . how much exactly?"

"I don't remember!"

"Perhaps I'll have to ask them in person then!"

"Fifty!" mumbled Alf. "The posh bird..she gave me fifty quid for the use of the castle today and on odd hours during the next month!"

"And the gentlemen of the press?"

"Those miserable buggers made it a tenner!" said Alf, as if his own business acumen caused him to be ashamed of himself.

His employer looked at him steadily and leaned back in the armchair near the Aga. "You're sure that's the sum total of it all?"

"Positive!" said Alf, nodding emphatically. "Oh, yes..definitely! . . . I'm not hiding nothing!"

"Well, I certainly hope not Alfred!"

Alf left a gap of three minutes or so while he pushed his hat about, and then perceiving from the long silence that the interview was at an end, left his chair and lollopped towards the door in the direction of the tiny kitchen where he regularly refreshed himself.

*   *   *

Donna was standing at the castle-gate bidding farewell to everyone. Her lilac silk coat with the fur trimmed hood glistened in the late sunshine like one of the light beings themselves. Everyone was well pleased, the results individually and collectively were impressive. So impressive that Donna was a little afraid of containing and managing the project in case it boomed and exploded out of all proportion and became too forceful in its own right. Especially where the press were concerned. She perhaps should not have been so hasty in letting West and his colleague have exact information about the castle location. She should have played them along a little first. Now they had enough information to arm themselves with proof from other psychics if they wished to, or simply to make things up.

She was in the act of seeing out Mr and Mrs Blackwell—who had enjoyed themselves so much in their various ways they were prevailing upon her to arrange another such event in the near future— when she was interrupted by Alf at her elbow, tugging at her sleeve like a recalcitrant child. She turned sharply and frowned in his direction, and then beamed her benefic smile back to the Blackwells before they had time even to notice her lapse of mood.

"..Listen, I've not got all day!. . . . I need to speak to you.." said the elf in crude oblivion of Donna's public, retaining his pinched hold of her silk coat between his finger and thumb. she shook her arm to loosen him and then pushed her elbow backwards, to repel him altogether. He moved sideways adroitly, dodging her sharp subtle offensive, while the Blackwells became curiously aware of him and wore perplexed expressions.

"I can't be waiting here all day!"

"*Alright!*" said Donna. "Just give me a moment!"

Alf stuck his hands in his pockets and strutted about the courtyard.

"We've come from Herefordshire . . ." Mrs Blackwell was saying, "and we could find a couple of prime sites down there..you could stage something in one of those.."

"Okay . . . let me know what you come up with!" Donna extended her hand to the Blackwells, like the lady of the castle four hundred years ago bid-

ding farewell to visiting allies. She watched the
Blackwells retreat to their Land Rover and then
turned impatiently to Alf. "What do you want?"

"You'll have to up the anti.." Alf said.

"I'll what?"

"You heard!. . . . I can't let you have the place so
cheap no more!"

"So cheap! . . . its an arm and a leg! . . . what are
you talking about?"

"Them newspaper chaps is all over now..and I
may be in trouble with my superiors!"

Donna lifted the silk hood over her head and
watched the nearby hills. A cool wind was rising and
blowing the creaking old sign announcing the castle
entrance to and fro and making Alf's hair tuft out
sideways in stiff strands.

"I tell you what . . . let me have a word with your
superiors!" Donna said at length.

"Can't do that I'm afraid!" said Alf, resolutely
confident.

"Why not?"

"They don't like to be bothered with folk.."

"Yes, but I'm not just folk! . . . I mean, I'm not a
mere sightseer..I'm a valuable business connection!"

"For me y'are!" agreed Alf, sagely. "Not necessarily for them!"

"Who is 'them' exactly?" asked Donna, frowning
into the distance and avoiding having to look at Alf's
more than usual unsavoury appearance.

"That's their business!" said Alf evasively. "Now,
I'm letting you know that you'll have to pay me twice
the agreed rate if you want this to continue!"

"You jumped up little squirt!"

Donna had blurted this out before she could stop
herself. Alf skipped towards her, animation enliven-

ing his delivery. "Look 'ere, missy . . . never mind your insults!..are you paying me or not?"

"I'll think on it!" said Donna, haughtily.

"Let me know by tomorrow lunch then.."

"Or else what?"

"Else you don't get to do no more of your stunts in 'ere.. that's what!"

Alf pranced off with the bumptious and nonchalant air possible only to people of his indifferent social ilk, and left Donna staring after him, quickly reappraising her position.

* * *

Gerald watched Donna covertly from a turret slit on a southerly promontory of the castle; her profile a study in pensive scheming. Then, slowly, he descended the stairs and psyched himself up for what would be a milestone in the decline of their affair, a political anti-climax in their business dealings.

She turned as she heard him approach, her brows raised in anticipation of reviews and observations of the days' event. Gerald nodded slowly. He never liked to speak first in these kind of confrontational matters. He waited to hear what the other would say and then reacted accordingly. Gerald was a classic reactor; he loved to imitate whilst pretending to innovate.

"What did you make of it then?" she asked smoothly.

"Which part?"

"All of it..the day in general!"

"Fine.. if you like that sort of thing!"

"But you don't!"

"Not much!"

"I'll carry on alone then shall I?"

Gerald hesitated. It was not exactly what he wanted to hear. It was not what he had in mind. But then again, what did he have in mind? His flair for reacting to stimulus was at a zenith but it was also without a lead.

"At any rate.." Donna said, watching him carefully, "you'll want your share of the proceeds!"

She brought a wad of notes out of her silk pocket and began counting off his half. It was a generous sum and he felt quite warmed at the thought of more of it following. "So..what are you doing?"

"Doing?" echoed Gerald, his vagueness a pea soup which befuddled his manner and confused others.

"Are you in or out?" she waited for him to assemble his thoughts as he idly stroked his beard in the way bearded men will, and when she had grown tired she said: "You didn't manage to see anything did you? . . . of your light beings!"

He drew his focus to the present and her words, his brow knitting with consternation and revealing all his misgivings. "You saw nothing of them..or anything of what some of the others saw!"

"Not today..no!" He looked guilty. She made it sound as if he had failed to reach an orgasm during lovemaking, or as if he were a novice teacher on work experience who finds his pupils better informed than himself. It was humiliation at its most classic, although Donna was not aware of that, or of making it obvious. She was aware only of a sadness for him next to her own blossoming and growing gift. But he did not know this and imagined her to be gloating over his failure. He was a failure now, as a psychical researcher and as a lover! As a husband and as a friend to Elaine!

He was not doing too well as a commercial photographer either!

"So, what is it then?..what is it to be?" she said, more gently. "Are you in or not!"

She was gambling; photographers with the penchant for this sort of thing were rare but Donna kept that to herself.—it had obviously not occurred to Gerald, and it appeared that she had the most powerful hand.

"I don't know." said Gerald who did not wish to seem like a pushover.

Donna deliberated, tracing patterns in the dry gritty ground with her toe, and then without warning walked away from him, leaving him to ponder on *where* he was exactly, and *who* he was in the scheme of things: her hired help? her business partner? her current lover or her unwitting stooge?

*   *   *

As she approached her car at the other side of the castle she encountered Guy West, talking into his little tape device. He was doing a large feature and it mattered little that he could not photograph or offer proof of any ghost like beings—he could talk about people who could. That was what journalism was all about. Otherwise he would have become a biographer or a technical author or some such.

He smiled at Donna cagily, as if he knew what the future might hold. And as if she did also.

"Fancy a drink?"

"Why not!" she replied off-handedly.

He was the kind of man you wanted to drink with, simply to see what he would come up with and what he would say. He had that kind of fascination—the sort which makes it possible to live a life without commitment.

"I was thinking we should come to a better financial arrangement!" he told her as they walked towards his car. "It makes better sense!"

"It probably does!" Donna agreed, her mind working rapidly.

They ignored the stares of the elf as he rounded the corner with his giant mug of whatever he used to quench his thirst. Donna allowed Guy to open the passenger door of his car for her, as if they were not twenty first century equals with money and corporate objectives at the forefront of their minds. Even before she fastened the safety belt in his small Mercedes, her mobile began to ring as other interested people tried to secure places on the next psychical phenomenon events aimed at capturing etheric beings for posterity with camera. She had advertised skillfully and discreetly in the right places, in the way which would be expected of her. And, as always, less was more!

*   *   *

"That little bastard is trying to extort more money out of me.." Donna said to Guy as he caressed her shoulder in the booth of the French restaurant, savouring her, the way men did at the stage of seduction when all was possible but nothing was granted.

"Which little bastard?" he said, his eyes on her mouth as if he were about to pounce on it and kiss it.

"Alf!..the caretaker!"

"Oh, that repulsive toad!" Guy might have given the remark more derision except for the sight of

Donna's mouth within his vision, possibly even his reach, soothing him and making him sound as if he were hypnotised and merely repeating words.

"I'm glad you feel the same way about him." Donna said, as if the scrutiny of her mouth were not taking place, pulling herself back fractionally and into the safety of the wall.

"Anyone in their right mind would feel that way about him.." Guy croaked, his voice pendulous with arousal.

"Shall I pay him then?" she asked nonchalantly.

"s'up to you! . . . why pay him more than we are paying him?.."

"I know!"

"Of course.." Guy managed to bring his eyes away from her dusky pink mouth, "if we amalgamated you wouldn't have that problem.."

"What?." she looked at Guy sharply, her voice breaking the sleepy ambience. "Join forces with you lot?"

"Yes.."

"Never!"

"Why not?"

"Against my principals!"

"Which principals?"

"The ones that dictate I do not give away my power!"

"You have to give away power sometimes in order to gain it!"

"Who said that?"

"I did!"

"Oh? . . . I thought it might have been someone important!"

Guy West had the sort of soft yet firm facial features which she liked best. It was a well-defined face and it was gentle but it was not flabby or babyish or podgy. His eyes had the sheen of patient satisfaction in pleasure. She stared back at him with her own pale eyes.

"Aren't I important enough?"

"You might be!"

"When will it be decided?"

"Soon.."

"Wonderful!"

He swooped down on her mouth and took it between his teeth, like a playful terrier, and she allowed it to happen, welcoming the sensation it brought to her.

CHAPTER NINE

GERALD WAS NOW quite frantic, barely able to keep himself in the alpha state necessary to access his light beings. He was fighting the urge to panic; after an hour of vigilant watching he could see nothing whatever. Every trace of the girls had vanished for him. For him! But not for others it seemed. He felt cheated! He realised, absurdly, that he was taking it as a personal insult. Perhaps he was insane.

He entertained the notion fleetingly as he sped down the stairs from the promontory turret to the first floor chamber. But then they always said that if you were truly insane you did not know it. Perhaps he was only marginally insane. Perhaps it came under the heading of being deluded! If so, he was an unwilling accomplice to Donna in the business of deluding others. Donna did not care She cared only for making money. She was unscrupulous! Yet she had the sight. How come that she had the sight if she were so unscrupulous? Was it not given only to those who were spiritual in their outlook! Obviously not. For Donna was clearly not a spiritual person. She was a scheming and hard-headed woman with the wiles and the power to succeed against the odds.

As Gerald was absently inspecting the font in the middle of the first floor chamber he caught sight of one of the female light-beings out of the side of his eye—the strongest of their circle. The one he had seen a few days previously. Relief flooded through him, together with a strange sort of gratitude. He focused on her intently and attempted to fix her, so to speak, to the spot where she seemed to stand. She smiled at him again with that wistful and Mona-Lisa like smile, and then she wavered and flickered out like a badly projected hologram.

Try as he would he could not get her back. Half an hour he tried, until his neck ached and his eyes watered and he was cold and drained. He left the castle, utterly defeated. He was desolate. He had never felt so desolate since he and Elaine had agreed not to meet all those years ago.

He wanted to go and be with Elaine, but it was harder now than it had ever been because of her migration to Glossop, which was some distance, and anyway she found it harder to leave her sister's at the drop of a hat because her sister questioned her and made her feel guilty about Gerald. It had cast an entirely different light on their liaison.

Gerald leaned against the wall in the cold night air and looked at the sky, clear for once, and with a sprinkling of stars that shone on the dark velvety background and made one want to utter euphemisms about the Galaxy and the wonder of it all.

He closed his eyes and recognised a pain of the emotional kind. It passed through him like stomach cramp, reaching a crescendo and then lessening as

he acknowledged it, to be followed by a dull empti-
ness that was in its way worse than the pain. He had
been wrong to become entangled with Donna, he
could see it now. He had lost Elaine because of it. He
had gained nothing whatever from it. It had only
served to complicate his life in ways which did not
bear thinking about.

He moved slowly to his car and wondered where
he should go. He seemed to belong nowhere. On
nearing the vehicle he de-alarmed it and as he activated the mechanism on his key-ring he was flung
sideways to the ground.

A dull thud to his rib-cage told him that he had
been kicked and he looked up to see Graham Ridley in the act of swinging his foot back to take a second aim. He rolled over, and over once again, and
then scrambled to his knees. His ribs felt as if they
were broken.

Ridley lunged at him and pulled him to his feet,
holding him by his coat collar, swearing and rasping
and panting and behaving as people behave when
they are letting go of long held rage by means of
physical violence.

Gerald was not a fighter—he had no defence
against Ridley except his size; he was a good three or
four inches taller than him. With this in mind he
shoved his right shoulder into Ridley as he lunged
with his fists and Ridley lost balance, but only for a
second and then he was back again, gripping Gerald
by the arm and swinging him round and hitting him
a dense blow to the right side of his face and then
positioning himself to throw a second punch.

The one thing Gerald knew was that the jaw was
fragile and very easily broken; he had learned it once
on a compulsory first aid course to which he had been

assigned while an apprentice many years ago. Adhering to this, he moved the whole of his body back and sideways so that Ridley's fist would miss his face. He succeeded in dodging the second blow but wricked his back in the event, feeling it jar and scream along with his bruised ribs. He was one mass of pain. He pushed Ridley with outstretched hands and Ridley caught his right arm and spun him round and got him in some kind of wrestling hold. He was done for, his breath reduced to short pants. He felt his knees buckle and he flopped like a shop dummy into inertia.

Ridley was holding him up, not quite ready to see him unconscious or on the floor. Wanting him to fight and to respond, wanting a protagonist, a partner for his testosterone overload. "You scum.." wheezed Ridley, "you bastard! . . . scum bastard! . . . you slimy twat! . . ."

Gerald cried out as his left arm was bent upwards and back.

"Years it's been going on..fucking years!"

"*Get off me!*" Gerald was aware that he was partly pleading and partly commanding.

"*How do you think its going to end? . . . eh?..how do you think its going to end?*"

Gerald slipped totally from the other man's grasp and fell to the floor. No doubt Ridley might proceed to kick him to death in the grounds of the castle and no-one would be the wiser. He closed his eyes on that thought and prepared to let fate have its way. And then he heard a shout, and too muddled and weak to determine what it was, it took him several minutes before he realised that the elf had appeared from nowhere and was coming to his assistance.

*   *   *

At this moment in time Elaine was ringing Gerald's mobile, which was locked in the glove compartment of his car. She allowed it to ring twice over its cycle, before the taped voice announced that the owner had not responded and it was best to try later.

Elaine had decided an hour before that if Gerald did not respond to her call this evening she was giving up on him. She replaced the receiver in the village phone box and looked wanly out at the dark and gloomy visage of shop windows, dimly lit or shuttered. Only the grocery/off-license showing signs of life.

She left the phone box and sauntered up the hill slowly, towards the church and the village hall and the war memorial monument. She measured each step, giving herself something to do and time to think. Leaves crunched beneath her feet because of the onset of autumn and soon the lanes and the village itself would look picturesque with the fall of the trees and the rusty hues of autumn.

She had made a huge decision. It felt like it had taken her whole being with it. She was empty and strangely numb. It was as if she had disappeared and did not know herself. It was lonely.

The affair with Gerald had been going on for too long. It had been all the time gaining in importance, so that she did not realise what a large chunk of her life it occupied! What a large proportion of herself she had given over to it! It was tremulous and frail, this part of herself. But she did not realise it until she had collapsed under it, until she had been made to assess it in the larger scheme of things.

If Gerald did not contact her this evening he

could not possibly value her, or what they had together. Her life might stretch out before her, full of
his carefully undetected neglect, his insulting indifference to their love. It was a bit like the game you
played with flowers and petals when you were a kid;
he-loves-me-he-loves-me-not . . . a sort of lottery. She
knew it was not a rational kind of decision, but it was
the way of the emotional instinct to find an outlet in
something so random.

She had reached the monument now and she
sat on the circular bench around the stonework
which allowed for rest after the climb up the hill
and a greater view of the village street beneath. When
she had been sat for a minute or two she became
aware of somebody else on the other side of the circular monument, the wooden bench vibrating
slightly with bodily movement other than her own.
Apprehensively, she peered round to see who it was.

A man she had seen once or twice previously in
the last day or so peered back at her and smiled.

Elaine looked away quickly, embarrassed and
alarmed, and then the next thing she knew he had
come to join her.

"Hello there.." He sat down some two feet away.

"Hello.." she responded stiffly and did not look
at him.

In the gloomy evening she could feel him staring at her. She became acutely aware of the bruising
on her face which she had concealed with cosmet-
ics, she thought he would not so easily see it in the
dark. An age seemed to pass and she wondered if
she dared get up and walk away. Perhaps he would
follow her. Maybe he was a maniac, there were undoubtedly a lot of them about nowadays.

"Its alright," he said, "I live next door but one to Amanda!"

"Oh!" Knowing that her relief was visible, Elaine felt guilty and a little stupid.

"I've seen you go in and out.."

She turned to look at him. She was not used to speaking with men other than her son, her husband, her bosses and Gerald. A person got out of touch with the art of casual conversation with the other sex.

"I'm Rod.." He held out his hand and she looked at it before touching it lightly with her fingers and then pushing her hands back into her coat pockets. Now she felt ridiculous; everyone knew how to shake hands, unless they were socially inadequate or hopelessly ill-bred.

"I take it you're staying with Amanda?"

"Yes, I don't live round here!"

"No.." Rod lit a cigarette and stared at the woodlands surrounding the south side of the village, "I expect you find it a bit quiet!"

"Yes..a bit quiet."

"I used to live in London.." he said, adopting that odd detached voice and manner which people use for making impromptu revelations about themselves to strangers.

Elaine turned to look at him, and he continued to stare at the trees so that she may do so safely.

He was about fifty with mousy hair and a shaggy look which reminded her of a bear or a large dog.

"How come you don't still live there?"

"Divorce! . . . expensive!. . . . I couldn't afford to stay..so I came back to where I hale from!"

"That's nice!" said Elaine, and meant it.

Rod laughed but did not explain what was amusing. "Its not a bad sort of place when you get to know it!" The insinuation was that she should get to know it, or that she may have to get to know it, and for the first time it occurred to her that she was on the brink of new life, that her usual expectations were no longer a foregone conclusion.

"I expect you must be a country lover?" she said.

He turned to look at her full on and she blushed. The word 'lover' brought her thoughts to Gerald.

In the gloom he could not see her face clearly, only that she was nervous and not at ease. "I am! . . . I much prefer it now. . . . I like the space.."

"Yes..the space!..there is more of that!"

"I often sit here at night," Rod said, "before I go for a pint..I like the air after being cooped up all day.."

"What do you do?" Elaine enquired.

"I'm trained as a civil engineer..but now I work with wrought iron..gates and railings and that kind of thing!"

"Oh!..that's creative then?"

"That's why I like to sit in the fresh air..if I've been welding or smelting all day!"

"I can see why you would.."

Rod looked steadily at Elaine. He took stock of her, noting the things he could only guess at when catching sight of her as she passed his front window. She was a gentle sort of woman, an unassuming sort of person, the kind you did not meet very often. She looked as if she were waiting for someone to write on her or bring her to life.

"You work for yourself then?" Elaine ventured, hoping to get him to look away again, at the trees or beyond.

"Yes..that's my place . . . up there . . . to the left of the old police station.."

They squinted into the darkness, following his pointed finger, as if they might see clearly.

"Is it a lucrative business then..wrought iron?"

"I have to say it is.." Rod said with modesty. "It surprised me when it took off the way it did . . . I thought it would be a stop-gap.. but its not bad at all!"

"And you sit here every night do you?"

"Not every night..some nights in the summer I drive out and have a pint! . . . In the winter, unless its freezing, I generally sit here for a while! . . . Its become a sort of habit..you know how I mean?..the kind of thing you do because it makes everything normal!"

"I know exactly what you mean.." Elaine sighed, thinking that things would never be normal again.

Rod looked at her, detecting the sigh, and the mood. A full ten minutes of silence prevailed, quite comfortably, while both of them followed their thoughts and different parts of the night landscape. It was far removed from Elaine's normal suburban surroundings. It was a different world and she could not say whether she liked it or not. Or whether she even cared.

At length Rod stretched, coming to life with careful movements. "I'm off for a pint now!. . . . King's Head! . . . perhaps you'd like to join me for one?"

Elaine looked at him fearfully, as if the invite was a temptation he had no right to offer but twice as welcome because of it.

"It is Saturday night, after all . . ." he assured her, and stood, patiently, politely waiting to be accepted or refused.

Elaine stood too, her legs stiff and cold, her eyes watering from the cool damp darkness. "Yes . . . okay..just one then.."

They walked slowly to the King's Head, not really wishing to arrive, but thankful to have moved the situation forward.

*   *   *

Gerald sat in someone's kitchen—too posh to be the elf's surely—and allowed him to dab TCP on his facial wounds.

"You sure you don't want an ambulance?" said Alf, screwing up his face to concentrate on Gerald's abrasions. "There could be untold damage under that beard of yours!"

"I'm sure!" said Gerald.

"Nasty bugger, that!.." said Alf with feeling.

"Yes.." Gerald agreed.

Alf tipped the TCP bottle onto a wad of cotton wool as if it were ketchup on a plate of food. "Nasty things beards!" he added absently, as if beards rated the same disdain as hooligans.

Gerald said nothing.

"What'd he want then?" ventured Alf into the long silence.

"A personal matter!"

Alf stepped back and peered at Gerald. "Well, I guessed as much!"

Gerald cleared his throat and shut his eyes, not to add further stimulation to Alf's thought processes. His head throbbed and his ribs felt as if they were broken. He wondered whether he could drive or not. He wanted only to lie down and go to sleep but he remembered that it was bad to sleep after head injuries. He recalled that tit-bit from his erstwhile first aid course. It amazed him what he had retained in the way of medical knowledge from that particular period and how clearly he recalled the instructor who had imparted the information.

Alf recommenced ministrations to Gerald's wounds. "You should 'ave yourself seen to properly," he said, "by a doctor at an 'ospical.."

"I'll be fine," said Gerald, "but thank you"

Alf tutted and screwed up his face to assist his concentration. "There's some rum goings on these days..there's no telling what's going to 'appen..there's no knowing from the moment you wake to the moment you close your eyes last thing. . . . and even then you're not safe!"

"No.." Gerald did not wish to prolong the topic; he was depressed enough without that. His face was stinging from the TCP. It felt swollen and sore and the size of a pumpkin.

Alf wandered off and came back with a cup of tea laced with some indefinable alcoholic distillation.

Gerald sipped it thankfully, although it made his neck and jaw hurt when he swallowed. It had crossed his mind that he may need some specialised treatment and may have chronic damage of some kind. But his hatred of hospitals, and his loathing of people questioning him on the subject of Graham Ridley lent him a bravery he would otherwise lack.

Presently someone knocked at the door of kitchen which was obviously part of a larger establishment and Alf went to open it. Gerald began to look around groggily and speculate on where he was since Alf had half carried and shuffled him to this refuge somewhere behind the castle grounds in the pitch dark. He ignored for a few seconds the voices of strangers and Alf's staccato croak, and then two policemen entered and stared amiably at the proceedings.

"Well, well.." said one, as if it were a slightly comical interlude from Gilbert and Sullivan, "what happened?"

"He was attacked!" Alf growled dramatically. The posh bird and this photographer friend of her's had breathed new life into the medieval relic and Alf felt himself to be taking an ever increasing starring role.

Gerald was mortified. "Who called the police?"

"Me, of course!" said Alf

"There was no need.." Gerald shut his eyes again so it might all just recede into his imagination where it belonged.

"I had to didn't I!" Alf's self importance was growing by the second. "I'm responsible for what goes on in the grounds . . . I'd be in trouble if I didn't report incidents!. . . . I mean, someone could sue and then we'd be up the creak if there wasn't the proper authorised papers..I remember three years ago when we had a party of.."

"*What happened sir?*" the first officer cut rudely across the elf and addressed Gerald.

"I was beaten up.." said Gerald and briefly opened his eyes.

"Better give us some details.."

"No need.." Gerald said. "It doesn't matter! . . . I'm sorry your time's been wasted!"

Alf was about to protest and struck an indignant posture in the middle of the floor before launching himself verbally. "Now look, Gerry . . ."

"*Do I take it you know the identity of the attacker?*" asked the first officer, again pre-empting the elf.

Gerald pondered mentally on the strange language used by the law which made things sound one level removed from how it really was. "Yes..I do!"

"So, its a personal matter?"

"Yes . . ."

"Has he taken anything?..money or goods?"

"No.."

"And you don't want to press charges?"

"No..I don't want the matter taking any farther!"

"You're sure?"

"Certain!" said Gerald.

"Has a grudge against you does he?" asked the second officer.

"Yes..he does!"

"And why would that be?"

Gerald hesitated and again shut his eyes, playing in his head with the phrase 'mind your own business'. But as law-abiding as Gerald's life had been he somehow knew the folly of antagonising police. "I know . . . I know his wife!"

The officers exchanged significant glances and then looked at Alf who was silent now under the influence of these revelations. "We'll be off then, Mr Spooner! . . . thank you for keeping us informed!"

Alf drew breath impatiently. "Can't you arrest him for causing an affray?"

Officer number one peeled paper from a strip of gum and stuck it into his mouth, grinning. "Its not a crime in this country to bang another man's wife, Mr Spooner!"

"*not 'im!*" Alf's grimy index finger pointed at Gerald, whose closed eyes had blotted out most of the proceedings. "t'other feller..the assailant!"

"I'm afraid not . . . our friend here does not want him arrested."

"No, but I do!..he might come back!"

Both officers grinned at no-one in particular. The second one could hardly keep his myrth in check. "Might he?..you're not banging her as well are you, Mr Spooner?"

Gerald was fragile and every sinew of his body was alive and raw and ready to react to the slightest provocation. He heard Alf tutting and muttering incoherently, before he slipped forward onto the work-surface next to the sink and entered into the vortex of the tunnel known as oblivion, which Alf on his return from seeing out the police took to be long needed sleep in the safe haven of his own beloved kitchen.

CHAPTER TEN

THE NEXT EVENING being the last Sunday in the month, Geoff Formby took up his usual position at the dinner table in the home of the founder and chairman of Heritage Matters. She observed him with a careful and languid sort of affection, her great age allowing her the privilege of unnerving personal communication within voice and manner.

Her daughter and son-in-law, her long time male companion, and the majority shareholder also were present. They awaited the serving of the second course, but they also awaited the arrival of Bill Brightwell. They discussed Heritage affairs in a pleasant and unruffled manner, moving to by-the-way topics leisurely and imbibing a good Sauvignon with relish, aware that they would be dozing off by the desert course.

The head of Heritage was Dame Ruby Wallstock, an American settled in Britain since her marriage in 1938 to a British diplomat and landowner. She wore clothes in the style of pre-war Europe, which suited her well because her eccentricity and legendary persona called for her to be outstanding as well as elegant.

Presently the butler entered, a young man of Irish extraction wearing casual clothes which included a jacket of the most extraordinary shade of blue linen. Ruby's daughter and son-in-law frowned at him as he spoke into her ear without heed to anyone else present, for they disapproved of him (he played loud rock music in his off duty hours in the attic quarters and smoked grass while he decanted the wine and cleaned the silver). They would have given a lot to see him slip up fatally and finally—contravening in some unforgivable way the protocol required of his position—but they were not holding their breath; everything he did was fine with Ruby as long as he spoke to her in his dulcet southern Irish drawl and not in the received accents he had learned at drama school.

"It seems Bill has been on the phone.." said Ruby, eventually, in her own slight accent left over from Michigan days many moons ago. "He's fifteen minutes away but there's a hold up on the motorway!" She seemed to address these remarks to Geoff Formby, as if he were responsible for all that took place within the Heritage staff lives.

"He'll be here!" said Formby, comfortingly

"Sure.." said Ruby, "but its whether we start the next course without him!"

"I don't think we should delay any longer, Mummy" offered her daughter, "otherwise we'll drink too much and regret it!"

"You're right, Grace!" said the major shareholder, appreciatively—he wanted to get away to enjoy a darts match and not be detained beyond nine-thirty.

"Okay".." Ruby nodded to the butler. "Con, serve us if you would!"

Con, whose full name was Conlan Kerrigan, inclined his head to Ruby, as to royalty, his eyes warm and respectful and full of the affection he held for her.

"And bring Perrier water.." said Ruby's daughter, "next time you're coming through!"

Con left the room with no signs of having heard.

"Did he hear me, Mummy?"

Ruby moved her dark eyes to her daughter. "Yes, Grace, he heard you!"

"Why the hell can't he say so then?"

"Because he's Celtic!" said Ruby, with asperity. "Unlike the English, they shoot from the hip!..that's why I like them!"

"Bloody rude, if you ask me.." Grace's eyes rested languidly on the table flower arrangement.

"For that matter, you should have been more civil in your request!" and then Ruby turned to Formby and asked: "Do you know why Donna can't be here?" as a way of changing the subject.

"He's the bloody butler after all.." said Grace, softly, to her husband. "What does she expect me to do?..kiss his arse?"

"Leave it!" said her husband, in an undertone which was picked up on by Ruby's male companion.

"I don't know why Donna isn't here!" Brightwell replied to the matriarch directly, and thought about Donna's increasing slyness in matters official.

Con had returned with a trolley full of tureens and hot plates and crockery and there was an almost collective and thankful sigh. He was joined by a young girl, also informally dressed in a pair of jeans and a white tee shirt, and together they began to serve the food.

At length Bill Brightwell bounced in. He stopped at the door and nodded to everyone in turn, bowing to Ruby, as always, in an exaggerated and humorous way which she had come to expect. Then he lurched forward and heedless of the current conversation thrust Sunday newspapers onto the dining table. "Have any of you seen these?" he demanded, sinking into the vacant chair next to Grace who looked at him serenely and awaited with anticipatory pleasure the diversion of new conversational material.

Ruby nudged her son-in-law urgently, so that he passed her a paper. There on the third page of the well known tabloid was the article Guy West had written about the castle and the photo of the ghost at the window which Heritage had hired Gerald Monkton to shoot for them exclusively. The bi-monthly magazine simply called 'Heritage' had carried them only the week before. Of course, they looked now like the poor relative, the plagiarizers of top media information.

Ruby settled back in her chair, her white hair shining beneath the chandelier and her once beautiful face very tired and sad under the light. "That will be the reason for Donna's absence tonight then I suppose!" and she looked at the rest of the table for support or contradiction.

*   *   *

Guy West and Donna Lees were again dining together, in a restaurant nearer to Donna's apartment.

"Do you think this photographer will still do the business for you?..when he knows you've joined forces with us?" West enquired, helping himself to more bread.

"Yes..I shan't tell him..he'll be none the wiser..you need not ever appear!"

"Right!..but he'll surely read the papers some day!"

"Yes, but by then I'll have raked in enough to start the venture properly!"

"Which way's that?"

Donna leaned back and studied the ceiling, her arms and shoulders glowing with a slight tan, her blonde hair shiny and sleek in the candlelight. "I'll have centres all over the place . . . venture holidays for the psychically curious . . . retreats from the material world . . . tours of the astral plane..skirmishes with your ancestors in sunny climates. . . . that sort of thing.."

West laughed. "I don't believe you!" he said, flatly. "You're up to something more fly! . . . I don't know what but no doubt all will be revealed!"

Donna looked over at him and winked. He put his hand on her cheek and leaned over and kissed her. "They want a whole series of articles now!..now that the interest is there!..we could spin it out..I'm always in favour of breaks in the flow and then high profile stuff at interludes..never over-face them..keep them intrigued and waiting.."

"Fine . . . whatever!" said Donna, lethargically. "That's your department!..I'll just bring in the tourists.."

"Can't we go back to your place tonight?" said West, bored with shop talk.

"No!" said Donna "I'm not some easy lay!"

"You're not an easy anything.." said West, summoning the waiter for wine. "I'm not sure what you are yet..but I could have fun finding out.."

Donna laughed, shaking her head so that her hair fell like pale cream silk onto her bare shoulder, covering one side of her face, tantalisingly, giving her a gamine and girlish appearance, like an intoxicated Rubenesque cherub about to reach puberty. It was quite the optical illusion!

West stood to go to the loo and staggered a little. They were both somewhat drunk and the world had that appeal which it held only in short bursts, when one allowed oneself to be totally off-guard and off-duty and heedless of the morning alarm call.

*   *   *

Ruby headed the little party back to the conservatory for a couple of hands of whist and some informal chat. Only the majority shareholder broke the faith. They poured over the photographs of the castle which had been drenched in eerie mist and atmospheric splendour, touched up by Guy West's colleagues to seem like somewhere else entirely. There was no evidence of ghosts in any of the other photos but by the time you had read the text you were convinced you had seen more than one.

"This shows nothing.." said Geoff Formby, his rimless spectacles oddly at variance with his rugged face. "It reveals nothing whatever..it's all in the content!"

"Of course," said Ruby, "what did you expect?"
They all looked at Ruby for further inspiration
"We can sue her, you know.." said Brightwell.
"Who?" asked Grace.
"Donna Lees!"

"For what?" Ruby looked up sharply. "For what exactly?"

"That's right.." Formby leaned back into a chair, "we've no proof its anything to do with her."

"Don't be stupid, Geoff!" said Brightwell, hot under the collar. "Intellectual property rights!"

"I'm not being stupid, Bill, I'm stating the fact..we've no proof . . . it could have been what's-his-name!"

"Gerald Monkton!" said Ruby, surprising them.

Brightwell and Formby swung around. "Do you know him?"

"Of course not.." she bit into a chocolate mint. "I just read the paperwork you send, that's all!"

"It could have been Monkton!" Formby said, but thought of Donna that day in his office stating her intention to take the castle project away from Heritage and manage things herself. He decided not to mention any of the conversation to anyone.

Brightwell was saying: " . . . she's the one who contracted him!"

"That's right!" Grace said. "Shoot the messenger!"

Bill Brightwell continued, undeterred. "He was supposed to do that site for us..not any Tom, Dick or Edna offering him enough money.."

"Did he sign to that effect?" questioned Grace, aware that all were looking at her as if she should mind her own business.

"That was up to Donna!" said Formby. "I expected her to do the thing properly!"

"There you are then!" remarked Brightwell facetiously.

At this point, Edward, Ruby's long time compan-

ion, intervened by thrusting one of the other papers
under their noses. "Look here.."

They all gazed for a moment before the headline sank in. It was a large photograph of the dancing maidens in the castle. It was compelling, convincing stuff. It had a feature by Guy West and the
caption read . . .

**'Giddy Girlie Ghosts. . . . a hoax or a Seventh
Wonder?'**

"How have they concocted this?" Ruby stared with
fascination at the photo.

"Perhaps its genuine!" Grace said. "It is a castle,
and it is old. . . . and after all, people have been seeing ghosts since time immemorial!"

"Yes . . . but not capturing them on film.."
Brightwell swilled brandy around a balloon glass.

Geoff Formby cleared his throat and waved a cigarette packet vaguely at Ruby, soliciting her sanction
before lighting one. "Its Donna's cherished ambition
to get some hard evidence and see it on paper!"

"I did not know she had an interest in such stuff.."
Ruby was anxiously scanning for mention of Donna
in the sub-text. There was none it seemed..

"She keeps it fairly quiet.." Formby ignited his
lighter and sparked the cigarette.

"I knew she was cranky!" Brightwell rasped.

Grace swung round on him. "*Excuse me??* . . . I
resent that attitude!..I have an interest in those kind
of things myself . . . and it is not cranky! Your kind of
thinking went out with crinoline dresses!"

Brightwell was dismayed at the suddenness of this
attack. "In that case I beg your pardon." he said me-
chanically. But Grace continued to stare at him, milk-
ing the last of his discomfort before letting him off
the hook.

"Besides all that.." Ruby cleared her throat noisily and stared at Grace: Grace was like one of those retriever dogs; there was no pulling her off once she had the scent, "we can look at this in many ways..but it must be decided what to do next regards our part in matters! . . . We do look rather stupid!"

"We have no choice but to start an action.." Brightwell said. "We owe it to our readers!"

"Bullshit!" Grace took hold of Geoff Formby's cigarette packet without seeking permission and helped herself. "You owe it to your pride you mean!"

"Well, maybe its the same thing!" Brightwell strived not to show any reaction to Grace's attack, which made his voice sound quavery and stilted. "The pride we have in 'Heritage' requires that we don't be seen to be conning people!"

"I would have thought this suggested the very reverse!" Grace retorted. "The fact that their interest is supported by national papers!"

"Yes, but they pay more for our journal than they would for a newspaper." said Formby. "They at least want original information!"

"Better do more of this kind of stuff then," said Edward, "using this Monkton chap!..Go to other places!..Continue the theme without the papers getting onto it!"

"Impossible if Donna Lees is in bed with the enemy . . . so to speak!" Formby flushed a little at his crude phrasing.

"Not much short of the truth, I wouldn't have thought.." muttered Bill Brightwell and Grace laughed raucously.

"Let's think about this carefully . . . let's sleep on it!" Formby countered, letting slip more unconscious bedroom associations brought on by thoughts of

Donna Lees and his own marital situation. "Its too important to rush at it!"

"Sure..but we also need to move if we are going to act against the paper!"

"We cannot just act against the paper, Bill!" said Ruby, quielty. "We need facts!..such as how they got hold of this..for all we know they may have stumbled upon it accidentally, like Monkton!..It is a tourist site, open to the public . . . anyone can go in and take photos!"

"I suppose Donna can't be trusted to tell the truth on it?" Edward enquired, and it was unclear whether he were stating a fact or asking for answers.

"No," said Ruby, with haste, "she can't! . . . that's not the road to go down . . ."

"What is then?" Grace lit her cigarette, at last, with Geoff Formby's lighter, and he smiled tolerantly and watched the trail of smoke curling upwards towards the glass domed ceiling through which the night sky held fast moving cloud and very few stars.

"As I see it, we do not need to do anything!. . . . we just leave things! . . . none of this can do us any harm!" Ruby said.

Silence prevailed and Con came in with the girl and began replenishing glasses and clearing coffee cups.

"It can do us no harm whatever!" Ruby repeated. "Just think about it!"

They did. Grace stubbed out her cigarette and immediately helped herself to another and played again with the lighter. Bill Brightwell watched her with covert interest; he disliked her intently, almost as much as he disliked Donna Lees. Grace's husband fiddled with his watch—a high-tech artifact given for his birthday by Grace—checking the time in Munich

and Istanbul where he did a lot of his business, secretly uncaring what happened to Heritage Matters
and its ghosts. Geoff Formby drummed his fingers
on the arm of the chair, following his thoughts along
the top of a huge mirror on the one solid wall which
joined the conservatory to the main building, making it look twice as big as it was. His image was re-
flected back at him dimly from the bracketed lights,
and several lamps which were bronze statues of
Greco/Roman females scantily clad and holding
torches. These were quite rococo, and a bit vulgar in
his estimation. But then he inhabited a different
world from Ruby and Edward, and found that his
wife's taste in sedate and unremarkable fixtures
suited him well enough. Edward patted Ruby's arm
absently and seemed to doze off.

Eventually the telephone rang and everyone sat
up and glared at each other. It was obviously going
to be Donna Lees to enlighten them on political
matters. After several rings Conlan Kerrigan came
in and answered it. "Its your niece in Boulder!" he
said to Ruby.

Ruby spoke to him sotto voce. "Ask her to ring
back in an hour, Con!..say I'm in an urgent meeting!"

Con relayed the information and left the room
again, his feet making no sound in his expensive train-
ers.

"You're right, Ruby!" Formby was the first to
break the ice. "There is nothing we need do!"

"At present!" interjected Brightwell. "Nothing at
present!"

Ruby inclined her head to Brightwell in complicity. "No..unless anything else transpires we will do
nothing"!"

A general agreement took place.

"I could have supplied that brainwave fifteen minutes ago.." said Grace's husband, under his breath, for his own and Grace's benefit. Grace smirked at him and blew the cigarette smoke into his face without thinking.

*   *   *

Gerald had booked himself into an hotel and stayed in his room until the next afternoon. It was better than going home to face Marjorie. Granted, he had something of an awkward few moments convincing the night porter that he was a decent sort of guest and not some kind of itinerant; his disheveled appearance and blooded face gave the appearance of a fugitive on the run from a serious crime. He told the porter he was a photographer doing shots of the castle for an architectural journal and had taken a fall from one of the turrets, rendering him unfit to drive the long journey home.

The man had accepted this story, reluctantly, sizing Gerald up and down with disdain.

Gerald was naturally irked. By the time he got the key to his room and let himself in, he was feeling badly used and humiliated. But it was still preferable to facing Marjorie. He phoned her instead. Fortunately she had gone to her History Society meeting and he was able to leave a message on the answering machine without speaking to her. He told her he was working in Wolverhampton and would not be back for a day or two.

He stayed around the vicinity of the hotel for the next eighteen or so hours, talking to other guests in the bar and picking up opinions on what people thought of the recent ghost sightings at the castle. It appeared that the photograph he had sold to Guy West on the quiet had now been published in one of the Sunday papers. It was a pity he could not claim any glory or credit for this at the moment, but he was not sure of the legal strength and the convictions of Heritage Matters and where he stood. Besides which, he did not want to draw attention to himself at present; his face was black and blue and he walked with a decided limp. When he sat or moved it was with the stiff deliberation of someone badly crippled. People always gawped and held over-long morbid fascination with anyone in that state who said they had met with an accident: not unnaturally they were loath to believe there was an innocent explanation.

At around six p.m. he decided he would drive back to the castle and take a look around. Parking the car he caught sight of the elf, emptying dregs from his mug of tea onto the patch of grass next to the pay-gate. He stayed very still in his stationary vehicle, hoping Alf would not see him. He was grateful to Alf for his help the previous evening but he did not welcome a further interrogation on the ins and outs of his private life.

Alf presently locked his hut and sauntered off towards the rear of the castle in the direction of the building to which he had taken Gerald after the assault. Gerald alighted from his car and walked into the castle, quickly ascending the staircase to the upper chamber.

It was already growing dim, the sun having disappeared some hour ago. The late September evening held distinct signs of encroaching winter in its light and temperature. He had perambulated the cham-

ber twice when he turned to catch sight of the circle
of girls. They were twirling and rotating as they had
before, and he was surprised by their sudden appearance and did not at first notice that that their clothes
were different. They were not wearing their usual
tunics but some kind of leggings over which were
short shift tops, tied around the middle, blouses of
some kind beneath the shift-tops. It took him a moment to realise they resembled Joan of Arc and that
ilk of female.

Their dancing today was more frenzied, the steps
more clipped and defined by wider foot movement.
It was as though they were doing some kind of war-
dance.

He watched for several minutes, wondering
when they would notice him, or if they would notice
him at all. The strongest of them was clearly in evidence as she glided by him each full circle. She alone
seemed to spot him—she smiled as she passed, some
three yards from him. Her smile today was no longer
omniscient and wistful. It did not hold that Mona
Lisa like quality. It held a cynical comment and
seemed to speak of malice and suspicion, and she
was not at all the same personality she had been on
the other occasions when she had graced him with
her presence.

As he stared after her, the tempo of the dance
suddenly changed and they seemed then to whirl
around the chamber in a frenzied manner, their fer-
vent gyrations jaggedly disturbing the otherwise tranquil twilight.

Passing him, they thrust their faces towards him
in turn and glared, making eye contact with him,
each one turning her head to ensure exact contact
at the exact moment. There could be no doubt he

had been singled out and seen by each of them. Their eyes held some kind of subtle and restrained menace. The temperature in the chamber fell and a freezing wind entered and blew the various bits of litter and debris around the walls and floor.

Gerald was now very shaken. Unnerved, he fell back against the cold stone wall, weak and trembling. But still they whirled and leered, and it seemed to him that they came closer with each rotation of the circle. He closed his eyes and felt himself break into a sweat. His angelic, dancing, medieval maidens had metamorphasised into a troop of Amazon warriors!

Then something worse happened. As he opened his eyes again he saw that they were all assuming male visage. Their feminine contours and features were changing rapidly into hard masculine form . . . unshaven, bearded even! Scar-faced! Muscular! Hairy arms and legs exposed beneath rough jerkins!

They were chanting in deep voices, but their language was foreign and he did not know what they were saying. And instead of dancing they were jumping about, their arms flaying upwards and outwards. Until eventually, in some unknown time frame, they saw him once more. They stared at him with one accord, their expressions intimidating, their intention united in one sinister joint motive which was strengthening and growing in the atmosphere.

They were going to kill him.

Gerald felt himself fade and grow weaker. He breathed deeply in and out a few times and felt the strange sweet nausea of shock and fear envelope his body. He tried to will them away, will himself to run, but he was too exhausted and injured after last night and Graham Ridley.

The circle of ghosts swam before his bleary eyes and he slid down the wall and lost consciousness.

*   *   *

When he came to, he thought he had been dreaming. The chamber was empty and the wind had subsided and it was almost pitch black. He did not move, even though he was freezing cold.

He spent a good twenty minutes going over things, and because he had a temperature and the groggy feeling which goes along with fatigue, he did not know whether he had been dreaming or not. What was worse, he knew that as time went on he would be less sure. He would never know whether he had dreamt the grizzly proceedings or whether he had had the ultimate in paranormal horror experience. It would be an all time mystery that he would never solve.

CHAPTER ELEVEN

AMANDA STARED AT Elaine and opened and closed her mouth a few times, in that time-honoured way of the genuinely gob-smacked. "*You went for a drink with Rod Yates?*"

Elaine said nothing. It was not the sort of question which begged a reply.

"You went for a drink with Rod Yates!" Amanda now tried it as a statement. It was no better. it made her feel ill. She had liked Rod Yates for nearly two years, to no great avail. She was beside herself with fury and not about to let it show.

"He asked me to go to the pub!" Elaine said helplessly.

"You did not have to agree to it!" Amanda was sanctimonious. "After all you are married.."

"In name only.." said Elaine and clamped her lips together tightly as if the words might try to find their way back into her mouth.

"But what about Gerald?"

"What about Gerald?"

"He'll be a bit annoyed, won't he?"

"I doubt whether he'll find out. I think its over between us.."

"Over! over? . . . after twenty years?"

"Yes." said Elaine, simply.

"I never heard anything so stupid!" Amanda's exasperation was muted to mere scorn.

Elaine bowed her head and stared at her hands. Amanda had suddenly turned into their mother.

*   *   *

Gerald went back to the hotel and re-booked his room—this lot was costing him a small fortune one way and another—but all he wanted was to lie in peace and recover, in a strange place where no-one knew him but at the same time his every need was met by an autonomous room service.

He had been lying in bed with a large brandy and a cup of tea for maybe fifteen minutes when the mobile phone began to ring. He was always forgetting the blasted thing, always leaving it on at bad times, or leaving it off at worse times. Checking the number on the screen he perceived that it was Donna.

"What the fucking hell are you playing at?" she said, obviously not about to mince words.

"What do you mean?"

"I mean that picture in the newspaper!"

"It's called free enterprise.." said Gerald, airily, but with an edge of malice.

"It's called shafting your colleagues..that's what its called!"

Gerald sighed and shifted his weight from his painful ribcage, groaning a little as he did so.

"Gerry, I would not have believed it of you.." She

had suddenly changed down a few octaves into a helpless and betrayed female, and Gerald found himself gaining satisfaction from it and said rather glibly. "Do you want to call it a day then, Donna?"

"Our affair, you mean?"

"No, our business liaison!"

Donna considered matters. If she ditched him now she may not get another photographer with his talent! Did that matter? Did it matter if the person operating the camera could not see the Light Beings? Was that perhaps preferable? It was very hard to know without trial and experience.

"You do realise we're booked for another workshop on Saturday? . . . heavily booked!.."

Gerald sighed. "You mean, you're booked! I don't remember talking with anyone about it!"

Donna stared ahead at the people entering the restaurant where she was lunching alone. "Okay..turn down a few hundred quid if you wish!. . . . photographers are ten a penny anyway! . . ."

"*How much?*"

The rising of Gerald's voice had been an involuntary process which he regretted, but it was too late.

And anyway, that consideration was lost next to his annoyance at being dismissed as *just another photographer.* Had she been in the room with him he felt he may have strangled her.

"I think you heard me, Gerry!" she said, with an infuriating patronage he could not now afford to have any reaction to. He remained silent and knew that it would be taken for compliance.

"I'll fax all the details and the location through to you then!" said Donna, more calmly. "I'll do it later today!"

"I may not be back home before then!"

"Really! . . . not de-camped for good have you?..not upped and left for what's-her-name?"

"I'm having a bit of a break..by myself!"

"Of course, darling! . . . I tell you what, ring my land-line tomorrow evening and I'll give you all the info then!"

"I'll reflect on matters.." Gerald had adopted that pathetically pompous demeanour, like Charles the First considering which shoes he should wear to saunter to the guillotine.

Donna swallowed hard on her furious disdain: "Listen, you self-opinionated loser..if you don't ring me by eight tomorrow evening, you will not be there at all!..is that understood!"

"I am the one with the claim to the dancing maidens.." Gerald offered weakly, his voice reedy and excited.

"I don't give a shit, Gerald! . . . you annoy the hell out of me . . . you always did! We are talking major concerns here, and you are too stupid to see it!..I will not allow you any more rope to screw me around! From now on..we'll do it my way!. . . . You could not organise a piss up in a proverbial brewery! . . . I am the brains of this particular outfit..not you! Without me you would have produced diddlysquat..and you know it! . . . You self-deluded wanker!..If you want in on the rest of it you can fucking well tow the line . . . which means getting directive tomorrow! . . . Is that clear?" Not waiting for a reply, Donna rang off.

Gerald's eyes were glazed. He stared at his mobile, mildly, but he thought that between Donna and himself it was now war!

*   *   *

Elaine sat with Rod in the pub the following lunch-time and listened and gazed at him as he spoke. He was the sort of person she wanted to listen to. Just listen, without talking much herself. He made her feel peaceful. He made her want to simply appreciate him, the way one appreciates a mellow sunset or a familar painting.

" . . . I thought you might show up last night," he began tentatively, "I waited until nine and then left.."

"I would have.." Elaine hesitated, and he lowered his head as if to hear what she was not saying. "But Amanda is displeased about it..you and me going out.."

"Oh!" said Rod, plaintively.

"She dislikes the idea..she made me feel.." again Elaine hesitated, "well, she made me feel ashamed..like a slut or something . . . a married woman being unfaithful to her husband.."

"She can't make you feel like that unless you feel like that already!"

Elaine looked at him. He was right! He was clever, like people who don't flaunt it but know all the answers anyway. "Yes..I know!"

Rod squeezed her hand, and then went to get more drinks.

*   *   *

Marjorie could see Graham Ridley approaching her house from her lounge window. She recognised him as he turned into the driveway on foot, even though she had not seen him for a good few years, since the revelation of her husband's affair with his wife, in fact.

He had obviously left his car on the avenue, in case he had to make a quick getaway. She waited for him to ring the doorbell, concealed behind the right-hand drape of her dark green velvet curtains.

When they were eyeball to eyeball he gazed at her in a mournful, insolent manner, like one of those people who sell things door-to-door without much hope of closing any deals.

"Is he in?"

"No, he's not!"

"Did he report me?" He was avoiding her eyes, she noticed.

She did not invite him in and stood obstinately holding her door five inches away from the frame, almost obscured by it except for her face. "Report you?" She felt herself growing very hot. "Report you to who and for what?"

He raised his eyes to her's. She obviously did not know then.

"I had a slight run-in with him!. . . . I hit him!"

Marjorie hesitated. "You'd better come in!" She opened the door wide and stepped aside.

"I thought the police may have got involved!"

"I haven't seen him since Friday morning!"

Graham's eyes flicked around the expansive hall, taking in the number of doors, and the strange am-bience of the place which was like a private hotel with chairs and magazines dotted about on small tables. Or an up-market funeral parlour that he had once had occasion to visit. And then he remembered that the pair of them worked for themselves from the house.

"What do you mean, you hit him?" Marjorie seemed to come to life after more digestion of his confession. "How badly?"

"I suppose you could say, I attacked him!"

She quelled a small sense of satisfaction at the thought of it and schooled her expression into mask-like neutrality and sniffed, as if things like this were not her concern and therefore beneath her. "Where is he then?"

"I don't know . . . I left him . . . in the castle!"

"What castle?"

"Barnard's Castle near Rotherham!"

"Oh yes!" Marjorie felt it best to pretend she was au fait with Gerald's activities; anything else was too demeaning and put her at a disadvantage. "That castle!. . . ." she turned her head to look into his eyes. "How bad was he when you left him? . . . have you seriously injured him?"

"He was asking for it wasn't he!"

"Yes, but how hurt was he?"

"I dunno . . . some little geezer came to his assistance . . ."

"And then what?" Marjorie snapped.

"I came away . . ."

"So, what are you doing here?"

"To see if he's seen sense yet!"

"He's hardly likely to see anything sensibly if you've knocked him for six!" She folded her arms and pushed up her bosom; a protective and belligerent pose which lent a comedic flavour to the setting.

"For all we know you could have killed him!" she said next, and a look of partial alarm spread across his features and quickly dissolved again. "I doubt it!"

"You might doubt it, but it remains a possibility.." said Marjorie, with dogmatic superiority.

Graham Ridley glanced around him, ill at ease, deterred from his focus. "No-one's been in touch have they?..the police or anyone?"

Marjorie paused, the power all her's! Though she knew it would be short lived; in not commenting, she relinquished it.

"They can't have been," said Ridley, "or you'd have known about all this!"

"You've gone too far!" she said. "Its all gone too far!"

"I told you that three days ago!"

She sat in one of the client waiting chairs and composed herself, preparing to tackle the insurmountable.

"If he's not here, there's no point in me staying.." Ridley watched her as he spoke; what did Gerald Monkton see in her to stay married to her? Or was there some hold she had over him that kept him from leaving!

"What would you have done if he had been here?..hit him again?"

"Possibly.."

Marjorie caught his opinion of her framed in his eyes: he was wondering what Gerald saw in her. Lots of people wondered that, some spoke of it and most kept it to themselves. It was a cross she had learned to live with. "What's *she* said about it all?"

Ridley blinked rapidly. "Dunno..she's left me!"

She vacated the chair, as if propelled by strings; her shoulders seeming to rise disproportionately towards her ears, like those of a puppet in animation. Her mind raced, reaching conclusions and exaggerated developments, knocked from its rigid grooves in this ephemeral saga and helplessly spinning. *Elaine free to be with Gerald. Gerald unable to resist being with*

*Elaine. Herself without a prayer! Financially inadequate
in hopeless and interminable estrangement. Unable to relieve the penny-pinching monotony. Pushed into some hor-
rible corner where she was under no illusion that she was of
little importance to anyone, and did not matter. Now that
she was no longer the aggrieved wife, but the divorcee. The
struggling middle-aged divorcee.* She turned her eyes
almost imploringly to Graham. "What are we going
to do?" she said.

Rubbing his knuckles against the back of his opposite hand he cleared his throat in stages. "No,
Marjorie, I said she'd left me . . . I did not say she
had gone to him necessarily!"

"I know what you said!"

He saw fleetingly where her fears lay as she stared
at him with her long-held disapproval, the way he
imagined prisoners stared at other prisoners.

"I'll put the kettle on!" said Marjorie, as to an
unwelcome guest.

*   *   *

"It suits you doesn't it?.." she said, standing with
one hand on the kettle. "It suits you to have it go this
way..her leave with him?"

"Its better! Something had to happen! It was common-sense!"

Marjorie said nothing and turned to face the window so that he would not see her mulish outrage.
She knew that her eyes were ablaze with hostilities,
she could feel it, as if they would at any second pop
from her head.

"You had better think about what to do if he does
call the police.." she said, and they both knew she
was playing for time.

"There's very little I can do!" Ridley moved his position, uneasily, his feet spread wide and his weight oscillating from leg to leg. "If he presses charges he presses charges..I'm not going to deny anything!"

"He won't press charges!"

"How do you know?..he's nothing to lose now?"

"I know him..it's not his style!" she was careless in tone. "I don't know what good you thought it would do anyway, physically assaulting him!"

"Neither do I . . . but at the time I was convinced I had to do something!..as it turned out she went anyway, probably because I hit her too!"

Marjorie turned and looked at him warily. "Is there anyone else on your list then? Or have you finished?"

He blinked in a partially shamed manner, accepting the tea she gave him in a white china cup with gold scrolling daintily decorating the rim and handle. It was fragile in his hand and felt as if it couldn't be lifted to his mouth without untold risk to its delicacy.

"She must be with Gerald!" said Marjorie suddenly, pronouncing the worst to get it over with.

"Not necessarily!"

"Where else will she be?" Marjorie was dissembling rapidly. If Elaine left Graham and did not go to Gerald, Gerald would be undone. In the absence of Elaine he would not have an anchor, he might do anything. He might decide to start life over afresh, totally, in every way! Of course, it seemed difficult to imagine him doing that, but people did strange things all the time. Life was rife with it!

"Where else might she be?" Marjorie repeated, a little more desperately.

"How should I know?" said Ridley. "And what

makes you think I care? ..I only came to see how the land lies."

Marjorie drank her tea in long and regular sips, bracing herself gradually. "The land lies the same as it always did!.. this is a blip, that's all..

"A blip!!" Ridley managed a laugh, short and sharp. "I don't know about that!"

"Things will go back to the way they were . . . its a blip!" she repeated.

"Marjorie, I don't want them back the way they were!..I want it sorted!"

He shifted his weight again and felt something soft and pliable beneath his heavy tread and then heard a yelp. He looked down to discover he had trodden on a dog.

Marjorie swore and moved to her old highland terrier, swooping down on it like a an overweight eagle. He muttered apologies. Embarrassed by his own clumsiness, he dropped to his haunches and examined the dog with her. Not too enamoured with humans, he had a better opinion of animals.

"Clumsy idiot!" she snapped..

He took the rebuke in his stride. "Listen, you cannot just keep on ignoring them.."

Marjorie lifted her dog and examined its foot, giving no sign of hearing him.

"You cannot keep pretending it'll go away.."

"I know it won't go away..but so what? . . . It doesn't bother me!"

"Then it should!" said Ridley with emphasis "Its not natural!"!

"Natural?" Marjorie swung round to look at him, the dog held against her generous bossom. "Don't talk to me about what's natural . . . you don't know

my position or what I feel . . . you know nothing of
my feelings on the matter or my private life !"

"Look, Marjorie, you're affected by this just as
much as I am! You . . . we!..need to think about the
future!"

"The present is enough for me, thank you!"

Her demeanour now was distinctly deflated, helpless even. "I think you'd best go. . . . if you've said all
you came to impart!"

"There's more to it, you know!"

"More to what?" She threw back her head sharply
and waited, poised for the shock of further disclo-
sure.

"He's not just involved with Elaine . . . there's
some other piece!"

"Piece!" Marjorie echoed. "What do you mean,
piece?"

"Woman! . . . he was with her the other day . . . I
saw them at the castle!"

Donna Lees! Marjorie smirked sardonically and
looked sidelong at the view of the garden from the
window. "What was she like?"

"Blonde..good-looking..very smart in appearance!..younger than Elaine!"

"I know all about her!"

The satisfaction in her statement pushed Ridley
beyond endurance. "Well then, like I said, you're
not acting naturally!"

"Do you imagine Gerald and I still have romantic
notions about each other?..do you think it matters to
me who he beds and who he sees? . . . how naive are
you?"

"No, Marjorie, you're the one who's naive . . . if
you think that one day he won't go off with some
other woman!"

He was unsure how it happened; it happened so rapidly. All in a few seconds Marjorie had crumpled. She had sunk onto one of the kitchen chairs, staring at her hands, as if he were not present. . "Are you okay?"

"Just buggar off!!"

"Look, I didn't mean to upset you!..I thought you should know the score..it's not just about Elaine and him, or me and Elaine, it's more complicated than that!" Ridley stared at her and waited.

"I've asked you to go.." Marjorie said, her tone one of formal hopelessness.

"If I were you, I'd see a solicitor!"

She turned her head away, presenting a granite profile. It was a pathetic sort of gesture, it told of her undignified struggle for position over many years; a forlorn sort of obduracy that had gone out of date with horse drawn carriages. In any other situation it might have been heart-rending.

He had reached the front door when he heard her say: "What do you think we should do then?..seeing as you're so wise in these matters!"

He stood very still for a couple of seconds, wondering if she had actually spoken. She was watching him, her dignity returning slowly in a defiant and begrudging sort of way, wrapped in a peculiar essence of despondency and braced by years of stoicism.

"Do?"

"Yes . . . what do you want us to do?"

Chewing the inside of his lip, Ridley considered things while letting his attention rest on Marjorie's florid features. "I don't know..I'll have to give it more thought!"

Marjorie nodded, as if he had out-lived his use-
fulness and out-stayed his welcome. He half expected
her to wave her hand, as if she were royalty dispens-
ing with service.

CHAPTER TWELVE

SATURDAY MORNING DAWNED and Gerald drew up at the castle. He could see Donna's old Porsche parked to the front of the grounds. He was quite dreading it; this second ritualistic public relations exercise in respectable ghost hunting. The alternative to horticulture or bird-watching! The thinking mans' answer to leisure activity within the urbanely adventurous middle classes! It was liable to become a veritable fad in years to come, the way the sighting of unidentified flying objects had become in certain parts of the world. He pursued his semi-cynical thoughts as he entered the castle, wherein a group of twenty or so people turned to peer at him. Whilst Donna smiled at him, radiantly, bathing him in acknowledgment of his obligatory status within the proceedings—her public persona already well in place.

Gerald looked at her sardonically, a look which a good few people registered before he had time to wipe it off his features and replace it with a light, modest smile.

"Better late than never.." said Donna, patronisingly, "we can now make a start!"

"I got stuck on the Motorway.." Gerald lied, and began unpacking his equipment.

If the truth were known, he was terrified of a repeat episode of the last time he was in the castle alone. Perhaps he ought to warn Donna, in case the combined energy of a group fuelled the already aggressive psychic forces personified by the maidens when they transformed themselves into men. But perhaps everyone else was safe! Perhaps it was just himself they were out for! Anyway, it was there own look-out; If they came onto sessions like this they must take the consequences. Deeply absorbed in his thoughts, he failed to notice a young woman at his elbow until she spoke: "Help me with my tripod?" Her voice was softly demanding.

He was about to say: 'and what is that other little magic word?' when he noticed that her feet were not quite on the floor. He stared down pointedly, and then he looked up to see if others had noticed. The group were concentrating on what Donna was saying.

The young girl tugged his sleeve. "My tripod.." she said, somewhat in a growl.

He continued to stare at her feet, which were still not earthed, then he raised his gaze to meet her eyes. They were translucent and looked right through him. She was one of them! Whoever they were!

"Show me!" he said, and she turned and moved to the staircase.

He spoke to Donna in a loud voice. "I'm going down to the ground floor for a moment!"

Donna broke off, frowning at the rudeness of his interruption. "What on earth for?"

"To assist someone!" he said cagily.

"Who?" said Donna, and her audience frowned at him too, of one accord. "Who else is downstairs?"

It was apparent to Gerald as he kept apace with the ghost, that no-one had seen her except himself.

"I'll be back in a jiffy!" he replied over his shoulder, and even as he descended the stairs behind the girl he wondered why Donna was not privy to any sight of her.

No sooner had he and the girl rounded the bend in the shallow circular staircase, out of sight of the assembled group, than she moved with precipitous ease to the eastern side of the ground chamber, seeming to glide without effort through the middle distance. And then turning to face him she assumed a welcoming expression, intimating that he might follow her.

Gerald was non-plussed, a little apprehensive, but he plodded carefully over to where she was. The light from the gaping aperture in the masonry lent her a quite ethereal quality, although anyone observing her from a distance would have no problem in believing her mortal. Unless they looked closely at her feet. Her feet were still not on the ground and it was hard to understand how she gave the appearance of standing firmly with something stable beneath her. It was a preoccupation not to be dismissed, this fascination with her feet, and Gerald stared at them again, long and hard, making out some kind of footwear which was of itself timeless, if a little down-market. A sort of ankle high boot, in a scuffed and faded leatherish material, worn out of shape by months or years of weather and expedition. He tried to make out if

there was a heel on the boot or not, and what it could
be made of, when suddenly she took herself, like a
large bird, some five yards further into the room.

She turned towards the aperture of now bright
sunlight, for the day was fine and clear, and he saw
that she was welcoming newcomers. In came the
males he had seen only the other day. Bringing with
them the same awesome feeling of testosterone overload and aggressive warlike countenance, they moved
randomly past the girl and gathered around Gerald,
staring at him menacingly. He could not believe he
had fallen for such a direct manouvre. He was caught
between the surreal and the downright unknowable.
He strove to keep a deadpan face and reveal nothing of his inner feelings. "Where's this tripod?" he
said, stupidly, to the girl.

*   *   *

Upstairs, Donna was in full flow, explaining how
it was necessary to meditate before beginning on any
photography, in order to align your vibration with
that of the light beings. Some people had not medi-
tated before, and some had. It was an effort trying to
get them all to one level of intention and concentration. "I'll go and get Gerald!" she announced, wondering if he were out to sabotage the proceedings.
"Please continue to breathe deeply and relax your
body and mind.. focus your intent inwardly before
focusing the camera outwardly!"

She smiled to herself as she crossed the floor;
she was pleased with that last phrase, it might easily
become her by-word if she said it often enough. So
that years from now it would be quoted by others
doing similar things, while she was forgotten, the way

all innovative people generally were forgotten when the imitators jumped onto the band-wagon!

As she began to descend the stairs she could hear Gerald talking in a rapid and stressed tone to whoever was with him. She stopped and peered around the bend cautiously. He was avidly shaking his head and attempting to edge his way round the walls, his hands behind him.

"What are you doing?" Donna was anxious not to be heard upstairs.

"Can you see them?"

"See who?"

"*Look, woman!..for Gods Sake!*"

She adjusted her vision and concentrated, and then dimly began to make out shapes. Warriors or something, looking like the kind of rabble who might have followed Robert the Bruce on his campaigns! Long straggly hair and unkempt beards, filthy clothes in primitive materials, bear arms daubed with oil or pitch and God only knew what other substance.

"They want to kill me!" said Gerald in a hoarse whisper.

"Well, they can't!"

"Too bloody right!.. .I haven't harmed them in any way!"

"No, Gerald, I meant its impossible..you're not in their realm!"

"It feels like I am!"

"Tell them to go.."

Gerald laughed nervously, and said in shrill tones "Please go!"

"Ssssh.." Donna ran down the remaining step "you'll frighten everyone!"

"You can see them too, can't you?"

"Yes, vaguely!"

"You can see how hostile they are?"

Donna sighed impatiently and closed her eyes. "Tell them to go, Gerald!"

"I just did"

"No..I mean, seriously, from your inner being..command them to disappear!"

Donna was well informed, it seemed. She may have been taking lessons from some occult expert. Or maybe she had that kind of knowing all along. He watched her curiously, his body shaking involuntarily with the fear and the severe drop in temperature.

"Tell them!" Donna snapped. "We have a seminar to run ..we can't be fooling around with them!"

"Who's fooling around? . . . I'm terrified!"

"Don't be stupid, Gerald! . . . just tell them in no uncertain terms and move beyond them!"

"Can you see their weapons?"

"Somewhat!"

"Try harder..they're not to be underestimated!"

"*Gerald!*..you're going to be no good to me at all ou keep bottling out like this!"

He was standing as if mesmerised. Their collec- 'll was greater than his. Donna saw nothing else nd ran down the remaining stairs and stood in itre of the room and clapped her hands two times. "Be gone now!" she said loudly, and for Gerald's arm pulled him through the nale light beings.

he turned around to stare, they had all 1. "That was very good, Donna!"

mmon sense!"

en of the upstairs group had appeared the staircase to see what was happening. "A little etheric trouble-shooting.." quipped Donna, "not everything out there is benefic!"

The reaction this brought forth was profound, and as always there was a great clamouring to go down below and see what it was that was so uncivil and unsavoury.

"All in good time." chided Donna, her schoolmistressy demeanour coming on her naturally as the only means to control these Saturday affairs without them becoming chaotic.

Gerald looked at her with grudging admiration. The woman was without equal in her ability to manipulate situations.

"Let's now regain our composure.." said Donna.

"And see if we can get exposure.." quipped one of the men in the group, already at his camera.

"Yes, exactly!" laughed Donna; the proceedings were underway nicely, with just the right dash of curiosity and unrest to intensify the interest.

*   *   *

Gerald felt that he had lost his grip totally now, on his life and his psychic experiments. He had clearly given his power away to Donna, and lost his understanding with Elaine. Elaine had not contacted him since he had taken her to her sister's. And everytime he tried to ring her at Amanda's it was the answering machine or Michael saying she was out. Out! Where the hell could she be going? They were lying to him obviously! There was something wrong.

Gerald needed to take time to think about everything, which was what he had planned to do earlier in the week, before being beaten up by Ridley. He felt his mind wandering off to other matters, even

as he was supposedly directing people on camera
angles and lighting. He desperately needed to go
for a pee, but he was afraid that if he went downstairs alone the motley crew from the dark ages would
once again make threats upon his life.

"If we could get footage of those guys we saw
before it would be marvellous.." Donna suddenly
appeared at his left and whispered in his ear.

"Oh, yes.." he closed one eye and looked through
the viewfinder towards the north window, "no
doubt! . . . You could make a killing with that one!"

"No pun intended I hope.."

He straightened and looked at her.

"Well, according to you, they were out to get you
personally!"

"I assure you they were!"

"Perhaps you have whatsit with them.."

"What?"

"You know, the Sanskrit thing.!"

"Karma!"

"Yes, that!"

"I don't care what I have with them..I'm not about
to risk life and limb tangling with them!"

"Gerry, they're ghosts!" Donna's eyes sparkled
with probing fascination, their milky grey depths
seeming pearlescent in the meek sunshine glistening off the chamber walls. She was still very attractive
to him, but not in the same way as Elaine. He had
fallen for that old temptation that men were prey
to; the passing thrill of an exciting new woman.

"I'm not so sure!" he replied at length.

"What I mean is, they can't harm you!"

"I'm not so sure!"

"Oh good heavens! . . . you're supposed to be

photographing light beings not writing a script for a Spielberg movie!"

Gerald's mobile rang. He visibly jumped with shock as it trilled Colonel Bogey from his inside jacket pocket. He was worn down by three weeks of high drama and his physical stamina weakened by one event after another. He was hoping it might be Elaine as he took out the phone, but it was Marjorie. "Where are you now?" she enquired, in an almost polite way.

"Working.."

"Yes, but where?"

"At the castle!"

"Do you suppose you'll be back soon?"

"Probably tonight . . . why?"

"I'm just checking!" Marjorie sounded as if she'd taken acting lessons. "Its nice to keep in touch now and then!"

"Yes, fine.." Gerald said, inappropriately, startled by this out-of-character dialogue, and he heard Marjorie put down the receiver at her end.

"Let's go downstairs.." Donna said, confidently, "to the ground floor, but with the group!..That way you'll have back-up if they appear!"

"Its not a comical matter, Donna!"

"Of course not, but one needs to keep a sense of humour!"

Gerald sighed. There would be no getting out of it now. They would all demand to discover more about the darker side for themselves, and probably demand their money back if not satisfied.

"Ok.." Donna turned to the group. "Come on, everyone!..We will go down to the ground floor and begin to see if we can sight the Picks or Galls or what-ever Gerry and I saw a while ago!"

The murmurings and clamourings were reminis-

cent of a schoolyard, or a group of tourists given free
wine with their lunch. Gerald watched on in desultory manner. There was another one of these events
planned for Wednesday week in Derbyshire, and a
whole series of them throughout the nation on sub-
sequent Saturdays. Perhaps this would be the last one
he did! Perhaps he would eschew the temptation of
the roll of notes! Perhaps, and perhaps not! It might
be that he would not be strong enough to do that
without a course of hypnotic suggestion.

They had all begun to move towards the stairs
when the elf appeared at the top of them.

"Where you lot off too?" he demanded.

Donna assumed her loftiest manner. "Not now,
Alf, please . . . I've no time!"

"We havn't discussed the business of my terms
yet!" said Alf, shamelessly.

Donna grabbed his elbow and yanked him to the
side of the chamber. "Listen, we will reach harmonious agreement at the end of today..but not now . . ."

"How do I know you'll keep to it?.."

"You don't . . . its called trust.."

"Trust?"

"Yes . . . its what fifty nine percent of business is
founded upon!"

Alf looked non-plussed "But..I don't think I.."

"Alf.." Donna dropped her voice to a mere whisper, "I'm not arguing! . . . go away or this will be the
last time I use the place.."

She peered at him questioningly—at his unshaven, grubby face, the remains of his breakfast jam
around his elfin chin. "Think about it . . . there are
lot of places like this, you know!"

Alf heaved in his breath and clamped his lips together angrily, but with notable reflection upon her words.

"I'm right aren't I? . . . and you know it!" concluded Donna, again addressing a schoolchild. "Now leave me to work and we'll talk business later!"

Alf turned on his heel and partly hopped and partly shuffled out of the chamber, in his strange everyday gait which someone today had already likened to Charlie Chaplin. He was some way down the stairs when he realised that although what she said was right, not everywhere had the kind of spooks she needed. He hovered on the brink of turning round, but then thought better of annoying her.

"Is he one of them, by any chance?" someone asked.

Donna smiled beatifically at the lady, and tried to soften the amusement of the group at this ludicrous suggestion. "Not as far as I know. . . . but he might be, I suppose!"

"Can we get on now, folks!.." Gerald said in a loud voice. "Time is of the essence!" He moved stolidly with his camera to the stairs and heard a male voice say: "That's rich from someone who turns up three quarters of an hour later and keeps disappearing!"

Gerald ignored this and carried on, his equipment balanced precariously on his shoulder and upper arms. He felt he had never been subject before to such a ridiculous and compromising working situation. He thought he would give it half an hour and then skive off and leave them for a further two, re-emerging after lunch some time. If they cared to make skits and comment on it, let them! He was calling the tune, not them.

*   *   *

The morning went off reasonably well, Gerald
felt, within the balance necessary. It was nicely surreal without being glaringly sinister or macabre. And
whilst Donna might be open to anything, up to and
including re-runs of 'The Exorcist', he did not welcome weird or freaky occurrences. Besides, there
was the spiritual angle to be considered. His light
beings were good guys, he had been entirely convinced of that, until the appearance of the dancing
maidens and their alter-egos or male entourage.
They had obviously slipped in from the dark side,
but it naturally begged the question of what else
might take similar advantage.

With these eclectic fears partially in mind, amid
the other more pressing and human problems in his
life, he went off to lunch, alone. When he returned
two hours later, he was greeted by looks of derision,
ranging from slight contempt to open dislike of his
behaviour. He had been attempting to get in contact with Marjorie, to no avail, and then with Elaine,
again to no avail, and this had meant buying a card
for his pay-as-you-go mobile, since the phone box
nearest the pub in which he had lunched was
vandalised.

The groups' collective census on his behaviour
might have been worse had it not been for the fact
that just after the lunch break two of the group had
sighted a monk in the lower chambers of the castle.
The speculation about this was quite understandably
of more interest than his careless conduct and lightning absences.

Donna informed him immediately of the sighting, to detract from his short-comings and give

people something else to concentrate on. "Penelope and Jean both saw it!" she told him, pausing while Gerald acknowledged Penelope and Jean in person. "Perhaps you should tell Gerald yourselves, ladies.."

Penelope and Jean were both in their fifties and not the frail or impressionable type of female. They were, on the contrary, rather robust and unimaginative, and could not grasp the nuances of what they had seen weighed against what they knew of common physics: the fact that matter cannot disintegrate in the face of more solid matter; a person cannot walk through a wall.

"But this is not a mortal person." Gerald explained.

"Oh, yes.." said Penelope, "he was as solid as you are..I . . . we..saw him and heard him moving.."

"That has nothing to do with it!" said Gerald.

They stared at him, awaiting further and—what was most galling—more convincing explanation.

Gerald was not at his most patient. He stared back at them, as if merely pausing to hear any other comments.

They continued to look at him mutinously. "Well, where are these creatures from?"

"They are not creatures!" he said, in constrained aggravation.

"If they are not human beings and not creatures, what are they then?"

Where had Donna found these troglodytes! He turned to address her personally. "You did make it plain that people need at least an awareness of metaphysics, did you?"

"Yes, Gerald!" Donna raised her brows warningly; he was not to offend the patrons.

And still Penelope and Jean were staring at him,

their faces masks of stony and implaccable challenge, awaiting his erudite summary on matters that were supposedly his domain.

Gerald, put upon, felt it time to embellish nature and garnish the esoteric. He closed his eyes and looked heavenward, then breathed rhythmically for a few moments before holding up his arms in the way evangelists and mystics have done since time immemorial, his palms uppermost to the sky as if receiving holy inspiration, or checking for rain in as wide as possible a radius.

All the group had gathered round now. They looked on a little sceptically but with riveted fascination, in an atmosphere conducive to hearing a pin drop.

Donna too closed her eyes, she sensed that the light being was now in the chamber above (where mortals could not tread for fear of crumbling architecture). Unlike Gerald, Donna did not question these phenomena too closely. She saw it simply as yet another astonishing fact in life, of which there were many—whether mundane or supernatural. The cosmos was nothing if not surprising, and to see one amazing revelation was not dissimilar to seeing another.

Gerald opened his eyes and drew breath. He smiled. Everyone shuffled expectantly. Then he closed his eyes again briefly before opening them wide once more and allowing his features above his beard to radiate benign and gentle surprise, rather like a parent who sees that the child is walking unassisted after falling down in the act of trying to run.

"I see that they are with us today.."

"Who?" enquired the bold and forthright Penelope.

"The Great Father Fraternity!" said Gerald.

There was a hushed and palpable pause while this was assimilated.

"And who are they?" said Jean at length.

Gerald gazed at her as if she should wait until the penny dropped. They were certainly not a performing circus act, nor were they a European football team. It was quite obvious to anyone who they were!

"A group of holy monks!" supplied a youngish man to the right of Penelope and Jean in a modest and soft tone.

"Discarnate of course!" added Gerald.

"Oh.." said Penelope, and it sounded as if she had been momentarily put in her place.

"And what are they doing?" asked Jean.

Gerald allowed himself a slight chuckle; the parent again, indulgent to the antics of the cherished off-spring. "Actually they are strewing rose petals!"

There was a communal silence, an unspoken mixed reaction.

"What on earth for?" Penelope queried next.

Gerald hesitated—it was possible that Penelope and Jean were a double act hired to heckle, the way theatre managers in Shakespeare's day hired hecklers to ruin the performances of rival theatres. "To demonstrate their love for you!"

Donna drew breath audibly. Gerald was going too far. Perhaps he had taken something at lunch. Or regressed to his hippy days under the duress of his current life problems. He would be sporting a bandana round his head next and inciting everyone to hold orgies.

"But why would they want to do that?" asked the young man next to the 'double act'.

"Because.." Gerald hesitated, "that is how it is in the higher realms!"

"How do you know?" responded Penelope, on cue.

A barrage of inane questions began and he fixed a long-suffering smile like the Pope on a walkabout. Presumably though the Pope had attendants around him to fend off the morons and save him from being harangued with unanswerable esoteric questions.

"Can they see us then?"

"Yes!"

"Why don't they show themselves to others besides Jean and Penelope?"

Jean sprang forward a few feet, defensively, as if in a union meeting or a civil demonstration. "Hang on, I only saw one..not a troupe of them! . . . no-one's mentioned *them* in the plural except Gerald here!"

"Perhaps you should try looking for them!" Gerald remarked.

"So, this is rather like a game of hide and seek?"

"No, not at all!"

"Why are they strewing rose petals if we can't see either the petals or them?"

"Its symbolic!"

"Does that mean they don't really exist?. . . ."

"I can't answer that"

"How do they know we deserve all this love. . . ."

"That's irrelevant!"

"Should we have a séance and sit in circle or something?" Penelope suddenly interjected.

"I don't think so!"

"What's the difference between a séance and what we're doing?"

"The intention and the motive!"

"Can you be more specific?"

"No" said Gerald, losing patience **"I can not!"**

Fortunately, one of the females had been to the rented toilets, situated in the grounds of the castle. She ran in panting from exertion. "I've seen another of them .."

"Another of who?" Donna demanded—it was time she took control!

"The great father thingy..a monk!"

This time there was unbridled enthusiasm and without waiting for instruction, permission or guidance, the group moved as one accord to the stairs and descended in leaps and bounds. Whilst Gerald subsided against the wall. "What a fiasco!"

"Rubbish!" Donna tied a scarf round her throat. "Its what they're here for! . . . I thought you were a believer..not a charlatan!"

Unable to comprehend what he had heard, Gerald came to life. "A charlatan!..who are you calling a charlatan?"

"You! . . . mocking their witness and decrying their enthusiasm! . . . and as for that business with the rose petals, I've never heard anything so feeble!.."

"Donna, you may be very clever but there are realms that you obviously do not have access to which I do!"

Donna lit a cigarette she had been holding for two minutes and prepared to follow the group. "God, Gerald . . . talk about a ham!.."

"How dare you!" Gerald retorted angrily, but his voice had that reedy effect which betokened his inconfidence and belied his outrage.

"To think that you once told me you were an open minded investigator! . . . and once also accused me of being an *uninterested commercially oriented onlooker!*

It would seem the tables are turning, Gerald, as they always tend to do!"

Strolling from the chamber in her cream suede boots, Donna watched him sidelong and noted his bitter and hang-dog expression. She would have to get rid of him before the next seminar. He was too much of a liability, not to mention a damper on proceedings.

*   *   *

Downstairs and some twenty minutes later, Penelope was in tears. There was natural surprise, because when people like Penelope crumble it always has a more sentient effect. Several of the group were attempting to comfort her.

"Whatever is it?" Donna said.

"She saw the Monk!" said Jean.

"Oh? . . ." Donna was at a loss. "And did he frighten her?"

"She thought she recognised him!" said one of the men sensibly, since everyone else thought this information too sacred or private to be related.

Donna sighed impatiently at Penelope. She felt more than ever like the teacher with teenage pupils who are at the age to close ranks and to have rebellious secrets. She felt, in short, excluded, and it bothered her more than she would have imagined. She fought hard to get a hold of her poise and confidence and to transcend her own irritation. "I'll fetch Gerald!"

"And what's he going to do this time?" asked the young man with Jean and Penelope in jocular tone, "organise an identity parade?.."

Donna held up her hand to silence the explosions of merriment. It was deteriorating into a

shambolic comedy of errors. "Derek, I don't think
there's any need for irreverence.. or sarcasm!"

"Sorry, Donna!" said Derek, "But you have to admit he's a bit of a flake!" and flushed a little, feeling
flattered by Donna's direct and alluring attention.

"I'll call him.." Donna moved to the staircase.
"Gerald.." she shouted, fetching a slight echo back
on herself around the cavernous place . She had no
intention of going up to Gerald; she knew when she
had scored a victory and was not about to undermine
it. "We need you here!"

"He's probably having to fight his way through all
the petals!" said Derek sotto voce for the entertain-
ment of the group, although he did not look at any-
body as he spoke, and who could deny it was a free
country! Donna turned to glare at him, causing him
to flush deeper.

Meanwhile, three of the younger women in their
mid-twenties found it all so amusing they were con-
vulsed with silent laughter, and Donna knew from
experience that they would not be able to contain
themselves now and would go from bad to worse.
Especially when Derek recommenced his drollery.
She had once witnessed a similar debacle in an historic chateaux in France while conducting a tour.

When Gerald appeared, he at once recognised
in Penelope the signs of 'psychic shock'. No doubt
some unfortunate half-sighting had given cause to
exaggerated responses, and everyone present was
infected by the tremors. It would be best to segre-
gate her from the group, but of course that was impossible.

"She thought she knew this monk.." Donna informed him, "but that is unlikely isn't it?"

"I don't know!" Gerald was huffy. "I cannot an-

swer those kind of questions! . . . there is no reason
why she would not recognise him..it could be past
life ancestral, or even this life ancestral.."

"How do you mean?" demanded Derek.

Gerald patently ignored him, until he repeated
his question. "How do you mean, Gerald?"

"Look.." Gerald swung around from his camera,
"I am not here to give you a lecture on metaphysics!. . . . go and research things for yourself!"

There were some gasps of horrified indignation,
but he did not care. Donna moved next to Gerald
and kicked him succinctly on the ankle. He sprang
back and stared at her. Her expression was little short
of murderous.

"I don't know what we've paid our money for!"
Derek was saying, but to nobody in particular.

"Let me make it clear," Gerald said, rattily, "I am
not here to supply a family tree for every etheric sighting you may see! . . . simply to instruct you on the
process of how to film them!"

"He was merely asking a civil question!" one of
the other men adjoined.

"And I am giving him a civil answer.." Gerald replied, his voice a touch reedy, as his alarm and anxiety rose. "I have no idea whether Penelope genuinely knows this monk or not! . . . she is responsible
for herself!"

Penelope was now gathering herself together.
She moved into their midst as if to distract them from
the possibility of a wrangle. "I thought it looked like
my grandfather!" she said, somberly.

"Was he ever a monk?" enquired Jean.

"No!"

"Well then!" said another woman close by. "There
we are!"

"Where exactly?" Derek asked.

"Case of mistaken identity!"

"Not necessarily!" said Gerald. "He might have shown himself in one of his past lives!"

"As a monk?" said Jean, eagerly.

"Yes!"

"Why would he do that?" Derek re-positioned his tripod, as though expecting Penelope's ancestor to be attracted by the publicity and appear on the staircase.

"There you go again!" said Gerald, "asking questions which have no validation in etheric terms . . . your thinking is too logical!"

Derek caught the sympathetic look Donna cast him and lowered his voice. "He doesn't like me does he?"

"Take no notice.." Donna smiled brightly as she spoke, almost through gritted teeth. "Don't take it personally, Derek!"

"He's getting my goat" said Derek, quietly.

"Then don't let him!"

Gerald turned to look at them "Is there something you want to say to me?"

"Not much point is there!" said Derek. "Seeing as you always jump down my throat.."

"So, do you suppose Penelope's grandfather is a member of the great father thingumy?" asked one of the women.

"*Fraternity!*" supplied Gerald in irritation.

"Yes..do you supose he's a member?"

"I have no idea!"

Derek looked at the woman. "See.. no point in asking him anything!"

"I wasn't addressing you!" said Gerald.

"May as well save your breath.." Derek added.

"If you are not prepared to think for yourselves and be a little open and reflective about what you see, you should not have attended" Gerald announced, imperiously.

The general silence appeared to hum with vituperation. It was broken only by some strange squeaking sounds—the young women, handkerchiefs pushed to their mouths, while they pretended to cough, their shoulders shaken by spasmodic and irrepressible mirth.

"Maybe you should take a break now!" Donna told Gerald. "I think you are a little overwrought!"

"I don't know what from.." said one of Derek's male cronies, "he's not exactly over-worked and burning off energy . . ."

The atmosphere was growing very contentious and Gerald could feel it, when suddenly one of the men ran up the stairs in panic. "They tried to kill me" he said, breathlessly.

The little posse waited, to see if this were more comedic relief. But he ran across to them and sank down against the wall. "Some thugs in loin cloths, and tattered clothing . . . they looked like something off a film set . . . Anglo Saxon tribesman or something.."

"What? ghosts?" Donna demanded.

"No..they were solid..one of them threw a knife at me! . . . Then this wizened little chap came and yelled at them!"

"*Alf!*" Donna looked over at Gerald, aghast, and Gerald looked smug.

Donna had gone pale. "Where is this knife?"

"Down there I suppose..near the porta-loos!"

En-masse the group moved to the window and peered down.

"Something shiny on the ground down there near the pay-gate.."

"No sign of any tribesmen though.."

"Let's go and see.."

"Hang on.." Donna assumed her most authoritative manner but to no avail. There was a surge to the stairs and they moved excitedly but with careful tread to the lower regions.

"Now look..!" said Donna, like a mother with unruly children.

Gerald had begun packing up. "Not my fault.."

"Where are you going?"

"Home!..you don't think you can get this back ontrack do you?"

"You can't just go home!"

"I can and I am.."

"Shouldn't we find out what Alf knows about them? . . . he obviously can see them!" It was apparent as she gazed from the window that someone had located the weapon and was holding it up for the rest to see, it was a crudely fashioned knife or blade of some kind.

"You can if you want, but even you may be out of your depth, Donna!"

"You are supposed to be an expert on these matters!..that's what you're doing here! . . . but just as things get interesting you bottle out!"

Gerald slung his camera bag over his shoulder and picked up his coat.

"Gerry, if you leave now, you will never work on this project again!"

"Tough!" said Gerald and snapped his tripod shut with a flourish. "You can send me a check for today!"

"And you can kiss my arse!" said Donna, resisting the need to panic at what she should do next.

CHAPTER THIRTEEN

PULLING UP OUTSIDE Amanda's cottage, Gerald wondered how he would open his dialogue with Elaine. He was aware that he was not actually favourite with her now, or she would not be ignoring his calls.

He waited at the top of the steep steps leading to the cottage. Eventually the door opened and revealed Michael, who gaped with morbid stare; this, his second opportunity to observe the 'philandering bastard' at close quarters!

"Is Elaine in?"

"No..she's out!"

"Where is she?" Gerald asked, without preamble.

Michael continued his dull appraisal of Gerald's face.

"Look, do you know where she is?"

"Who is it?" he heard Amanda call from inside the cottage.

"It's..it's.." Michael could not think of the right descriptive phrase in the polite sense. "Its Aunty Elaine's friend!"

Amanda appeared in person and looked sourly at Gerald. Michael stepped back to his bedroom and the television.

"Come in!" said Amanda, "but she's not here!"

Gerald stepped into the small enclosure of the hall and followed her into a room which was the lounge, disproportionately narrow and low, like the stem of a letter L., with its casement windows and its dark interior, the antithesis of what he was used to at his own modern, airy residence.

He could not help but stare around him; the professional photographer overtaking the anxious lover in terms of awareness.

"Sit down!" said Amanda, briskly, and he did so.

"I don't suppose you know where she is?"

"Of course I know where she is.." Amanda's eyes began to blaze, lit from within by emotions unknown to him. "She's with him from next door-but-one . . ."

"What?" Gerald was bemused, the words conveyed no meaning even though he heard them correctly.

"She's gone somewhere or other with Rod Yates!"

"Who the hell's Rod Yates?"

"My next-door-but-one neighbour!"

Having made the revelation from hell, Amanda vacated the room, like an eddying wind, and left him sitting there, sorting out the words from the thoughts and the meaning from all of it. A little while elapsed and she entered again, carrying a small tray with two mugs of tea. She plonked one down next to him with negligent disregard, so that it spilled over and ran along the walnut inlay of her occasional table. She seemed not to care, or even to notice.

Gerald took a sip from the mug, before any more catastrophe could befall it; he had not eaten or drank much in the last two days, due to pressure of life.

"So?" Amanda glared at him over her own drink. He stared back at her dully.

"What do you think?"

"About what?"

"About my sister and Rod Yates!"

Gerald stroked his beard. "I don't know that I rightly understand what you're saying.."

"How thick are you!" said Amanda. "I'm saying that Elaine and Rod Yates are an item!"

"An item?" he echoed weakly.

"Yes..they're romantically attached! . . . he's filling his boots! . . . she's gracing him with her favours!. . . . how many more ways do you want me to describe it?. . . . At this rate they'll be shacked up together before you can look round!"

"I don't believe it!" Gerald said, and his voice seemed to come back to him from afar.

He heard Amanda laugh. It occured to him that he and Amanda had never met before, but they had sort of waved that fact under the extenuating circumstances. It felt as if he had known her a long time now.

"You probably don't want to believe it!" she said. "Otherwise you might have to take a good look at yourself!"

Gerald turned his gaze sharply to hers' and frowned. He did not really welcome this confrontation but could not avoid reacting to her words; anything else would have been stupid. He hated confrontations, but he supposed this one was inevitable. He waited, until she chose to speak again.

"Two bloody years I'v been cultivating a friend-ship with Rod Yates!..two years! . . . and then Elaine comes along and moves right in on it! . . . How do you think I feel about that?"

Gerald opened and closed his mouth and felt helpless.

"Its not even as if she'd gone out of her way to look good, the way I had! . . . she didn't!..she just sauntered about in her jeans and a sloppy old sweater, those bruises half covered with make-up, and some-times not even any make-up on at all!.."

Gerald closed his mouth firmly and stared at the china plates adorning the walls—scenes from old rural England—he just could not catch up in his head.

"Talk about there being no justice!" said Amanda.

He found his voice. "It doesn't sound like Elaine!"

Amanda gaped, her eyes awash with untold and furious passions. "Oh, doesn't it!"

"No..she's usually so..so.."

"So what? . . . dull?..dim? . . . unattractive?.."

"No..just..just so . . ."

"Loyal, I think you mean! . . . I think you mean she was so loyal!" Amanda sat back in the chair with a little plop, in a satisfied manner. "And so she was to you! . . . and to Graham!. . . . and to everyone really!..That's the worse part, I know what a good soul she is!. . . . she's my own sister, so its hard to hate her!"

Amanda and Gerald fell silent in joint agree-ment, the mystery of Elaine's departure from loyalty uniting them in the gloom of the long, low cottage room, lit as yet by only one early street light at a distance.

"And where were you, I may ask?" Amanda's voice suddenly invaded the quiet space, so that Gerald started visibly and shuffled uncomfortably. "Where were you when it was all taking place?" She stared at him, her eyes oddly tranquil compared to her tone. "Strutting round some bloody castle!"

"I was working!" His voice was patient, but touched even so with an edge of dignified resentment.

"Working!. . . . not for the last however many years you weren't!"

"That is not..not.." he tailed off, unable to finish.

"Not what?" Amanda coaxed. "Not my business, were you going to say?"

"No, I was going to say . . . not relevant!" lied Gerald—even now he could not say what he thought, and despised himself for it.

"Of course it's relevant!..do you imagine this would have happened if you'd got on with life years ago? Do you seriously think she'd have looked at another man, the way she adored you?"

Gerald turned a beetroot colour. Despite his resolve to autonomous choice he was partly ashamed. He half rose, and then sat again.

"Its all your bloody fault!..you've ruined everyone's lives!"

"Rubbish!" His expostulation spluttered stupidly from his mouth, his voice high and squeaky. Pathetically, he heard himself elaborating. "You can't say that. . . . its not logically correct!"

"I can say it, and I have!. . . . and don't give me logically correct!..what are we all going to do now?"

"I don't know..I'm not God!"

"No, you're not! . . . you're some sad, suburban Don Juan, deluded about your own prowess with women!"

"I don't live in suburbia!" Gerald said, more stupidly than ever. And then he found the stamina to rise, and did so, but with his knees a little bent. "I'd better go!"

"Yes, I suppose you had!. . . . I expect she might be next-door-but-one if you want her!..or in the King's Head, round the corner!"

Gerald floundered in the sum total of his life's lack of moral stamina and daring as it came at him headlong and thunderously, rolling over him in one fell reaction against direct participation.

"But you won't do that will you?" Amanda said, reading his thoughts. "You won't do anything so bold! . . . you'd rather lose her than face it!"

"Its not the right time!" he said.

Amanda laughed. "Not the right time!..what are you waiting for..their wedding day?..are you going to stand at the back of the registry office and object when they ask for objections!"

Stiffly, he walked to the door, his knees still a little buckled, stooped like someone aged.

"I'll think about things!" he said, leaving Amanda perched in her chair, like a tense contestant in a game-show.

"That's all you ever do, Gerald!" He heard her words as he stepped out of the front door to the top step. The use of his name seemed an audacity in the circumstances. "And if you ask me, that's all you ever want to do!"

*   *   *

Outside, he wandered to his car. Not without a sense of the ironic, he realised he had left it next-door-but-one. And as he walked towards it he saw that Elaine was standing at the window of that house looking down on him.

Stopping in his tracks, he beckoned to her—a little weakly, it had to be said, but nonetheless it was clear that he wished to speak with her. She did not move, and presently she was joined by a man, presumably the said Rod Yates, who also stared at him. They appeared to be a couple. As if they had been together for years.

She was wearing the hairband she wore only at her most informal, scraping back her hair from her forehead and pinning it behind her ears: It gave her the 'at home' look which completed the picture.

Gerald felt out of himself now, as if he were no longer who he had always been. He expected it was a reaction to pain, or shock or something. It was a strange, disembodied feeling, and it made him think of his light beings. . . . the girl with the tripod, her feet some way from the floor!

He thought he understood then what death might be like: an entrance to a realm with sudden surprise—a level of being which was not connected to anything but tethered to what you had known; a ragged rope dragging a trailer full of useless yet priceless possessions that you could not let go of. And maybe you walked, or stood, forever, in the timeless infinity that was the supposed Universe . . .

He was still looking at Elaine, and she at him, but the man had gone. Either from discretion, or disinterest, he had disappeared. Gerald beckoned to her again, this time more forcefully, mouthing the words . . . 'let's talk, come out..'

A further full minute elapsed, suspended in this apprehension of potential outcome. Then, like a curtain going down on a small stage, dropping without ceremony—clumsily forbidding any poignant charm or grace of movement—the white lace drape in the window belonging to Rod Yates dropped back into position and Elaine had gone.

He waited, unable to move, pretending that mere seconds had passed when he knew it to be more like five minutes. Pretending that there was still some hope. Until it was not possible any longer to cling. She was not coming out. Not now!

*   *   *

Disbelief rooted him to the pavement, and he looked several times up and down the street, before going to the car. It was then that he discovered he had left his keys in Amanda's cottage.

Could the 'Powers That Be' dish up any further upsets and ironies? The realisation that he was being tested is some way, or even reprimanded, fleetingly came to his mind, and then vanished. He thought of himself as quite upstanding. Pure in reason, even. It did not do to become unwittingly self-reproachful. Life was never so simplistic.

With a sinking heart, he rang Amanda's doorbell again.

She answered almost immediately. She had been watching his progress from her own front window.

"I left my car keys on your table.."

Amanda turned and walked into the depth of the house, leaving him to follow. It was when they

were in the lounge that he saw that she had been
crying. He felt bad, but not as much as before.

"So, you tried to see her?"

"Yes..she won't come out..I can hardly force my
way in!"

"No..but you could come back!"

"*He* was with her..this Yates chap!"

"Naturally, its his house, but they're not joined at
the hip! . . . he'll have to go out sometime!"

"What do you suggest?..that I camp outside!"

Amanda did not reply. She grabbed the keys and
threw them over to him. "You're a very literal person
aren't you, Gerald? I thought you'd be more subtle
somehow..but I see you're not! . . . You're like a lot
of people I know, you have ideas above your station!"

That she was annoyed was inevitable, but what
she said and the way in which she said it was not ac-
ceptable to him, and therefore he had no insight
into her words. They did not concern him, did not
relate to him in any shape or form! She was just letting off steam. He resented the fact that she could
presume to know him at all when she had so little
acquaintance with him. He walked once more to her
front door.

"What I mean.." Amanda resumed, coming up
behind him, "is that you have too many notions of
how things ought to be! . . . and no idea of how to
make it all come about!"

Gerald thought it best to say nothing. It behoved
him to exit graciously, even inclining his head in
acknowledgement of her words, to imply that her
rights were with her own opinions. He felt the bigger for doing so. But Amanda saw only an arrogance
born of indifference to real meaning and despised

him then for all time! The impression was indelible now, as impressions at times like these tend to be.

She took up a watching position again at her window. She was holding off her pain and sadness (which would probably hit her in a while) with anger. The question of whether to take on the serious acceptance of the betrayal of her sisiter with the man she had hoped would develop feelings for her in the way she knew she was developing them for him? Or whether to shrug it off and put it down to the twists of fate for unknown reasons? Even to give them her blessing! It was not a decision to be made lightly, if it was, in fact, a decision at all!

It took some application to the subject. It meant carrying it around, becoming absorbed in it, until it had clarity. It was a daunting task, but the whole of her future and her family's future depended upon it.

"Stupid sod!" she said to no-one in particular, watching Gerald walk to his car.

Now that she was alone, Michael came into the room. "Who are you talking about?" He lollopped over to join her. "Oh, the philandering bastard, you mean?"

Amanda tutted vaguely and put her arm about his shoulders. "Mike, what a thing to say!"

"That's what you called him the other week!"

"Hmmm.." she was distracted momentarily by the U turn of Gerald's conspicuous red car. Once he had gone forever the total responsibility for the situation would be hers. "Well.. I was most probably being accurate.."

*   *   *

Gerald drove back to his home in zombie-like
lethargy. He felt he had left his body and was resid-
ing somewhere else, on another planet perhaps. It
was the strangest of sensations and one he had not
experienced since he and Elaine had been forced
to split the first time, all those years ago. It was as if
the usual signs of life had no meaning, as if he had
been de-sensitised, or de-personalised, or one of those
things. It was like the jaw felt after a local anaesthetic at
the dentists, only it applied to the whole of him.

The house from the outside looked much as it
always did: the arc lights were on over the back pa-
tio, he could see them as he swung around into the
circular avenue, his own house second on the left.
The porch was illuminated and Marjorie's car was
on the driveway in front of the double garage. This
was somewhat strange, as she always put it away as
soon as she had finished using it for the day. It was
now nearly ten o'clock at night and if she were in
then she was surely not going out again.

He parked and alighted, and then he saw that
his belongings were out on the driveway, tidily packed
in several suitcases; his overcoat, and a c.d. collec-
tion in a cardboard box nearby. Rushing up to the
front door he knew an unaccustomed surge of fury
as he rummaged for the key.

Marjorie was in the hall fiddling with magazines
for clients forced to wait there.

"What the hell are you doing?"

"Sorting my waiting-room mags!" she said
nonchalantly.

"No, I mean my belongings! . . . out there on the
drive!.."

She stopped fiddling and stood erect. "Oh, those! . . . I should have thought it obvious!"

"Obvious?..well, yes! but what do you think you're playing at!..this is my home as well!"

"Yes, but you're the errant partner so you're the one who has to leave!"

"Leave!..what for?"

"Because we have to divorce!"

"Marjorie.." He advanced towards her, his face very red and contrasted against his dark beard. "You can't just evict me . . . I have rights!"

"So do I..and I know what they are!..I don't have to stand for your infidelities!"

"But you've always known . . . I mean . . . we have an understanding on these matters!"

"Do we?"

"Yes. . . . you knew after . . . after the breakdown of our . . . of the conjugal part of matters . . . you knew that I would be..be . . ."

"Sleeping around?"

"Yes!. . . . no, not actually sleeping around! . . . I mean, you knew that I would make my . . . my own arrangements!"

"Oh, God, Gerald!" Marjorie too was florid of complexion as she slammed down two or three of the mags and glared at him. "How insensitive you are!.."

Gerald was involuntarily shamed into avoiding her eyes.

"*Making your own arrangements!..*"

"Well, how do you want me to phrase it . . . I'm being as delicate as I can!"

"Oh, yes, delicate alright! . . . with Donna Lees! . . ."

Gerald turned away sharply, coming into close

eye contact with the brass wall plaques, reminiscent of an olde worlde inn rather than a domestic residence. What appalling taste Marjorie had.

"That's over now!.." He stared at the plaques, about which and before their wall-mounting he was never consulted.

"Oh is it?..how convenient!..unfortunately its too bloody late, Gerald!"

Summoning something of a normal persona he walked into the kitchen. He could not quite believe that Marjorie was actually going to divorce him. It must be some kind of a ploy or a freakish whim based on female hormone change. It surely would not be an actual probability!

He dared not think too much on Elaine's desertion; it was like a seering hot blade in his mind which repelled him every time he mentally approached the memory. He felt he might be in shock, or in one of those traumatic emotional black-holes into which people descended, never again to emerge.

Marjorie followed him and watched as he poured himself a drink of mineral water from the fridge. He thought of nothing at all, his mind was mercifully blank. He did not register much beyond Marjorie's unrest. It was more than her usual unrest, but harder to fathom. It seemed to take the form of a curiousity mingled with a morbid resolve of some kind.

He began idly sipping the water, and as he did so he wondered idly—*everything Gerald did, he did idly*—how she had found out about Donna! But then she may have no hard evidence and only supposition to go on, perhaps from his business dealings over a number of weeks with Donna Lees.

"So where is she then?" Marjorie asked of his implacable back.

"Who? Donna?"

"No, Elaine!..I couldn't give a damn about Donna!"

Gerald put the glass down onto the fridge-top and walked from the kitchen door as if she had not spoken, intent on following the path round to the outer entrance of his studio.

"Gerald..I asked you a question!.." Marjorie followed, hard on his heels. "Where is Elaine?..Graham Ridley keeps calling here and he wants to know. He has a perfect right to know!"

"He has no right whatever. . . . he hit her!"

"He told me!"

"And you have sympathy with him?"

"I never said I had sympathy with him, but there are other considerations besides their scuffles! . . . he is her husband!"

In his mind's eye he could still see the brass wall plaques; tasteless and crass, especially to one of his professional propensities. "This wasn't a scuffle!..this was domestic violence!" He went in to the studio and closed the door on her.

Thinking again of the plaques, and other similar domestic abhorrences; he never had been consulted, in all of their married life! The affront this presented to his professional accomplishments was sudden and unlooked for: never once had she requested one of his more acclaimed pieces of camera work for the wall. Or requested him to go and photograph some specific object of interest and aesthetic value to her own taste. Oh no! That would have been far too risky, it might have given him some false impression of his own worth! All this was nearly as bad as the thought

of Elaine's desertion, coming as it did in the same
sickeningly unexpected manner.

He rummaged through his recently developed
films, looking again at the shots from the castle—the
whirling girls, their leader, the strongest, in singular
glory, a one-off study closer to. And then suddenly
he caught sight of a new photograph he had not
seen before, something he did not think he had shot
himself. He snatched it down from its peg where it
hung drying, and gazed at it. It was a circle of men,
dressed in ragged, rough garb; sacking and coarse-
weave wool, their hair long and matted. It was the
tribesmen from the castle. But he had not taken
photos of them, he had been too off-guard to reach
his camera.

Assiduously he frowned at the stills, vaguely aware
of Marjorie knocking on the door and demanding
stridently to be given attention. He examined all the
shots and then the ones he had taken some time
ago. Amongst those drying he discovered that the
most recent one of the dancing maidens had disappeared, but when he checked the numbering he
found that the tribesmen were reproduced on the
shots which should have contained the girls. So, they
could shape-shift on paper too! Or maybe he was
just going mad!

"Are you going to hide forever from the realities of life?"
Marjorie was asking in a voice which would no doubt
be heard by any neighbours interested enough to
listen. She was unaware of her own vocal prowess in
these matters, and no doubt felt she was being mod-
erate of octave.

He continued to look at the tribesmen until the
knocking grew aggravating in the extreme and in-
truded on his esoteric speculations.

Openning the door he intended to quieten her with words, but as he did this she put her bulk against it and pushed her way through, closing it firmly behind her. He stepped back, momentarily revolted by her at such close quarters and in such a frame of mind.

"Where is Elaine?"

"Its not my business!"

"Don't talk such rubbish!..whose is it then, if its not yours?"

Gerald leaned past her and attempted to re-open the door so that he could push and maneouvre her out. But she hit his arm just above the elbow, knocking his hand away from the latch. He moved back, swearing lightly. "Leave me in peace, Marjorie!"

"Not until you tell me where Elaine is and make signs of leaving the premises!"

"I have no intention of leaving the premises! . . . I'll sleep in here!"

"How long for?"

"Until I make other arrangements!"

"When will that be?"

"I don't know! . . . just get out and give me some peace!"

"Where is Elaine?"

"Why are you so interested?"

"I need to tell Ridley when he next appears!"

"Let him find out for himself!" Gerald turned then to look at his wife, to discover why she was suddenly so concerned with keeping Ridley informed on the subject. They had obviously been hob-nobbing together! As he stared at her he noted the subtle change of her expression as she moved, on the balls of her feet like a criminal intruder, and darted in a sideways move towards his work-table, where she picked up the proofs of the light beings and held them aloft between her fingers and thumbs as if to tear them. *"Tell me!"*

Gerald was unable to believe her pantomimic audacity. And then suddenly—as suddenly as the realisation about the brass plaques—he had had enough. He saw the next months roll out like so much of his negative film: acrimony, stealth, accusation, humiliation, failure . . .

Marjorie had begun to tear the proofs, carefully and slowly, so as not to actually complete the task before he gave in to her demands.

He picked up the brass bell which had once belonged to his father's printworks (in the days when reception areas were mere lobbies and necessitated the summoning of a human). He saw, fleetingly, Marjorie's expression of frozen horror and mutinous hatred before hitting her over the head with the bell.

She staggered, round-eyed, dropping the film and rotating her arms like someone skating for the first time trying to maintain their balance, and then she crumpled to the ground in a heavy, disjointed sort of heap.

Gerald took up his films, examining them for marks and spoilage, seeing them mercifully in tact. He leaned over Marjorie and, finding her still breathing, went out and closed the door behind him.

When he had taken his belongings upstairs to his bedroom he carried the films with him to the car and reversed out into the avenue once more and drove away from the scene of the crime.

CHAPTER
FOURTEEN

DONNA DROVE INTO the parking space right outside Bar Espanol, which could have been reserved
for her by some interested and magnanimous party
but was in fact a rare fluke of timing. Checking her
appearance in the rear-view mirror—more for good
luck than for genuine doubt about herself—she already had her hand on the door handle to make a
swift exit. She was ten minutes later than the time
she had agreed to meet Guy West. Of course, it mattered little; men always waited, in fact it did them
good to wait: one might even say they expected to
have to wait, and anything else disappointed them!
One could say that, but one rarely did, out loud at
any rate!

Guy West pushed a gin and tonic in front of her,
as if it were a piece on a chess board, his mouth set,
his eyes uncompromising (he obviously could be the

exception proving the rule). He watched her take a few sips and then handed her a menu, again as if it were an obligatory process rather than a pleasurable gesture.

Donna frowned, receiving the menu with her eyes fixed on his face. "Are we in a hurry of some sort?"

"The sooner we order the sooner we can get down to business!"

She held the menu to one side as if to aggravate him. "Has something significant happened?"

He went into his inside pocket and retrieved a photo packet.

Inside were shots of the ancient tribesmen who had been responsible for the debacle on last Saturday's event! The latest in the series of light beings!

Bloody Gerald! He had done it to her again!

She looked back at West. "What do you want me to say?"

"You cannot exclude someone with this sort of talent from the deal!"

"But..he . . . I don't understand.." She snatched up the film again from West's hand and began to study it. "I'm too shocked for words! . . . He can't have taken this himself, he didn't have time!"

West watched her patiently, inviting more comment.

"He saw something, he said, something which would fit the description of what you're showing me but he did not have his camera with him!. . . . and then when everyone rushed outside to see them he wanted nothing to do with it!"

"I don't understand what you're talking about Donna.." West said placidly, "can you cut to the chase!"

"All I mean is, he left the castle before he had time to take any films of these particular ghosts.."

"Well, somehow, they are here, in this magnificent shot!"

"When did he give you this?"

"He didn't *give* me anything, I paid him for it!..handsomely!"

Donna waved her hand dismissively. "Yes, but when?"

"This morning . . . he phoned and we met!"

"Slimy bastard! . . . you shouldn't have agreed without speaking to me!"

"And have him sell them elsewhere!"

"But why should he?"

"Because he's desperate! He would go somewhere else now soon as wink!. . . . He looked as if he was on something to me!"

Donna turned from sipping the aperitif. "He looked like that on Saturday too! . . . He's often like that recently, it means nothing, Guy!"

"My point, Donna, is that you can't entirely trust someone in that state! . . . You never know which way they'll jump!"

"Guy, if you want him in count me out!"

Guy West looked at her seriously, raising an eyebrow, an unspoken question about whether she really expected him to make that choice under the circumstances.

"He's too good at this to be passed over!" West told her.

"Only with my organising skills!"

"Yes..I know..but the fact remains.."

"Fact, my arse!" said Donna and shrilled to the waiter to bring her another drink. "I can't stomach his patronising ways and his self-deluded egotism! . . . he's a flake, like Derek says!"

"Derek! who the hell's Derek?"

"Oh, a punter on the last event..but he had Gerald sussed!"

"Nevertheless, Donna, find a way to work with him. He does the business and that's all that matters!"

"Don't tell me what to do, Guy! I have other evidence that he can't procure!"

Guy raised his pleasant brows and she studied them with detached satisfaction and heard him say: "Such as?"

She reached into her bag without looking and retrieved a bundle wrapped in kitchen towel which she pushed along the table towards him, the way government agents did it in films.

Intrigued, West carefully unwrapped the paper and found a crudely fashioned knife or cutting instrument made of some kind of antique metal with a curiously polished veneer. He was for a moment more fascinated with the nature of the metal and its finish than with the exact meaning of the object. He had never seen any such material; it was either foreign or hand-crafted. He stared at her, his brows raised in query. "A weapon of some kind!"

"Ssshh!" Donna admonished, then looked around at other clientele guardedly.

"You haven't killed him have you?.." West found her stealthy cunning amusing. "Old Gerald!.. you haven't done for him between my buying the photo and our meeting tonight?"

The waiter delivered her gin and tonic and she grabbed it off the tray with asperity, her face blank, as if West had not joked and there was not a priceless artifact in white kitchen paper which the waiter watched with only passing interest as he turned to leave; he assumed her to be one of those persons whose parsimony led them to taking home the bread rolls.

Another few deep swigs of her drink and she leaned forward and modified her manner to a more intimate level. "Its an aport!.." she pronounced, and West's silence invited fuller explanation. "An aport is a.."

"I know what an aport is!" West intercepted. "I'm not a complete philistine! . . . Just give me the griff on this one!"

Donna began to speak in a tone so low it was a whisper. "These same tribesmen dropped it on the ground after apparently threatening one of the group!"

This information was a little heady even for a journalist of West's experience and zeal, ready to suspend disbelief in the face of huge readership. He rolled his tongue around the inside of his mouth, frowning, straightening his wrist watch—'playing for time' she thought wryly, smiling slightly at her own unspoken wit.

"Are you sure, Donna?"

"What do you mean? Do you mean, 'am I lying'? No, I am not!..Someone fetched it in while the group were present! There were witnesses! They only let me keep it because I said it was going for analysis!"

"That's what I will do with it, with your permission of course!"

"Ok. . . ." Donna took little tiny sips of the drink, thoughtfully—her lipstick glossy—eager for the liquor. West was aroused just watching her. "Ok..but I want something in writing!"

"We have to be open to the fact that it could be from anywhere..it could be a hoax, for example!"

She put the drink down, sharply. "I admit, I didn't

think of that! . . . No..no, I doubt its a hoax, Guy!"

"Let's hope not!" he smiled at her invitingly, seeing her melting from the ice-maiden of the public relations world to a woman desirous of affection.

The waiter hovered and they ordered the food and waited for him to leave the table.

"If handled rightly it could be worth a fortune to us.." Guy produced the weapon from its paper package and toyed with it gently. "Does Gerry know about it?"

"No, he doesn't." She took the relic from him and held it in her palm, like an offering. "He left before we found it, and I don't want him to know! He pulled out on me and made it clear he'd had enough!.. We don't need him now!"

West took back the instrument and began wrapping it. "Its obvious that someone's got to produce these kind of photos..and unless you can find someone else, make peace with Gerry!"

"I don't want to work with Gerald Monkton!" said Donna, haughtily.

"You haven't got another name have you?" Guy teased, "like 'Prima', for example!"

Donna crossed and uncrossed her legs beneath the table and lit a cigarette to displace the growing fury she felt rising in herself; a feverish kind of feeling intonating all sorts of future upset. "I do have the right to say who I wish to work with, Guy! . . . I am the one organising, and it is my baby!"

"It's gone beyond that now..it's in an entirely different league, and you.." West pointed one casual finger, "are not putting up the money for the castle! ..You are not hiring the whole shooting match and footing the bill! . . . It may be cheaper to buy the bloody castle than to meet that little bastard's terms!"

"Alf the elf! Pity he can't meet with some kind of accident!" said Donna, callously.

West looked as if her were considering the idea, his eyes calmly caressing her hair, his mind elsewhere. The starters arrived and they picked up cutlery and napkins.

"What have you done with those prints ultimately.?" Donna enquired.

Grinning, Guy West reached under his seat and brought out a copy of the Sunday paper he worked for. On the second page was the picture of the tribesmen, following up on the feature figuring the dancing maidens. It was massively impressive editorial and coverage.

Donna gaped at him, she had not seen the paper this day and had been busy arranging venues in the south of England for the furtherance of the project. He raised his glass to her in a theatrical gesture. She laughed, throwing back her luminous fair hair and revealing her perfect teeth.

* * *

Gerald had spent the night in Alf's cabin, behind the castle. It was obvious now where Alf spent most of his working life, but where he went after that remained a mystery. The cabin was rough, it had to be said, seldom cleaned or tidied, but it contained a sort of bunk effort, on which Alf slept. Gerald was glad not to look a gift horse in the mouth and took the offer of a bed for the night. Alf had made himself scarce after offering to loan his cabin to Gerald, and not returned until the following morning at about eleven o'clock.

Many tourists had arrived and were looking round

the castle, obviously as a result of the publicity photographs, and Alf had the job of collecting the amazing number of tolls from people who were willing to
pay, and of discouraging others from admitting themselves via the aperture in the masonry. Many more
were still arriving while Alf took a respite from this
task to visit the cabin, and they would no doubt gain
entrance for free, but Alf seemed unbothered by
the fact.

It occurred to Gerald to wonder why Alf did not
now seek to employ assistance, but this was only a
passing wonderment in light of his other concerns.

"You want some bacon?" he asked, generously.

Gerald was suspicious. "Where are you going to
acquire bacon?"

Alf tapped his nose and wandered off towards
the rear of the grounds.

Gerald huddled under the dirty blankets and
allowed his mind to rest on Elaine, and then on
Marjorie. He had not shaven since the day before
yesterday, nor bathed, and he knew he now resembled a vagrant and a down-and-out. He cared
little. His life seemed devoid of a future and had
plummeted into one endless present in which time
hung suspended and did not require the little nice-
ties like bathing and shaving anymore.

Eventually Alf returned with bacon sandwiches
and a mug of tea and Gerald ate with a desperate
hunger but little appetite.

Alf watched with morbid interest."You in trouble
again?" he enquired, carefully.

"Could say that!"

"God's Teeth!..I never knew anyone like you for
attracting trouble! . . . Ever since I know'd you you've
'ad trouble, and that's not been above five minutes!"

"True, Alf!..very true!"

"What you going to do?"

"Depends!"

"On what?"

"What happens next!"

Alf groaned and made for the door again. The conundrum of Gerald's affairs taxed his brains to the limit. "Where's the bird?" he asked over his shoulder.

"Which one?" said Gerald, absently.

"The one you took them photos for!"

"Donna! . . . dunno!..don't care!"

"Mind you, she seen me right.." Alf rubbed his thumb and finger together to indicate finances "I'll say that much for the wench!"

"She knows which side her bread is buttered!" said Gerald, bitterly.

The day beyond the greasy cabin window was turning decidedly winterish for mid-autumn; gloomy pewter clouds hung low over the horizon of hills and cold blasts of air swirled litter and dusty earth around the grounds.

"What exactly is this trouble?" Alf ventured, holding open the cabin door against the rising wind.

"You probably don't want to know!" Gerald replied, his mouth full of the food.

"Not 'im again is it, the feller whose wife you've been messing with?"

"No, not exactly!"

"Not done 'im in 'ave you?"

"No, but you're warm!" said Gerald, and chewed the last of the bacon sandwich thoughtfully.

At the pay-gate and beyond the confines of the castle proper, a massive crowd was converging on the place, resembling a cast of extras for a Hollywood epic.

* * *

Later that day the staff of 'Heritage Matters' gathered at Ruby Wallstock's, even though it was not their designated Sunday. It was Monday evening, and it felt very odd to them, as if time had lurched into some weird rhythm that had nothing to do with their normal lives at all. Such is the result of ritual and habit! They were attended by Conlan Kerrigan and the girl commis, and a cold buffet had been served in the conservatory. The only ones missing were Ruby's daughter, Grace, and her husband.

They all examined the Sunday papers more carefully. Especially the one which carried the picture of the tribesmen and the castle, having had their attention drawn to it by Bill Brightwell who was the first to enter the house. Formby was late, due to an extraordinary meeting called for the shareholders of 'Heritage Matters' demanding to know what was going on.

Donna Lees' name appeared quite often in this latest editorial written by Guy West. It clearly stated that she had once worked for 'Heritage Matters'.

"*Once* worked for us!.." Ruby echoed, spectacles on the very end of her nose. "Havn't they got that wrong?"

"She resigned on Wednesday!" Formby said, quietly.

As if stung, Bill Brightwell stepped back from the marble table under the lighted torches held aloft by the Greco/Roman females. "No-one told me about that!"

"I havn't had chance.." Formby opined, "I was in Bristol on Thursday, and Friday you were out on site!. . . . Anyway, there was no particular crisis or urgency caused by the event!"

"That's a matter for opinion!" said the majority shareholder, contentious as ever.

"What could you have done?" continued Formby.

"Not the point!" retorted Brightwell.

Ruby straightened her aged back rather stiffly. "Is she not working any notice?"

"No . . . except for tidying loose ends!..She doesn't expect to be paid any more money though."

Conlan Kerrigan entered bearing a tray with the best cognac; an avenging angel with telepathic powers and mature nurturing skills. He wore an enigmatic smirk as if he had distilled the liquor personally and was immensely proud of it, knowing the solace it would bring in the disquiet of the contemporary business life.

"Wonderful, Con!" Ruby held her bejewelled hands together in frozen applause. "Now gentlemen, we said last time that we would act if anything further occurred!. . . . do we today feel this needs to be acted upon?"

"Yes..but there isn't much we can do.." Bill Brightwell picked up the cognac the instant Con set it in their midst, "if we are honest about it!"

"Oh, I don't know.." said Edward, "we could employ people who would tell us!"

"Do you mean legal people?" Ruby enquired of her partner.

"Yes..or public relations!"

"Very costly.." Brightwell said.

"Its what is done though.." Edward accepted

brandy from Geoff Formby, "in these kind of circumstances!"

"Maybe, Edward, but we need to decide first whether we want to let the matter drop or make more of it.." Ruby touched Edward's arm gently; she disliked having to thwart his suggestions.

"That is something we will find difficult to decide on!..that is the gamble!" said Formby.

The night beyond the conservatory was very dark owing to a day's rain and overhung skies. Nothing much was to be seen beyond the huge glass walls. They all stared even so at the darkness, seeking distraction or inspiration from other quarters. The brandy helped; it oiled their mental wheels which were not particularly going anywhere, but coasting soothingly into alternative directions of thought.

Suddenly the silence was broken by the majority shareholder who jumped up from his perusal of the local newspaper. "Look at this . . . *Local photographer sought for attack on wife!* . . . isn't that what's-his-name..the chap contracted by Donna to get these ghost films?"

Being nearest, Ruby snatched the paper from him and stuck her nose into the printed sheet. "Yes, yes . . . Gerald Monkton . . . it says so here . . . *Monkton, a well known commercial photographer is alleged to have struck his wife with a blunt instrument before fleeing their detached residence in the Plumley Vale district. Police are asking anyone who knows of his wherabouts etc etc . . .*" Ruby frowned at them over her spectacles.

"Is the wife alive?" questioned Formby.

She ducked her head down into the paper again, scanning the print rapidly "Yes . . . *Marjorie Monkton was said yesterday to be in a stable condition after recovering consciousness.. *"

There was a pause and Con replenished glasses. "What else does it say?" Brightwell enquired. Becoming suddenly revolted or impatient with the matter, Ruby passed the paper to Brightwell. "Here..you read it!" She snatched off her spectacles hastily and rubbed her eyes. "What are we going to do?"

"About what exactly, Ruby dear?" Edward turned in his seat with concern. "That woman's plight is nothing to do with Heritage!"

"No, Edward, I know! I wasn't referring to that!..I mean, in general!"

"It says here, *Marjorie Monkton, was discovered by Graham Ridley, whose wife is rumoured to have been having an affair with Gerald Monkton for many years! . . .*" announced Brightwell.

"Good God!" said Ruby. "I thought you said he was having an affair with Donna Lees!"

"I only surmised that!" said Bill defensively, "from my own deductions!..things she said and so on when she was discussing the budget with me!"

"Things like what?" Formby asked; he did not want Donna to become more tarnished than she already was but he could not resist finding out.

"I don't know . . . just certain comments!"

"Can't you remember any of them?" Formby lit a cigarette without first asking Ruby, such was his consternation . "You must have some ideas to have made the remark at all!"

"No..I haven't!" Brightwell said, testily. "Just certain feelings I gleaned . . . insights, so to speak..you know how one does!"

"No, I don't know '*how one does*'.." Formby was becoming equally tetchy.

"What the devil are you saying?" Brightwell

turned to Formby, colouring.

"Its what you're saying that's the crucial point here! ..I'm saying, unless you have facts to back up your theories keep them to yourself.!"

Brightwell laughed derisively. "We all know that Donna was your choice of candidate, and that in your eyes she could do no wrong, I was never in favour of having her on board at all, but now there is is this..this..debacle! You might as well stop fighting her corner, Geoff!"

"None of it means she has had an affair with Monkton! The chap is obviously some kind of a degenerate!"

Ruby scraped back her chair, a grating sound which jangled the nerves and broke the flow. "Look, for heaven's sake..let's stick to the question in hand, gentleman, please!"

Brightwell blew out his breath heavily and turned his head in great annoyance to stare at the night darkness beyond the windowed walls. "I am all too happy to do that, Ruby, but if a person can't make an idle comment.."

"Idle comments are sometimes salacious!" said Formby. "This isn't the time for idle comments!"

"Let's just leave things a while longer and go to our beds!" Edward's manner was consoling. "This is a very frustrating and really quite futile situation. . . ."

CHAPTER FIFTEEN

HUDDLED BENEATH THE grimy blankets of Alf"s primitive personal dwelling, Gerald pursued his life in a vacuum of timeless hours. How long he had been there he was unsure. He did not even bother to check his watch, or note the darkening of the day. Periodically Alf brought him sustenance in the form of bread and soup, or tea and crumpets, or toast and jam, or the odd glass of beer.

He felt the lack of Elaine keenly, as one might feel the lack of a limb; the memory of where she had been within his system held a long lingering presence, an ache for which there was no beginning or end. Of Marjorie his feelings were benumbed and confused. He scarcely knew if she were an object of past affection or of hate. She was that unspecified thing, a familiar and accepted adversary! There was the questionable fact that he had possibly murdered her and it lay second in his thoughts to the fact that he had changed the course of his everyday existence.

The rights and wrongs of the situation were simply not to be addressed—they were too abstruse.

He was aware of Alf entering, the door creaking a little as always, the cold draft blowing around the bottom of the cabin, lifting ever so slightly the hairs on his arms.

Alf began rummaging around in an old chest containing two shallow drawers where he seemed to keep his belongings. "Police 'as been!" he announced dully, "asking for you!"

Gerald looked over at him, his eyes heavy and unhealthy, his stare that of a vacant and wandering soul. "What did you say to them?"

"Told 'em as 'ow I'd not seen you since last week!"

"And did they believe you?"

"Don't see why not!" said Alf, closing the chest. "They took 'emselves off at any rate!"

"Thanks, Alf..I owe you!"

Alf made indistinguishable sounds in his throat, possibly of agreement or complicity, and said next: "Course, it won't stop there . . . it'll only buy you time . . . they'll be back!" He straightened an old and worn cloth which covered the chest in a vain attempt to emulate a decorative item. Gerald watched miserably. It seemed to him the item might at one time have hailed from the Far East. "You were in the army, were you?" he asked Alf.

"Navy!" said Alf shortly, summoning a vestige of pride which was so fleeting it might have been missed. "I was a naval man!" He straightened his shoulders, dignifying the statement with a remnant of the appropriate posture.

"Really!" Gerald politely forced an interest which may have been more genuine if not for his own state of wretchedness.

"That's right.." continued Alf, absently. "twenty odd years!"

"Interesting!..I wouldn't mind hearing a bit about that..later!"

"Later..yes!" agreed Alf, without conviction, and vacated the cabin with a swift and almost graceful movement spurred by the thought of someone being impressed by his own neglected history.

Gerald's beleaguered brain began conjuring with the question of why Alf would risk lying to the police on his behalf. Perhaps he detested the police! Or perhaps he had his own more convoluted and covert reasons! But what would they be?.. .At this point in the equation Gerald fell asleep from the sheer effort of trying to maintain too many thoughts at once.

*   *   *

When Marjorie regained consciousness she knew almost at once that she was different; that part of her which was not directly within her immediate control was feeling and perceiving differently. She lay for some time, a little apprehensively, trying to fathom it out. She remembered clearly what had happened to her, even down to the way the bell had nearly slipped from Gerald's hand as he swung it on its upward arc; the way his fingers twitched to stop it slipping from his grasp. The way the transistor radio he left permanently switched on in his studio had been blaring out that stupid advert for insurance where the woman's husband is amazed to find she has seen to the task before him and the woman gloats! What a very meaningful choice of ad to accompany her brush with death. *A gloating wife!* Except that she did not possess an admiring husband!

She remembered everything. Even so, she knew she was different. It was odd, the way she kept on recalling the events of the Saturday night, and even so expecting Gerald to visit her with a bunch of flowers.

They had sent her a counsellor yesterday, an expert on domestic and marital violence, but she had pointed out that she would rather have an expert on 'homicidal mania' and refused to talk to them.

She watched the goings on in the ward, mutely, and assessed her past and present situation. Her mother had been to see her. But her mother (a lively and outgoing seventy something, with so many friends and associates she needed a personal secretary) did not understand what it was to be Marjorie. She was unsympathetic, and always had been, to her problem with Gerald.. Her mother it was who had warned her against marrying Gerald when they were young . . . 'He's too compliant..' she had told her, 'he's altogether too meek!'.

Marjorie had enjoyed these remarks, in her naivety. 'Its just that he loves me so much!' she had declared, not caring how true it might or might not be. 'He's frightened of you!' her mother had replied. 'It'll lead to trouble in the end!' And recently she had been just as scathing: 'You're unsuited, Marjorie, its always been the case, and I don't know why you just could not accept it years ago, instead of turning life into this fiasco!..money isn't everything you know!' Usually Marjorie seethed when she heard such phrases, and especially from her mother. *She wondered amid her anger and denial from where her mother got these avant garde modes of thought. It was hardly seemly*

*for someone of her generation who had lived all their lives
in suburban England and not the outer regions of Gautamala
or the bohemian quarters of Paris.* Now she felt differently, and she could not be bothered to seethe. And
in the space where she normally seethed she allowed
herself to see the truth. She could no longer be bothered to cover it or deny it.

The police had visited her the moment she regained consciousness and asked her questions, finally
announcing that they were charging Gerald with attempted murder, when they could find him. Helpfully she had given them Graham Ridley's address
and told them about the affair with Elaine, making
out that she had known nothing of it until recently.

She saw the young Nigerian nurse approaching
her bed, smiling that wide and white-toothed smile
and raising her brows expectantly, so that Marjorie
had too smile ever so faintly back because it was contagious.

"Hello, Marjorie.." The nurse said her name so it
rhymed with 'jamboree' " . . . how you doin' today
girl?. . . . visitor for you!. . . . a nice young man!..your
cousin!"

Marjorie did not have a male cousin. She attempted to sit up a little in the bed and the nurse
darted forward to discourage her, taking advantage
of the opportunity to say more softly: "He got to say
that darlin'..he don't get in otherwise.."

Clearly, thought Marjorie, the nurse was under
the opinion that this male visitor was a romantic interest. Perhaps it was Gerald, incognito. She clung
to the nurse's arm fearfully, gazing up into her large
brown eyes with her own small blue ones. She opened
her mouth to speak but could not form her phrases
to her liking.

"..Don't worry . . . I'll stay near enough to watch.."
The nurse assured her, and then held her hand
firmly for a few seconds before going off to fetch the
visitor. Marjorie felt herself beginning to shake, lying thankfully beneath her covers, her head swathed
in bandages. She did not care that she was shaking,
only that it was symptomatic of these deeper changes
within her.

The ward was getting busy and noisy now. Visiting hour had approached. Signs of outside life were
in the corridor and everywhere. There was a thrum
of activity, like an airport or a theatre before the curtain. Marjorie listened to it with interest for a minute
or so, and then the nurse came back with Graham
Ridley.

*   *   *

It was very embarrassing for Graham Ridley, more
than for Marjorie, because Marjorie was lying in bed,
undeniably the victim, whereas Ridley did not know
what he was. Possibly the villain! but possibly the un-
suspecting by-stander in the whole proceedings!—it
depended on the way you looked at it, and he had
never bothered much to look at life through any window other than his own! It made him vulnerable and
uncertain, and it was affecting his job, which involved
being confident and selling things to people.

He sat picking at his thumb-nail and now and
then at the grapes he had brought for Marjorie.
Whilst Marjorie watched him with an unblinking gaze
of minor trepidation.

"It shouldn't have gone the way it did!" Ridley
stated the obvious.

Marjorie drew breath and twisted a little uncomfortably in the bed. "I couldn't get him to leave the studio . . . so I thought I'd provoke him a bit and I picked up a couple of prints and began to tear them!. . . . They were only of some actors or something like that, out of doors, dressed like medieval thugs. . . !"

Ridley turned his head away so as not to have to reveal his feelings.

"But he doesn't seem to care about Elaine any more! ..the whole thing seems to have changed and I can't understand it!" Marjorie pronounced.

"That's because she's found another bloke!" said Ridley, and he was embarrassed and dejected and couldn't look her in the face.

"What?" Marjorie attempted to sit up but slid immediately back down, weak with the effort. "I don't believe it..when?"

"According to her sister he lives a few doors away and they're at it like knives!"

"I don't believe it!" Majorie said it as if she meant it.

"Its true! ..I waited around and saw them leave together . . . and Gerald knows! He went to talk to her but she wouldn't see him!"

Marjorie's pallor became paler, she felt weaker. Ridley sat like someone removed from the circumstances.

"But . . . what?.." Marjorie tailed off. "Perhaps its as well that I didn't try to get him to fall into that electrified pond, after all!"

Loudly, Ridley made shushing noises at her so that other patients looked at them. Marjorie glanced about her and then at Ridley. "No-one will hear us!"

"Marjorie, you are not to mention that to a soul

now . . . do you understand? Otherwise you will be an accessory to attempted murder!"

"That's what they want to charge *him* with! Attempting to murder me!"

"Did you hear me, Marjorie?." Ridley leaned in very close to her and she tried to shrink back, but the pillow resisted. ".. you must forget all about the pond now!"

"Yes, of course I hear you!" Marjorie lay as one stupefied and gazed into the distance and thought about the garden and Graham's labours and ministrations with seemingly innocent bits and pieces of apparatus near her disused and stagnant garden pond, which Gerald had flatly refused to help her modify or fill in.

Eventually she ordered her thoughts. "Have you removed that wiring and stuff yet?" she said vacantly.

Ridley shushed her a second time, looking at her as if he loathed her. What was he doing sitting with her then, all this time!

"I could be referring to anything!" she said lamely, her voice a shadow of its former vibrance.

"Doesn't matter . . . you must be careful!"

"Well, have you?" she repeated, in a subdued and soft tone

"Not yet. . . . I will do, when the hub-hub has died!"

"Supposing they find it?"

"They won't..and even if they do it'll look like negligence resulting from normal neglect and possibly storm damage accruing to that disused shed next to it . . . it'll seem like natural dereliction because of the overgrowth of the garden and the sheer decay of the woodwork and the overall dilapidation!"

Ridley sounded like an effects specialist for a film studio, or a corrupt loss adjustor.

"Do you make a habit of this kind of thing then?" asked Marjorie listlessly.

"No.." He stared at the woman pushing the tea-trolley, "but I do sell conservatories, patios and garden accessories!"

Marjorie lay still, as if it had all been made perfectly clear.

"It wasn't supposed to be this way!" Ridley reiterated, in a voice almost inaudible. "He wasn't supposed to do for you!"

Marjorie nodded, making her head ache.

"I can't believe its happened this way!"

"No.." she looked down at her hands on the pristine white sheets, the rings on her wedding finger.

"It was one of those things that was either going to come off or it wasn't . . . but I never thought he would try and do for you!"

"Neither did I!"

"Look . . . I'm sorry it happened the way it did!"

Marjorie regarded Graham serenely.

"I'll get off and leave you to it now, I don't want to tire you out!"

"Have they got him yet?"

"They can't find him!" said Ridley. "He's done one!..not that he's much of a chance, they'll pick him up! . . . unless you change your story!"

"Do you think I should?" Marjorie was becoming uneasy, it was not a decision she wanted to make. She wanted them to avenge her without her consent or obstruction.

"I don't know. . . . that's your decision!..I suppose it may be best all round!..less prying!"

"Yes..I never thought of it that way! . . . Oh, I don't

know.." she turned and twisted and became ruffled and animated.

The nurse arrived and took her arm and felt the pulse. "Marjorie. . . what you up to?"

Ridley stood back, feeling guilty and out of place. "I'll come again in a day or two!" His tone was for the benefit of the nurse, but rang falsely.

Marjorie waved her free hand vaguely (in that way which reminded him of royalty dismissing service, but less arrogantly now) for she could think of nothing sensible to say.

CHAPTER
SIXTEEN

DONNA DIALED FRANTICALLY Guy West's mobile number. It rang twice and then his message service came on. "Donna!." she said, cryptically, "Ring me as soon as!" She turned her car in the direction of the castle and drove there too quickly. The police had been to see her with regard to Gerald.

At the castle Alf lurked shiftily and waited for her to alight her car. "Suppose you've come looking for him, 'ave you?"

"Why?..is he here?"

"Yes.." said the elf, shortly.

"Well, where?"

"Not so fast, missy!. . . . there's some explaining and negotiating to be done!"

"Don't tell me you want paying for this as well!"

The elf's beady little eyes flashed angrily and he puffed himself out in readiness for confrontation

when Donna's mobile rang and she cut him off totally while she fished it from her bag and answered
it. "Gerald's on the run from the cops . . . he attempted to murder his wife!" she told Guy West.

"That's all we need! . . . you'd better find another
photographer then!" West's voice was heard in the
breezy air surrounding Donna's mobile phone.

"Not as easy as you may imagine!"

"I told you that a week ago, if you recall! . . . and
you didn't seem worried at the time!"

"No-one seems to know where he is." she said,
by-passing the topic of West's superior insights.

"He's here . . . with me!" Alf said into Donna's
face.

"What?" she held the phone at arm's length and
then rammed it back to her ear. "The el. . . . I mean,
Alf, is just telling me that he's here at the castle!..
presumably hiding!"

"I'm on my way there now!" said West, and terminated the call.

A coach was pulling up and spewing a party of
people into the grounds. There was no end to them
now, they came and went at all hours.

"What did you call me?" Alf demanded of Donna.

Donna pretended to look bemused. "I beg your
pardon?"

"To your associate, on the phone then..what did
you call me before you said my name?"

"Nothing!" said Donna sharply, her face closed
and haughty.

"Yes..you said 'the el'..and then broke off! I'm
not deaf!"

Removing a tissue from her bag, she affected to
blow her nose, dabbing it daintily and sniffing, as if
affected by chronic hay-fever. "No, what I was about

to say was 'the herald' . . . 'the herald says that Gerald is here' . . . but then I thought better of it and used your name.."

"The what?.." Alf ignored the roaming visitors entering the castle freely. "The herald!..what the 'ell's that mean?"

"You know, castles and things always had heralds at one time!"

"Yes, but do I look like a bleeding herald?"

"No..no, but you might if you dressed accordingly! What I mean is.."

"Any road, you said 'el'..I distinctly 'eard you!..it sounded like 'elf'!"

"No, I said the start of the word herald but I may have just dropped an aitch.. which is not like me, I have to admit.."

Alf had turned his head and was gazing at her from the side of his eye in that way which was disconcerting in its accusatory meaning.

"Anyway, where is Gerald?..you'd better take me to him!"

"Not so fast!. . . . how do I know he'll want to receive you?"

"Don't be silly, Alf! this is as an extenuating circumstance and I.." A man and a woman appeared next to them and the man spoke loudly into the middle of Donna's statement. "Where's the loos?"

"Excuse me..we're speaking!"

"The loos!" repeated the woman, as if Donna had not uttered. "We need the loo..and so do a few other people!"

"There aren't none yet!" said Alf, and the couple stood back as one, aghast. "'aven't delivered 'em.." Alf confirmed.

"What'll we do?"

The woman addressed this remark to her husband, and Donna stepped away from them and signalled to Alf to join her.

"Tell you what," Alf said to the couple, "they'd better go to the nearest pub . . . a couple miles up the road towards Rotherham!. Or else they can use the lower field over there, where there's trees and privacy!"

"I think we'll use the trees!" said the man.

"Yes . . . good idea!" Alf began marching off towards the field. "Come this way for the quickest!"

Donna called after him. "Alf, where is Gerald?"

Alf carried on ushering the couple, his retreating back suggestive off disinterested unhelpfulness.

"Alf, just tell me where he is and I'll find my own way!" called Donna.

Again there was no reply. Donna gritted her teeth and made an expression of tolerant outrage tempered by mild desperation, as if she were being filmed by an unseen onlooker for an outside location drama. Then she hurried to the only part of the castle with which she felt familiar and climbed the stairs to the upper chamber and gazed from the window over the approaching-winter landscape, chill and rather devoid of colour on this October day, and wondered what exactly to do next while Guy West arrived.

*   *   *

Alf watched the tourists head off into the nearby woodland, chirruping to each other and lurching hither and yon in the long coarse grasses. Had he been in close proximity to them he would have warned them not to go near the disused shaft once connected to an ancient foundry dating back to Roman times, and to avoid the boggy area that was once a large pond into which a person could sink up to their thighs—lured unsuspectingly by the innocent looking ferns and wild flowers which flourished profusely on the moistened land. But he was not in close proximity and was observing from a window in his employer's residence.

"Where's this Monkton chap now?" asked the feudal personage.

"In the cabin, where he's been the last three days!"

"Not very safe!"

"I expect he knows that . . . he must take his chances, I've warned him!"

"And the other one? . . . the woman!"

"She's just arrived, looking for him!"

There were shrieks and shouts as several of the visitors succumbed to the bog and felt the cold slimy waters assault their vulnerable limbs.. "I should 'ave warned 'em" Alf said, in desultory manner.

"Who?"

"These 'ere trippers!..the portaloos haven't arrived..they're making do with the field yonder!"

"How many of them are there out there altogether?" asked the employer.

"Hundreds!" said Alf, almost proudly but with a manner of pained forbearance. "There'll scarce be an end to it now!. . . . not with them press folk at it!"

"Which press folk?"

"Blondie and her boyfriend!. He'll be along soon, I shouldn't wonder!"

"Which boyfriend is that? I thought Monkton was her boyfriend!"

"Not any more! . . . As far as I can make out, its this journalist chap she's taken up with!"

"I can't have it!" said the venerable one. "You must do something, Alfred!"

"Yes..but I can only wear one hat at once, so to speak!"

"Alfred!". The voice of his employer from the rear took on a sombre, draconian quality. "Who was it who attracted all this in the beginning! Whose greed is at the root of this latest debacle! Who set all this in motion and orchestrated it!"

"I didn't mean to make more than a few bob!" Alf oppined, his attention on the field.

"Whatever you meant, you've reaped the whirlwind..and I won't have it, I tell you!"

"I'll do what I can!" said Alf, looking at the spectacle of other tourists rushing to help their sodden associates.

"You'll do more than that!..you'll wind matters down and restore normality. Normality is all I ever crave, and I pay for it dearly!"

Alfred was about to defend himself a shade more stridently when the arrival of a police car onto the eastern slope of the castle grounds diverted his attention. "Here's the coppers again!" he said in a hushed and sorrowful way.

"Quite! . . . and you must see exactly what I mean when I say I won't have this!"

Turning his head from right to left, Alf was in a dilemma of which way to go first. Whether to lend assistance to the tourists in the bog and ignore the police, or to distract the police from the shrieking by approaching them first. Was it a criminal offense to allow visitors to the site to wander aimlessly into perilous reaches of the terrain? No, it probably wasn't! And if he did not get to the police quickly they may roam about and discover his cabin and find Gerald, and it was certainly an offense to harbour known criminals. His feet, ill-clad in their shoddy footwear, almost skidded on the shiny parquet flooring as he scurried to the door and made haste to intervene in the proceedings.

"And make sure you clear the whole estate, don't allow any stragglers to be left behind!" said the venerable one, languidly, to his retreating form.

*   *   *

Donna had now located an old cabin, which was locked but through the dirty windows of which she could discern a huddled figure lying in a make-shift bunk. It was perhaps Gerald. She tapped on the window and got no obvious response. She wondered whether to tap harder, but hesitated because if it was not after all Gerry but one of Alf's relatives or friends, she would be at a disadvantage when ever after dealing with the elf. Not to mention being labelled some kind of nosey parker, or worse! Creeping around and looking in on strange men while they slept!

She tapped a second time, more loudly, and the figure raised its head. In the dim inner light of the cabin she saw that it was Gerald. She beckoned, but Gerald made no sign of having recognised her and buried himself beneath the blanket. Mortified, she could only gaze numbly at the state he had gotten into! What exactly had been happening to him? She called out to him in a hissing whisper. "Gerald . . . Gerry..!" But the body stayed perfectly inert, the blanket over its head. Had she imagined it? Perhaps it was one of his light-beings, impersonating him! Trying the door she was not surprised to discover it locked.

She strolled about the periphery of the cabin, kicking up stones and twigs with the toe of her boot, lighting a cigarette, handling her mobile phone; wondering what she could do and speculating on how long it would take Guy to reach her. It was already late afternoon.

Through a clearing in the bushes and sprawling shrubbery she caught sight of Alf talking with a police officer outside a car, and she debated with herself on the topic of the law versus one's moral obligations to another person. She owed it to Gerald not to shop him at least, despite their altercations. He had never done her any harm personally. And he was obviously in hiding. Anyway, if questioned she could deny ever having looked into the cabin window. She was simply taking a stroll while she awaited her colleague, Guy West, and how was she to know what lay in other peoples' sordid hovels!

She slumped down against a stunted maple tree and rested her back. She hummed to herself from her favourite symphonies and allowed time to stroll past. If Guy arrived he would steer clear of the police and call her on her mobile from his and then they could hatch plans for meeting without being too readily seen.

*   *   *

"I haven't seen him since last week!" said Alf in his best accents, his eyes like shards of misted glass in wrinkled pastry cups, moist and strangely sub-human. "But that doesn't mean to say he's not here somewhere . . . look around if it makes you happy! My eyesight's not what it used to be!" Alf smiled, causing the little shards of misty glass to glitter as they grew somewhat larger with the lifting of his face into an expression of affability. He was rather pleased with his declaration; it subtly covered any untoward contingency.

He knew one of the officers was staring at him, in the way that lot did; unnervingly, trying to make a person reveal more than they wanted. Alf was accustomed to subtle intimidation and low key tyrany. He watched the nearby countryside serenely and listened to the shrieks of the loo-seekers as they cavorted in the swamp.

"If you haven't seen him since last week, how come you were spotted talking to him last night!"

"Who by?" Alf turned his head swiftly, the twinkling shards darkening like rain clouds.

""Never mind . . . you just were!"

"Case of mistaken identity!..I talk to hundreds of folk in these parts!"

It had been a trick question but the police officer watched him closely to see the reaction it brought forth.

"Some folk need to test their facts before opening their mouth," Alf said, "and need to keep their nose out of things that don't concern them!"

"Mr Spooner, its an offense to obstruct us in the course of our enquiries!" said the officer with the muted stare.

Alf was about to prevaricate further when the shrieks from the field were over-lorded by a louder groan of anguish, piercing in its intensity.

"What exactly is going on over there?" queried one of the law enforcers.

"Visitors!" snapped Alf, in throw-away manner.

"Stuck in the swampy part of the field by the sounds of it! . . . they were finding a private place to perform their ablutions!"

"Do you mean to say you haven't lent them assistance?"

"No! . . ." said Alf with finality. "They got into the mess they'll have to get out of it!..it's not my job to wet-nurse them!"

"But you're responsible for the castle security!"

"Them fields is off the castle grounds!" Alf had a triumphant manner, destined to provoke acrimony.

"We'd better go and see!" declared one of the officers, shutting the car door and locking it. "Mr Spooner, we haven't finished with you yet, so don't disappear!"

"I'll just sit here in the pay-hut then and read the paper!" Alf was reassuringly angelic. He waited until they had moved off well towards the field before dashing round to the cabin, moving and crashing through shrubs and briar, muttering loudly.

"You'll have to scarper.." he told Gerald, "they're here for you . . . I've diverted 'em but you've not got long. I can't do no more for you now!"

Gerald stood up, tottering somewhat. A dishevelled mess and a far cry from the man who had first appeared at the castle some weeks ago.

"How long have I got?"

"About twenty minutes to half an hour, I'd say! . . . They'll come and question me some more, but you'd best get out!"

"Alf, I appreciate all you've done and I won't forget it in a hurry!"

Embarrassed, Alf gave a naval salute, and left the cabin before Gerald was tempted to make further emotional links for posterity.

*   *   *

Guy and Donna sat in Guy's small Mercedes and kept watch on proceedings, taking it in turns to look through Guy's binoculars. Positioned on the western hill overlooking the castle and its grounds, they could see the cabin in which Gerald was domiciled, dimly through trees. Guy talked intermittently into his voice activated tape machine about other news matters whilst watching the land. Donna, sick of playing detective, had dozed off in the warmth of the car's interior.

The police had just arrived in the field with the shrieking multitude, for whom Guy held nothing but contempt (they were the kind of people who gave him the juiciest of his angles into football hooliganism and the like) when he saw the cabin door opening to admit the elf, who stayed a mere minute and came out again rapidly. Guy applied his full concentration to the cabin, adjusting the lenses of his binoculars, and suddenly the door opened once more, slowly, and Gerald appeared and shuffled off out of sight. Guy nudged Donna awake and presently they saw Gerald emerge from the surrounding woodland area and move to the castle structure.

"He's going in!"

Donna looked at Guy, rubbing her cheekbones to restore some vitality to her senses, frowning with disbelief. "He'll walk straight in to them! . . . maybe he's giving himself up!"

"No they've gone over to that field. They already looked in the castle!" Guy trained the binoculars on Gerald with avidly focused attention.. "There will be a lot of people in there . . . he may hope to merge with the visitors! . . . Come on, we'll go and see for ourselves!"

"But what if..?"

"What if what?" said Guy, looking at Donna suspiciously.

"Well, what if we get embroiled?"

"In what?"

"Its dangerous now! . . . He's a wanted criminal!"

"I'm used to tricky situations!" he replied, airily. "What do you think our job is based on, Ministry of Health regulations?"

"There's no need to be sarcastic!" Donna scrambled from the car. "And there's no need to be so flash either!"

West made a scornful sound and pulled her to one side, out of the visible observation of anyone watching from the castle windows. "You have to be a bit foxy, darling! You're not doing a P.R. stunt now!"

"Get your hands off me!" Donna made one of her outlandish faces for an invisible audience as she trotted after West who was crouching and sidling along the shrubbery line so as not to seen by anyone inside. "This is ridiculous.." she moaned, dragging her expensive and cumbersome bag through muddy soil and bracken. "We're not in the bloody jungle . . . we could be here for any reason!"

"Yes, we could, but the reason we're really here is the most important one to us, and we'll have to keep a low profile to achieve our ends.."

"Which ends?"

"Relieving Gerald of any further film footage before they read him his rights!. . . . doubtless, he's got it in the car, but he'll have hidden that!"

She was not au fait with all of the dealings brooked between West and Monkton, and the way they connived together recently made her blood boil, but to admit that openly was too demoralising. It was better to feign indifference. "How callous!" she said, but not very convincingly, as she scrambled in the wake of her journalist lover.

*   *   *

Gerald was utterly amazed at the numbers of people in the caste. The upper chamber, a veritable second home to him of late, was swarming with them. All shapes and sizes, varying ages, and from all walks of life. Had he not been in such desperate straits he may have found the spectacle distasteful. As it was, he was thankful for the cover it gave him, the safety in numbers feeling which that kind of crowd affords at times of heightened sensitivity to ones own identity. He was on borrowed time. And the question was what to do next! He supposed he would have to give himself up. But then again, he still played with tenuous notions of leaving the country and starting over. He knew little of how to go about it, but it was something he had read of people doing often enough in books, and it seemed a possibility, in the fevered anxiety of his over-wrought mind.

He hovered near the southern window and looked across the grounds. The police were coming now from the vicinity of the cabin, Alf tailing them. They had been here hours and now knew the location of Alf's private dwelling. He watched as they got into their vehicle and drove away. He was safe again, for the time being! Anyway, it was not as if he were one of the country's most wanted criminals. Although he supposed he may well be, given the exaggeration of the media these days.

His thoughts had scarcely touched on the media when by some strange coincidence he saw that Guy West was milling about near the pay-gate, binoculars around his neck, passing himself off as another visitor.

Gerald felt immediately that he was in danger from Guy West. His nose for news, and his connections made him just as much the enemy as the police. If he saw Gerald he would most likely tip off the police. Edging his way back down the staircase and around the side of the castle walls, Gerald decided it was best to head back to the cabin until West had gone. He was stealthily moving through the bushes which surrounded the cabin and kept it obscured from the vantage point of the castle windows and high-ground when he saw that Donna had now joined West. He slunk quickly towards the cabin door, and as he entered the place for the last time it occurred to him to wonder at the strangeness which prompted Alf to live in such a way and in such an eccentric place, and what motivated him and why.

*   *   *

"Not found him yet then?" enquired Alf of Donna and Guy as he waved his arms around at passing tourists, ushering them off the premises like a dishevelled smallholder with wayward hens.

"Not yet!" said West, patiently, as to a backward child.

"Not likely too either!" rejoined Alf, physically pushing two teenage boys towards the exit.

"Why do you say that?" said West.

"Because he don't want to be found!"

"Yes, but we're here to help him!" remarked

Donna, and Guy West shot her a look which reminded her there was no necessity for useless remarks.

"I expect you really know where he is!" West told Alf, with pained jocularity, as though he were a squire addressing one of the peasantry.

"You can expect as much as you like!" Alf coldly appraised West with the contempt of the inferior for the self-made superior. "No charge for expecting, I always say!" He turned away to attend to the flock; ushering and goading and urging them from the confines of the castle.

"Loathsome little prat!" said West, quietly. "He'll take us right to him next. . . . if we're patient!"

Donna nodded and dropped her tortoiseshell shades onto her nose to shield her eyes, even though there was no longer any sun.

Feeling he could trust the last dozen folk to depart unaided, Alf made his way out of the castle perimeters towards the steep hillside. He did not risk going to the cabin, because he knew that West and Donna would follow him, and he did not want them or anyone else knowing its location. It was bad enough that the police knew of it.

*   *   *

The venerable one saw all, missed nothing, and knew everything.

"Has the multitude dispersed, Alfred?"

"All but a couple," Alf replied, "and they'll be gone soon!"

"What about the press folk?"

"Down by the pay-gate!"

"Waiting for what?"

"Gerald Monkton!"

"Ah.."

"But he's not to be found!"

"He's gone back to your shack!"

Alfred looked at his employer soberly. "I told him to leave there!"

"He went back in some fifteen minutes since..I saw him from that window, through the telescope!"

"Oh?" Alf's grizzled features puckered with great bewilderment.

"No doubt because he has caught sight of Donna and her boyfriend!"

"I'l have to get rid of 'em!" Alf said. "I'll have to force 'em to leave!"

"Get rid of Monkton while you're about it!"

Alf indulged in a few moments of scratching while he cogitated; his head, his neck, his inside wrist, raking his broken and blackened finger nails across the various parts of his anatomy with the concentration of a nesting rodent. Finally he nodded at his corporate benefactor, pulled his woollen hat about his head for improved comfort and departed again.

*   *   *

When he entered the hut he saw that Gerald had lost all and any shade of confidence for the outer world. "Guy West is out there!" he told Alf.

"So what?"

"He'll report me to the police!"

"Not right away, he won't!"

"Yes but.." Gerald could think of no further sensible protest and tailed off feebly.

Alf was watching him, with a keen and glistening eye which Gerald felt himself impelled to watch in return. The temperature in the cabin was dropping, or perhaps it was his own temperature. He felt as if he were about to black out. But he did not do so, he merely felt weaker and dizzy. And then as he stared, a phenomenon took place which over-shadowed all other immediate concerns.

Alf was changing before his eyes. It was as if he were dissolving or melting. He seemed to be spinning, so that the contours of his form were blurred. Gerald tried adjusting his vision and shaking his head to clear it. An age seemed to pass which was in reality only moments, and still this process was underway. Fleetingly, Gerald realised that Alf was shape-shifting. Not sure how much more mental trauma he could withstand, he shut his eyes.

When he re-opened them he was looking at the embodiment of the leader of the dancing maidens. The one with the smile, the one who had lead him from the upper chamber that day to fix a non-existent tripod, and down into the centre of the marauding tribesmen. The one whose photograph he had taken in solo.

She smiled with that vague omniscience which was charismatic and innocent at the same time.

Gerald hardly dare ask. "You're.. Alf?" His reverence for the proof of paranormal activity caused him to sound ecclesiastical in the oppressive gloom of the cabin. That he did not receive a reply did not surprise him. Such things did not bear comment. They merely needed remarking upon, paying them homage.

He stared now at her feet, which as usual were not quite on the floor, and she allowed him this space for adjustment, this settling of his turbulent senses, and then she beckoned him and spoke. "Follow me, Gerald! . . . and don't be afraid!"

He did so, without further ado. They moved from the cabin and through the grounds and into the castle, and all the while Donna and Guy monitored their progress, thinking themselves to be unobserved and covert.

*   *   *

"Its one of the light beings!" Donna kept saying, as they silently scurried towards the castle.

"The what?" said West, impatiently, his eyes on the prey.

"You know, one of the light beings.. from the photographs!"

"You're joking!" said West, scathingly.

"Of course I'm not joking!" Donna was irritable. She felt as if things were so sordid and surreal they were totally out of her control, and she had that universal common notion that she might in fact be asleep in bed and dreaming. "Would I joke about something like that?"

"Shush . . . keep your voice down!" West commanded. "We don't want them hearing us before we know what they're about to do!"

"You need to be very careful, Guy!..this is a light being! . . . this female is not one of us!"

"I keep an open mind.." said her current lover, as if she had revealed herself to be the possible source of an elaborate hoax.

"Do what you want!..but I'm telling you, if you're not prepared it'll blow your mind!"

"It'll have to be good!"

"Well, sweetheart, it will be!" She was getting fed up with West's know-all attitudes on life; they were boring and stymied. "But don't say I didn't warn you!"

"Donna, for God's Sake, keep it down! . . . In fact, better still, keep quiet! . . . We don't want to attract their attention, noise carries in these places!"

"Don't try to tell me about places like these..I was the one who discovered the place, remember!..not you!..There's this little maxim about teaching your granny to suck eggs.."

"*Donna!!.*" West turned from his stalking gait to glower at her, hissing her name warningly.

"Please yourself!" she replied under her breath, trotting some way behind him, her shades in place over her eyes to keep out unwelcome observations of her inner mood. "Don't say I didn't warn you!"

*   *   *

No sooner had Gerald entered the upper chamber with the maiden than she was joined from nowhere by her dancing circle who fell into place about her, the seven of them whirling and gliding gracefully about the enclosure, silently casting their spell of enchanting tranquility around the walls. Gerald watched for perhaps ten minutes before wandering to the eastern window. He had reached that stage in traumatic proceedings where he no longer waited to see what would happen next, or gave it any thought.

Looking down on the entailed land he saw that Donna and West were in the lower regions near the remains of the old portcullis, trying to look inconspicuous.

Suddenly the main maiden (and the erstwhile Alfred) spoke to him. "Stay where you are!" she said, scarcely breaking her rhythm or movement within the circle. "Do not attempt to follow us!" And one by

one they danced and whirled out of the chamber by
the staircase and down into the area of the portcullis
and into the chilly evening.

Gerald saw them emerge into the grounds and
glide in a line towards the fields, their feet inches
off the floor, treading air. He saw Donna and West
follow at a distance, stealthily, so that they thought
they would not be seen. He saw the girls drift on-
wards, oblivious of who had seen them and who had
not.

It was darkening now, and not easy to believe your
eyes, but still there was no doubting the visage of the
maidens and of the two mortals who followed. There
was nothing to be heard for quite a while, and then
the cracking of tree branches heralded the arrival of
West and Donna into the fields.

By squinting, Gerald could make out their forms
quite distinctly in the twilight, because the field at
its centre was open and free of plantation, affording
a view from an elevated position at the castle windows of its innermost circumference. Gerald watched
as they walked slowly behind the dancing girls, as if
hypnotised, in obedience to the ritual and not brave
enough to defy it, when suddenly there was a cry, a
male voice! and then a shriek, a female cry! But both
happened so close together that there was no time
for consideration. And then the forms of Donna and
Guy disappeared, swallowed, it seemed, by the dark
ground.

Gerald listened and peered intently for an age,
but nothing remained of the occurrence; the air was
so still it hummed, rent only by the odd late-evening
bird song, the maidens kept on dancing—the field
was empty and calm, except for their filmy presence.

Donna and West did not reappear. Gerald pondered, his mind numbed. A quarter hour went by, marked by a distant and almost inaudible chime of a church bell. The maidens now were barely visible— so dark was the landscape—but still a frothy luminescent outline was to be observed, dusting the backdrop of hillside and surrounding trees. Gerald waited, and the world waited with him in the quiet English countryside, undisturbed for centuries in these parts. The very land seemed to call forth his perception and insight, as though his mere mortal stupidity were something it witnessed without judgement, yet keenly; enticing him to transcend same by sheer force of will and vision.

Then suddenly it came to his mind that there was a disused shaft, from a by-gone foundry, Roman in origin. Alf had told him of it yesterday, and that it lay to the right-hand side of the field. It should have been closed up, but they had never got around to it. Alf had told him that sometimes they put up warning notices and then sometimes they took them down. It had not occurred to Gerald to enquire why this changeable behaviour was so. And even had it done so, who was he to question the idiosyncracies of other people!

He contemplated the fate of Donna and Guy West almost placidly. Sanguinely, he considered whether he should enlist assistance or notify authorities. And then he laughed at this folly in the face of his own personal catastrophe. Had it not been for Donna he would not have gone through any of the past weeks! He would still have his life, such as it had been, in tact. Still have Elaine, and his domestic arrangements. Still have his business interests, which would be bound to improve with time. Still be an expert in psychical research. Still have some semblence of self-respect.

He was in one of those moments when it becomes possible to see the sheer beauty of imperfection in the hum-drum and the substandard.

He was *still* laughing slightly when the maidens arrived back in the chamber, dancing and whirling.

The leading maiden stood to one side and beckoned him and he took a step nearer her, finding it hard to do so in the almost total darkness of the chamber. And then there was a whirring motion, like a fluttering of animated wings on large feathered creatures. He sensed rather than saw that more shape-shifting was afoot. He closed his eyes, and before he found the courage to open them he heard and felt a different atmosphere. Shufflings, gruntings, murmerings, the gross sounds of manhood.

The tribesman were in the place of the maidens. The chief maiden was gone. In her stead was the leader of the clan. . . . hostile, sweating, intimidating, without moving a muscle or issuing a command he was the archetype of primitive war. In his hand was a weapon, an axe or a spear, or a combination of both.

Gerald shrank back and felt the cold stone wall against his shoulders. He was losing his lifeblood now, it was draining away from him, like the swift effects of an anaesthetic to lessen sensation and pain.

The chieftain was towering over him in his superior position, mighty against Gerald's diminished stance. Gerald's eyes were fixed wide upon him without blinking. His ears poised to hear the mystery solved. Eventually the tribesman spoke, his face as real as anything Gerald had ever witnessed, the pores of his roughened skin, his strong facial hairs coarse and wiry, and he watched the man's mouth form words and his arm swing the weapon into a high arc above his head.

"It is better to die with honour than to survive in disgrace!"

Gerald digested the words slowly, trying irrelevantly to pin-point the dialect spoken, as the darkness engulfed him. He thought that in the main he might have to agree with what the man had said, but he needed a few more seconds to be absolutely sure.

As always, in this life of his, he had not quite made up his mind before time ran out.

Lightning Source UK Ltd.
Milton Keynes UK
UKOW04f0859240315

248413UK00001B/87/P